THE
MARRIAGE
TRAP

SHERYL BROWNE

Bookouture

Published by Bookouture in 2019

An imprint of StoryFire Ltd.

Carmelite House
50 Victoria Embankment
London EC4Y 0DZ

www.bookouture.com

ISBN: 978-1-78681-896-6
eBook ISBN: 978-1-78681-895-9

This book is a work of fiction. Names, characters, businesses,
organizations, places and events other than those clearly in the
public domain, are either the product of the author's imagination
or are used fictitiously. Any resemblance to actual persons, living or
dead, events or locales is entirely coincidental.

*To Drew for his inspiration – and my family
and friends for their fabulous support.*

I AM FALLING

KARLA

Her stillness is disconcerting for him. It's distracting him from this – this thing he's been planning to do for weeks. Jason isn't able to meet her eyes – too cowardly to see the bewilderment there, the pain. Two or three times, she sees his worried gaze stray to where she stands silently in the doorway, watching this final chapter in her marriage play out like a scene in a soap opera. This would be the calm before the storm, the prequel to tragedy, where the avid viewer, who knows this wronged woman's humiliation, her indescribable hurt, waits for her to plunge the long knife deep between his shoulder blades, as he stuffs his shirts into his suitcase.

They're not ironed, the shirts. She stopped doing that some while ago.

She will snarl contemptuously down at him, a combination of disgust and deep satisfaction in her eyes, as he crumples, a pool of his own blood flowering beneath him, disbelief flickering briefly in his deceitful, dark eyes, before the light fades.

This woman who stands here silently does none of that. She is detached, unreactive. This woman is me. I don't know her any more. The tablets supplied by my doctor – mild sedatives, that's all – for the endless nights when my mind can't find solace in sleep, they numb me, allow me, through the wooziness, to view things with clarity. I can't stop him leaving. My silence, this time, is not tactical, a ploy to manipulate him into backing down after an argument. There's nothing to say. No words left. No words that can keep him. No more accusations to scream, no tears I can cry that won't fall on barren ground. Jason has made up his mind. Even as I see his determined stride falter under the weight of his guilt, as he walks away from the dressing table with random handfuls of clothes, I know he won't be dissuaded. He will go to her: Jessie. Jezebel. The woman who is apparently everything I am not.

Jason hesitates, glancing around the room for anything he might have forgotten – small things, obviously. No doubt he will come back for 'the rest', whatever the rest may be. Material evidence of our time spent together. He will take what he perceives to be his, leaving me with the physical evidence, the scars on my heart, my mind. On my body from bearing his children, the children he will abandon. For her.

He walks across to the bedside table. His watch lies there, marking time – *tick, tock* – twelve years of my life, flushed down the toilet. It's the last thing he takes off at night, always placing it next to the framed photo. A framed photo of me. I'm certain he won't take that. Will he place the watch next to a similar photograph, I wonder? Will he compare us? If he lays his head down next to her, I'm sure he will.

'Will you stay with her tonight?' I ask him, eschewing silence for knowledge. 'Your perfect woman?' *Jessie.* I silently repeat it, recalling how the name rolled off my tongue the first time I mouthed it out loud. Meaning: Gift from God. This much I know. I smile insipidly. I won't give vent to the emotion bubbling up inside me; fuel the argument that would allow him to slam out of our house without saying goodbye to his children. His choice will be to do that despicable thing all on his own. I won't allow him to pretend he's doing it to avoid confrontation with me.

'Yes,' he answers uncomfortably, meeting my eyes, finally. The look in his own is anguished, full of remorse, as if seeking forgiveness, as if he should perhaps receive a plaudit for that one single scrap of truth. 'I'm sorry, Karla. I didn't want things to end like this.'

'Yes, you did.' I laugh – a short, bitter laugh of contempt. How am I supposed not to? He's not sorry. He's excited, anticipating his new life, with her. He will already be imagining what he will do to her. What she will do with him. What positions he will take her in. I know this. I know him. All of him. His every aspiration. His every fantasy. Can he truly be so oblivious?

'And you love her.' It's a statement, not a question. This much I know is true, too. His love for her is stronger than the love that should bind him to his children, to his wife, the woman he swore to love and cherish forever.

'I don't want to argue, Karla – not again. I should go.' He avoids the question. Does he imagine his answer will hurt me? That, with my mother disappeared, hiding away from the press who have relentlessly hounded my father, and with my husband about to desert me too, I can possibly hurt any more than I do?

His eyes are downcast as he collects his case and walks towards me.

I stand aside to let him pass. The knife behind my back feels solid in my hand. The only solid in the shifting sand. I'm tired – too tired to play this game any more. But a rational part of me clings on through the fog and the rage. The mother who, if she does this, will feel her children's pain as surely as her own, holds on to my waning sanity. I need to let him go. This is not the last chapter, I am sure of it.

'Will you still love her when you know all of her, as you imagine you know me?' My voice is strained, bordering on hysteria. I'm fighting hard to keep it at bay.

Pausing at the top of the stairs, Jason glances at me – a sorrowful glance, which pierces my heart like a sharp stab of the blade I am mentally wrestling with. 'I do know her, Karla,' he says sadly.

I doubt that, I think, as he descends. I doubt that very much indeed.

I follow him as I hear the front door open. Will myself not to lose control, to fall, as I dread that I eventually will. My name is Karla. Meaning: womanly; strength. I've googled it. I will stay strong.

CHAPTER ONE

THREE MONTHS EARLIER

KARLA

My mother's tipsy, I notice, as she leaps up with her 'girlfriends', gyrating excitedly and belting out the lyrics to 'There Goes My First Love' as she weaves through the tables towards the dance floor. The sharp-suited tribute band is good, emulating the smart moves and honeyed harmonies of The Drifters perfectly. My father's excelled himself, money being no object when it comes to celebrating his own first love's sixtieth birthday. Idly, I wonder whether he's been straying again. He usually splashes money around like it's going out of fashion when he has. I have no idea why Mum puts up with him. Largely, she ignores him. I imagine the only reason she's here is because he sent out the invitations to her sixtieth birthday party before actually telling her she was having one.

Glancing towards the bar, I see he's making a beeline for Jason, who's being served and therefore has no chance of avoiding being cornered. Seeing my father reach to shake his hand, regardless of Jason holding a glass in each of his, I shove my chair back and head across the room to rescue my husband from what's bound to be a work-related grilling, meaning he will be agitated for the rest of the evening. And who could blame him? It's a birthday party, for goodness' sake. Does my father have to be so formal with him?

Oh no. Approaching them, I rein in my own agitation. 'So, how are things in the ecommerce industry? Thriving, I hope?' I hear Dad ask, inevitably, his smile fixed in place as he appraises Jason, as if measuring him up. Why does he do that? Make it so obvious he doesn't rate him?

Jason takes a breath, visibly quashing his annoyance. 'Not exactly thriving, no,' he says, with a tight smile, 'but we're ticking along.'

That won't impress my father. I can't help but feel angry for Jason. He mentioned only this morning that the new software interface he's designed, and as good as sold to a major overseas client, has hit a major glitch. Having just two employees, and only one as skilled as he is, he said he'll need to get someone else on board if he's to have any hope of staying ahead of the game. With a major cashflow problem, though, that isn't going to be possible any time soon.

'I wish you'd reconsider approaching my father for a business loan, Jason,' I ventured, busying myself with the kids' sandwiches rather than meet his gaze, which I knew would be incredulous. Our last discussion on the subject had ended badly. Jason had flatly refused to entertain the idea. 'I mean, he wouldn't be doing you any favours, would he? It's not as if it's a personal loan. He'd be investing in the company, so…' I hurried on, hoping he would relent.

'*Investing?* Jesus…' Jason almost spat out his coffee. 'Have you any idea what you're asking? He'd be breathing down my neck 24/7, trying to control everything. Then there's Rachel and Mark to consider. They're not going to want to work for someone like him. No, I'm sorry; I can't do it, Karla. You know I can't. There's no way I'm going to be indebted further to him. I'd rather go bust than let Robert ruthless fucking Fenton anywhere near my company.'

'That'll help,' I sighed, as he dumped his mug in the dishwasher and headed for the door. Friday's being his busiest days, he'd already been stressed. I probably should have chosen my moment more wisely. I didn't dare mention that I'd already broached the idea with my father. I shouldn't have done that either – Jason's bound to see it as going behind his back – but what other choice do we have? Him burying his head in the sand isn't going to pay the mortgage. A mortgage my father has no knowledge of. When we got married, I'd been pregnant and Jason hadn't been earning much, so my father had paid outright for our house. He's so loaded, he would never miss the money, but the situation does little to alleviate Jason's frustration. There's no way on God's green earth he's ever going to go cap in hand to his father-in-law again, and my job as a personal assistant and officer manager doesn't pay enough to cover much more than the domestic bills. I never did manage to pick up my acting career. It's a horribly ageist industry, and I realised it was an unrealistic aspiration, particularly when, soon after having Holly, I fell pregnant with Josh.

I watch Jason now, noting the tense set of his jaw. He's definitely irked.

My father, seemingly oblivious and still standing in front of him like an immovable mountain, takes a leisurely swig of his whisky, and then, 'You should overhaul your finances, take a look at income versus expenditure.' He takes another swig and points his glass at him.

I'm only grateful smoking's banned. In times past, he would have been taking a puff of his cigar and blowing smoke all over Jason, infuriatingly.

'You could use my accountant,' my father goes on, regardless of Jason's now stony expression. 'This guy's on the ball. You'd be amazed at what he can chalk up to expenses. Why don't I give him a—'

'No.' Jason cuts him short. 'Thanks, Robert' – he forces a smile – 'but I'm happy with the accountant I have.'

My father arches an eyebrow dubiously, but doesn't comment, thank God. 'Well, if you change your mind…' Shaking his head in that despairing way he does, he reaches into his inside jacket pocket. 'Here, let me give you his card.'

Time to interrupt, I suspect. '*Dad*, it's supposed to be a birthday party, for goodness' sake, not a business meeting.' Relieving Jason of my wine glass, I shoot my father a warning glance. I've made him promise not to mention that I've spoken to him about a loan. I'll never forgive him if he does. 'Stop talking shop,' I urge him, 'and get over there and keep Mum company – or she'll be leaving tonight with her toy boy.'

Pushing the card back into his pocket, my father twizzles his neck, a scowl creasing his forehead as he glances to where Mum's improvising a slow jive to 'Under the Boardwalk' with the son of one of the band members, who's apparently their roadie. Wearing her black off-the-shoulder Bardot dress, Mum's a knockout. He's in ripped jeans and a T-shirt, but I have to admit, he looks pretty hot too.

Narrowing his eyes, my father looks Mum over, looks the young man up and down, and then… 'She should be so lucky,' he says, raising both eyebrows in wry amusement as he turns back to the bar, where he immediately homes in on the daughter of one of my mother's friends. He's leering at her, invading her space. I see the girl's discomfort, and feeling a rush of heat to my cheeks, I look away.

Jason has obviously noticed it too. 'Are you sure you're related to him?' he asks, his expression contemptuous as his gaze travels over my embarrassing father.

Unfortunately, yes. I sigh inwardly, so wishing my father wouldn't act this way. It doesn't seem to occur to him that he's doing it in front of me, his daughter. But then I've turned a blind eye to his deplorable behaviour before. Kept quiet about things I shouldn't have. One of which I will regret for the rest of my life. My sister would still be here to celebrate our mother's birthday with us, if I'd handled things differently.

Glancing again at my father, who's now draped an arm over the shoulders of the girl at the bar, I wonder if he thinks about Sarah with each passing milestone. About what he did, the lies he told. Does he see her when he looks at me? We weren't identical, physically or in nature. Sarah, with her freckles and rich auburn hair, was much prettier than me, I think. More extrovert, too – boisterous and confident where I was quiet and shy. He must be reminded of her though, surely, when he sees me? A sister robbed of her twin. If he does, he never shows it.

Shaking off the memory of the dark shadow that hangs over our family, I paint my smile in place and turn back to my husband. Sometimes, when the air needs to be lightened, I find the skills I learned at acting school come in quite handy. I'm not sure playing the role of peacekeeper helps my own frustrations, but it might keep my husband and father civil tonight.

'Ignore him,' I tell Jason. 'We're supposed to be enjoying ourselves.' Hooking an arm through his, I lead him away from the bar. I certainly don't want to be sitting miserably at the table, watching everyone else having fun, while my mind wanders sadly down memory lane – which it's bound to, now feelings of my rudely isolated childhood have surfaced.

We reach our table and I plonk my glass down, revving myself up to join the throng on the dance floor. Mum and the girls from the golf club are still 'getting their groove on'. The band member's son ought to be a little less keen, I can't help thinking. Mum might well take up his invitation to 'Come on Over to My Place', which is the current song the partygoers are throwing themselves into with gusto. The man has some moves.

'I think I'll sit this one out,' Jason says, with a half-hearted smile.

'Oh, Jase…' Disappointed, I sigh as he wearily sits down and parks his coke in front of him. I don't normally act like a teenager. With two children to look after, as well as working close to full-time, I'm too exhausted to walk up the stairs to bed half the time, but the music is contagious.

'Maybe later,' Jason says, reaching to ease the crick in the back of his neck. 'Sorry, I'm just a bit tired, I guess.'

He's bound to be. I feel a surge of sympathy. He'd slept badly, which is why he was in a mad rush and more stressed than usual this morning. I'm not surprised, with his business worries and bills we can't meet piling up. Nor am I surprised he's not in the mood for partying, but things haven't exactly been easy lately for either of us. It would do us both good to loosen up. Jason, though, his brow furrowed pensively as he runs a finger around the rim of his glass, doesn't look as if he's going to be moved.

'Right, well, I hope you don't mind if I do. A girl's gotta have a little fun, you know.' Wiggling my hips, which causes him to raise his eyebrows in amusement, I head off to join Mum and her toy boy on the dance floor.

Allowing the music to wash through me, I soon lose myself completely. For a short, blissful time, I am carefree, detached from the me who frets constantly, transported to a place where I don't have to worry about our financial problems, about my children, my father belittling their father. I concentrate everything on the dance.

It must be a good twenty minutes later when I feel Jason's arm slide around my waist, pulling me away from my slow dance with the toy boy and forcefully to him. I'd glanced across to him once or twice, but my father had joined him the last time I looked and the two were deep in conversation, so I'd decided to stay where I was. I'm sure my father won't break his promise not to say anything to Jason about our conversation, but still, seeing them together, I'd felt nervous butterflies take off in my stomach.

'I hope this is my dance?' Jason says, close to my ear, as he moves around in front of me. With the band now crooning 'Save the Last Dance for Me', and my husband looking classically tall, dark and extremely handsome in his blue linen-mix jacket and cream chinos, it might have been terribly romantic, but for the thunderous expression I see in Jason's eyes.

CHAPTER TWO

JASON

Driving away from the golf club, finally, Jason blew out a sigh of relief.

'Everything okay?' Karla asked, her tone slightly wary.

Jason nodded, though he supposed it was obvious he wasn't 'okay', since he'd more or less insisted they leave. He hadn't been able to help himself. After being cornered by her father, again, and then watching the guy his wife was dancing with appreciating the view – his eyes had been all over her – Jason had fervently wished he'd made a work-related excuse not to go to Diana's party. But it wouldn't have gone down well with Karla. Her old man, though, might possibly have mustered up a smidgeon of respect for him, putting business before pleasure – as he himself always had, he was fond of saying, which was bullshit. Robert Fenton might bang on about business acumen and work ethic, but when it came right down to it, the man had no ethics. Jason had learned that as soon as he'd met him. The man had made it clear he didn't consider him suitable husband material for his daughter from the outset. He'd wanted her to finish her acting degree at the Royal Academy of Dramatic Art – validated by King's College, London, no less – not throw her future away.

He'd wanted her to abort their child.

Jason still felt it now, the anger that had boiled up inside him twelve long years ago, when he'd overheard her 'caring' father trying to make her see sense. Fenton's study window had been open. Arriving at the front door, Jason had heard every word.

'I understand you want to be with him, princess. I know love isn't choosy,' he'd said, oozing understanding while backhandedly insulting him. 'I won't try to influence your decision, sweetheart, I wouldn't dream of it,' he'd continued, doing just that, 'but you can postpone motherhood for a while, surely? You're young. You have plenty of time to have children. Finish your degree before tying yourself down, hey? It's what you've always wanted. Meanwhile, you'll be giving Jason time to prove himself. He's hardly in a position to support—'

'He doesn't need to prove himself!' Karla had jumped aggressively to his defence. 'I love him, Dad. I'd marry him if he were penniless.'

'But love doesn't pay the bills, Karla.' Robert had sighed expansively. 'Does it?'

'We'll work it out! Jason has plans,' Karla had countered.

'To do what, exactly?' Robert's tone had been scornful, even then.

'Ecommerce,' Karla had announced, which had been news to Jason. His degree had been in computer science, and he had been toying with the idea of designing packages and websites for sports equipment manufacturers. Even then, though, he hadn't relished the idea of being stuck behind a desk. Being inclined to extreme sports, enjoying everything from scuba diving to paragliding, he had wondered whether there might be an opportunity in corporate events – preferably hands on, leading team-building exercises.

'I see. He'd have to be very savvy to make his mark in that industry.' Sounding unconvinced, Fenton had offered his invaluable opinion, he himself being an entrepreneurial genius who had grown his hugely successful plumbing and bespoke bathroom business from the basement of a dry cleaner's. After hitting £1m revenue six years after start-up, Robert Fenton, self-made man, was now worth an estimated £50m. Clearly, he thought his fortune afforded him dubious privileges – Jason still couldn't believe the man would make overtly sexual advances to a young woman at his own wife's birthday party.

'You're very quiet,' Karla observed, after several miles spent driving in silence.

'Yeah, sorry.' Jason ran a hand over the back of his neck. 'Just thinking.' He hadn't meant to give her the silent treatment, but the truth was, he was tired. Tired of her father preaching at him. Tired of Karla not seeming to want to listen whenever he tried to talk to her about how it made him feel: Useless, basically. Tired full stop.

'So what were you and Dad talking about?' Karla enquired, as they neared the house.

'Nothing much.' Jason tugged in a terse breath. 'He told me there was no shame in failure.' Turning into the drive, Jason killed the engine. 'I cut the conversation short at that point, for obvious reasons.' He'd been sorely tempted to tell the guy, once and for all, what he thought of him, and then suggest he piss off out of their lives.

'Oh God.' Karla winced. 'Did you argue with him again?'

Jason didn't much like the implication of that, as if he were somehow partly to blame for the fact that he and her father didn't get on. As far as Jason was concerned, he deserved a medal for being remotely civil to someone like Robert Fenton. 'Nope. I held my temper, you'll be pleased to know, excused myself to reclaim my wife from the arms of another man and then suggested we leave, which my wife was severely pissed off about. All in all, not a great night.'

Karla spilled out the passenger side as he shoved his door open and climbed out. 'Is that what that was all about?'

'What what was all about?' Jason headed for the front door.

'Your moodiness.' Karla followed him. 'You barely spoke to me on the dance floor, and you've hardly spoken a word since.'

'I couldn't hear myself speaking on the dance floor,' Jason pointed out, going in first and heading towards the lounge, where the TV was on way too loud. 'And I'm not "moody". I just have a lot on my mind.'

Correction: now he was feeling a definite mood coming on. 'Holly?' He swung his gaze in his daughter's direction. 'What are you doing up? It's way past your bedtime. And what in *God's* name are you watching?' He turned his attention to the TV, which the babysitter had paused, unfortunately freezing an opaque-eyed corpse rising from a post-mortem table.

Jesus. It would give Holly nightmares for weeks. Storming in, Jason shot the babysitter an unimpressed look as he relieved her of the TV remote.

'Dad!' Her expression indignant, Holly unfurled herself from the armchair as he hit the off button. 'I was watching that.'

'Bed,' Jason said, pointing the way.

Holly splayed her hands. 'But you and Mum let me watch Netflix.'

'Age-appropriate stuff, Holly. Which this is *not*.' Jason folded his arms and waited.

Clearly seeing there was no wiggle room, Holly folded her arms in turn and then, her face set in a petulant scowl, she flounced past him to the hall. 'This is so unfair,' she muttered, as she went. 'You're treating me like a child.'

Watching her disappear, wearing a fluffy leopard skin onesie and her feet adorned with furry white unicorn slippers, Jason shook his head in bemusement, and then turned angrily to their babysitter, who was looking sheepish. And so she should be.

'What the hell were you thinking, Megan?' he asked her, trying very hard not to lose his temper.

'She couldn't sleep,' Megan offered by way of explanation, as she scrambled up to stuff her feet into the pumps she'd kicked off and retrieve her phone from the coffee table.

Jason laughed, disbelieving. 'Excuse me?'

'It was just *The Haunting of Hill House*,' Megan said, with a discernible sigh, as if he was making a fuss about nothing. 'My little brother watches it.'

'I don't care what it was!' Jason lost it. '*She'll* be haunted. She probably won't sleep for weeks. There is *no way* you should have…' He stopped and took a breath. 'Look, forget it, Megan. It's probably best if you just go.'

Megan glanced down at her phone and guiltily back up. 'Do you still want me next week?' she ventured, as he pulled the money from his wallet and handed it to her. 'It's just that Karla said you might be going out.'

Dammit. He'd forgotten. It was supposed to be just the two of them, an attempt to make more time for each other, which they badly needed to do, since they seemed to be at loggerheads lately. He'd hoped they might be able to talk, properly. Not just about the suggestion that he approach her father for money – something, quite frankly, Jason would rather die before doing – but about the man constantly interfering in their lives. He needed her to understand, to at least acknowledge she was hearing him. He honestly wasn't sure how he would react if she mentioned the damn loan again. He'd have to think of something. Hopefully, Karla's mum could have the kids. Maybe he was overreacting, but he wouldn't call on Megan again in a hurry. Allowing his eleven-year-old daughter to watch horror stuff – whoever else watched it – simply wasn't on.

'We'll have to talk about it,' he said, his look hopefully telling her she shouldn't count on it. 'We'll let you know.'

Nodding, Megan shrank past him.

'I'll walk her home,' Karla said, from where she'd appeared at the lounge door.

'It's only half a street away,' Jason pointed out.

'Too far away at this time of night.' Karla gave him a look.

Jason felt a pang of guilt. She was right. He should have offered, but then he doubted Megan would have wanted him to walk her.

'Be careful,' he said, glad Karla had pulled her coat on over the short dress she was wearing.

'I'll be two minutes,' Karla said, her gaze lingering – and not in a good way. Was he missing something here, or was she looking at him as if he were in the wrong?

'I'll go check on Josh then,' he offered. And make sure he hasn't been allowed use of his iPad in bed, he thought despairingly, in which case he'd be busy gaming under the duvet and undoubtedly wouldn't be sleeping much tonight either.

'I've checked,' Karla called back from the hall. 'He's dead to the world.'

Well, that was something, Jason supposed. Josh was a light sleeper at the best of times, and he actually had been having nightmares lately, ever since the night Jason had been honest with Karla about the state of their finances. That was the first time she'd hinted he should go grovelling to her father to bail him out, and they'd ended up arguing. Josh had overheard – got it into his head they were going to split. He'd tried to reassure him, but the tension was still there. Kids picked up on it; Jason could testify to that. His adoptive parents staying together 'for the sake of their kids' had been a complete nightmare.

Sighing, more at his own ineptitude than anything else, he went upstairs anyway to look in on Holly, whose bad books he would definitely be in.

Yep, he was clearly in the doghouse where his daughter was concerned. She burrowed under the duvet when he knocked on her door and peered in.

'Night, Holly.' He walked across to her. 'We'll talk more tomorrow, yes?'

Nothing but a fidget from under the covers.

Jason waited a second, and then, 'Night, duvet,' he said, pressing a hand lightly on the bulge he guessed was her head, or else her elbow.

He doubted she would actually talk to him the next day – until approximately 10 a.m., that was. Saturday mornings were when he gave the kids their allowances. Holly wouldn't be slow reminding him about that. Smiling amusedly, Jason headed back downstairs, to find Karla coming through the front door.

'All settled?' she asked him.

'Settled,' Jason said, moving past her to pull the chain on the front door. 'If rather disgruntled.'

Karla didn't say anything, giving him that look he knew so well instead – the one that told him she wasn't happy with him.

Jason followed her to the kitchen. 'Am I to take it you're annoyed with me?' he asked, wondering whether it was the babysitter thing she was peeved about or just everything in general.

'A bit,' she said, watching him cautiously as he went to check that the back door was locked.

Finding everything secure, Jason came back. 'What, because I gave Megan her marching orders?' He knitted his brow. He hadn't, as such, not without discussing it with Karla first. But even if he had, surely she couldn't blame him?

'Not about that, no. You were a bit sharp with her, but she was well out of order.'

Jason nodded, glad they were on the same page about one thing, at least. But the financial situation they were in, which he accepted was squarely down to him and his business acumen – which was severely lacking, as pointed out repeatedly by her father – would remain a bone of contention between them. Jason had had no say in the matter when Robert had bought their house. He'd been grateful. He couldn't keep being grateful though. Nor could he contemplate asking him for further help.

He wanted him out of their lives as much as was possible, not further immersed in it.

Flicking the kettle on, Karla turned to face him, giving him a long, searching look.

'So?' he asked, guessing there was something she needed to get off her chest.

'I am a bit annoyed, to be honest,' she said, and hesitated.

'About the toy boy?' Jason eyed her questioningly. He wasn't sure it was him who should be defensive on that subject.

'No.' Karla shook her head. 'Although you did act like a bit of a dickhead.'

'Oh.' Noting her semi-amused look, Jason laughed uncertainly. 'Cheers for that.'

'Well, honestly,' Karla sighed, 'coming over all macho and proprietorial like that. I was only dancing with him.'

Jason nodded tightly. 'I could see that.'

'There was nothing to be jealous of, Jason.' Karla blinked at him, astonished. 'He was aged about two.'

More like twenty-two, thought Jason, though he didn't bother to correct her. And muscular and not bad-looking – not that he was any judge of what women found attractive in a man. The thing was, he had felt jealous, possibly because, with the problems hanging between them, he and Karla hadn't been near each other for weeks. The fact that he wasn't the provider he should be for his family was exacerbating his sense of self-doubt, he guessed. But then, Karla dancing with a man was one thing – she deserved to have a little fun, especially with him being as miserable as sin lately – but her dancing up close and personal with the man? The way he'd been holding her, it had got to him. Looking his wife over, he noted again how good she looked in the short, strappy dress she was wearing. She'd been more effervescent tonight. More like the woman he'd met, laughing easily, relaxed. Letting go on the dance floor was probably good therapy. They should get dressed up and go dancing more often. Except, he'd just as good as sacked the babysitter.

'So, it's not me cutting in to extract you from the guy's arms you're annoyed about then?'

Karla rolled her eyes; wide, sharp, sparkling-blue eyes, which looked even wider with make-up and mascara. When had she stopped wearing make-up around him? When had he stopped noticing?

'It's my father.' Karla dropped her gaze, her expression tentative when she looked back at him. 'This thing between you and him.'

Ah. 'Now there's a surprise.' Jason felt his hackles rising.

Karla pushed on. Jason really wished she wouldn't. 'I know he can seem aggressive and insensitive sometimes—'

'Seem?' Jason balked.

'Has it ever occurred to you that he might be genuinely trying to help?'

Jason quashed an immediate overwhelming anger. 'What, by telling me I'm a failure?' He stared at her, incredulous. 'Constantly reminding me I'm a disappointment? That helps, Karla. *Really*, it does.'

'Jason…' Dragging her long, tousled hair from her face, Karla sighed in despair. 'The only one who perceives you as a disappointment is *you.*'

'And you're not disappointed?' Jason asked, point-blank. 'Disillusioned with me, with your life, now we're struggling to make ends meet?'

'No, I am *not.* You need to stop doing this, Jason: blaming yourself, worrying yourself silly, refusing to reach out,' she went on imploringly. 'Yes, accepting help might mean that you're not Superman…'

Like Robert Fenton.

'…but that's not something to be ashamed of. There are people who are willing to help you. You have to let go of your own expectations of failure, though, and ask for that help.'

Your father's expectations, Karla. Jason didn't bother to say it.

Karla looked at the ceiling. 'Dad wants to help,' she said, looking back at him. 'Why won't you let him?'

She really hadn't been listening, had she? He did *not* want to go that route. How many ways could he say it? He might as well be talking to fresh air. Attempting to contain his agitation, Jason searched her face, and was perturbed by what he found there. Had she spoken to him? He narrowed his eyes, his heart dropping as he noted her sudden inability to meet his gaze. She bloody well *had*. Incredulous, he shook his head. She'd gone ahead and discussed her father loaning him money without *telling* him? In exchange for what? His soul?

So much for trust in a relationship. Smiling cynically, he quelled a rush of hurt and defeat. 'Why do you rate him so much?' He studied her, curious – genuinely so. He got that she was his daughter; that her affection for him might make her blind to his flaws, but she must realise some of what he was like.

'He's a bully, Karla,' he growled, his anger getting the better of him, despite his fervent desire not to allow Fenton to do this to him, 'a womaniser and a *fucking* sleazebag.'

Folding her arms, Karla blew out a sigh. She still wasn't looking at him.

'Don't tell me you haven't noticed his hands straying all over the place whenever an attractive woman comes near him?' Jason went on. He couldn't help himself. God only knew how her mother put up with him. If he were Diana, he'd take Fenton for what he could and be out of there like a shot.

'I might have known,' Karla mumbled eventually, her tone now considerably peeved. She pulled herself away from the kitchen counter.

'Known *what*?' Feeling more than a little pissed off himself, Jason watched her walk to the hall.

Karla stopped, whirling back around to face him. 'That *you* would do this. Anything to try to avoid the real problem.'

Jason squinted at her in disbelief. 'I'm not trying to *avoid* anything, Karla. Trust me, I *know* what the problem is: me, clearly.'

'Oh, this is ridiculous,' Karla snapped. 'I try to have a sensible discussion with you about our financial situation and you start acting like a temperamental adolescent.'

Well, that pretty much summed up her opinion of him. There really was no point talking to her, was there? Jason stared at her, disbelieving. 'Fine, whatever. Think what you like about me. What your father is, though – that's fact, Karla. Ask some of the women who work with him. Ask your mother's friend's daughter. He was standing so close to her at the bar, he was practically breathing down her neck.'

'I don't want to!' Karla glared at him, her eyes blazing. 'He's my dad, Jason! What do you want me to do?'

Jason had no idea how to answer that.

'There's nothing I can do, don't you see? But I *can* do something about this. About us.' She scanned his face, her expression now beseeching. 'Why do you do this every time I try to talk to you? I don't understand.'

Jason took a tight breath. 'No,' he said, more quietly, 'and I don't understand why you think I would want to be indebted to the man, Karla. Honestly, I don't.'

Karla said nothing for a second, and then, 'I can't do this, Jason. Not tonight. I'm tired.'

Me too, he thought. *Very*. He sighed heavily behind her as she walked away.

CHAPTER THREE

KARLA

I feel the dip in the bed as Jason climbs in beside me. Desperate to avoid further argument, or worse, obviously not speaking, I'm tempted for a second to feign sleep, but I think he probably knows me well enough to know when I'm faking it. But he doesn't know me, I remind myself. Not all of me. Not the secret I keep.

He's right about my father. Everything he says is true. What my father did to the person who was once closest to my heart opened my eyes to this fact years ago. The awfulness of it haunts my dreams. I wish I'd told. Made him tell. I was young, too young to realise the significance of Sarah losing consciousness when she fell, but my father would have. My mother would have. Had she not been by the bedside of my dying gran, she would have been there. She would have done something. I should have rung her at the hospital. The number had been there on my father's desk. I should have said something. *He* should have.

I wish I could go back. See my sister again, hold her. Tell her that, no matter how much we argued, I loved her. That I'm sorry.

I would have told, Sarah whispers in my head.

She would have. Had it been I who was unconscious, Sarah would have stood up to him. Always the more confident one, she wouldn't have allowed herself to be silenced by him. I was weak, but I gathered strength as I grew, began to see my father for who he really was: a man who would instil fear in a child. His own child. Who thrived on the fear he could instil in other people. I fought for my daughter. I fought for Jason. I will always fight for him, though he doesn't realise that's what I'm doing, trying to secure his future. Our future. I didn't fight for my sister.

Squeezing my eyes closed, I hear Jason breathing. He's lying still, flat on his back, staring at the ceiling. Sometimes he will throw an arm across his forehead and drift into a fitful sleep. More and more lately, he will toss and turn, pummel his pillow. When he does finally drift off, he will wake with a jolt, his own troubles haunting him. I so wish he would let me help him. Yes, it's my father's money, but it will be mine one day, after all. Surely putting some of it to good use now, when we need it, makes sense.

I feel him stir then, drawing a deep breath into his lungs, sighing it heavily out. 'Sorry,' he murmurs.

And my heart aches for him. It's not his fault. It's mine. I should have known better. Raising the subject of him taking a loan from my father was inevitably going to lead to us arguing. Jason wants to make things right, of course he does. But how can he? The bank has turned him down. We've already raised money against the house. He has no other options. He doesn't stand a chance of raising the capital he needs to clear his debts and get someone else with the relevant computer science experience on board.

'I know,' I answer. I want to tell him it's okay, but I can't. Things feel far from okay right now. I feel as if the sand is shifting beneath us. As if we're drifting apart, rather than reaching out to each other at a time when we need each other most. We've argued in the past. With two children, both now heading alarmingly quickly towards the dreaded teens, there's an argument on average once a day in this household. But we've never been distant like this.

Jason doesn't speak for a minute, and then I feel the mattress move under his weight as he turns towards me. 'I really am sorry,

Karla. I'll fix this,' he promises, sliding an arm around my midriff, easing me closer. 'I just have to work smarter.'

I place a hand over his. He has nice hands; strong, with long fingers and clean fingernails. I wish he wouldn't try to be so strong sometimes. Wouldn't try to do everything himself, as if he has something to prove. I smile ironically at the idiocy of that thought. Of course he has something to prove. In his eyes, he's in competition with my father. He always has been. But he needs to succeed on his own terms. To provide for his family. I get where that comes from, that it's some inbuilt caveman instinct – though I daren't say that to him – but it doesn't make me feel any better. I'm scared. Scared I might lose him. That my father will eventually win the battle he has waged against him.

'Bear with me,' he whispers, pressing a soft kiss to my shoulder, another to the base of my neck. His hand strays lower, moving around to trace the curve of my hip, and my heart flutters, like a frantic butterfly in my chest.

I can't do this. I try to quell a ridiculous rush of panic. Jason's a good lover – a tender, caring, adventurous lover. There's nothing I want more than the connection between us, the closeness it would bring, but now all I can see is my father. Worse, I can hear him, snoring as he lies by the side of my sister. And Sarah, I can't hear her at all. My panic rises, twisting my heart in my chest. Guilt, too; expanding unbearably in my throat. *You should have told.*

I couldn't. I catch Jason's hand as it slides over my pelvis, dipping below the waistline of my shorts. 'Don't, Jase,' I say, a shiver running through me. 'I'm so tired…'

I stop as he freezes, feel his frustration as he pulls away from me. Turning to him, I see the silhouette of his arm as he rakes a hand through his hair. 'Jason…' I reach for him, but he moves swiftly, rolling away from me. Sitting up, he plants his feet on the floor and yanks himself off the bed.

'Where are you going?' I pull myself up as he plucks his phone from the bedside table and heads for the door.

'Not far in my boxers,' Jason assures me, his tone short, as if he would quite like to go as far away as possible.

'Jason, don't,' I implore him. 'I want to,' I say weakly. Even I'm not convinced by the sound of my voice. 'It's just that I…'

'Don't,' Jason finishes as I trail off, a weary edge to his tone. 'I won't be long,' he adds, with a despairing sigh. 'I just need some space… to think.'

'Jase…' I climb out of bed, but he grabs his dressing gown from the door and heads out onto the landing. I don't want us to argue again – more than anything, I don't want that – but nor do I want to lie here worrying about him being upset, which he obviously is.

'Don't go down.' Reaching the landing as he gets to the top of the stairs, I implore him. 'Can't we just cuddle?'

Smiling wryly, Jason glances at me – and then quickly past me, towards Josh's room, as his bedroom door squeaks open.

'I heard a noise.' Josh emerges, blinking nervously, and my heart sinks. He looks more like a startled owl with his glasses off than he does with them on. My ten-year-old boy. He doesn't take after Jason, with his broad shoulders and toned chest. Josh is slightly pigeon-chested, if anything. Small for his age, he's an easy target for the bullies at school, and picked on by his more robust sister, who, though just a year older, is growing like a beansprout. He's vulnerable. Perhaps he is more like his father than I imagine. I don't want to upset his little world.

'It was just Daddy and me talking,' I reassure him – a small lie. 'Come on, let's tuck you back up and then I'll go and fetch you a drink.'

'I'll see to him,' Jason says. 'You're tired.' His eyes flick briefly in my direction, pointedly. 'Come on, mate. Let's go and make some hot chocolate. I'm not sleeping so well lately either.'

'Sucks, doesn't it?' Josh says, with a world-weary sigh, as he trudges towards him.

'And some.' Jason smiles, wrapping an arm chummily around his shoulders.

I watch them go down, my heart beating a worried pitter-patter in my chest. Why can't I oust the feeling that something is looming over us? Something that will blow our little family apart?

'Were you arguing?' I hear Josh ask his dad as they reach the hall, his voice small and uncertain. And my stomach clenches inside me as I realise my sensitive boy senses it too.

CHAPTER FOUR

JASON

'All good?' Jason asked, as Josh scrambled back into bed.

'Yup.' Josh nodded quickly, looking happier for the man talk they'd had while they'd made hot chocolate together. Jason hadn't lied to him. He told him that yes, he and Karla had been arguing when they should have been sleeping – about his working hours, he'd said, rather than their sex life, or lack of. He'd assured Josh that they would make up. He wasn't sure they would, however, unless he caved in and did what Karla wanted and went grovelling to her father. Josh had seemed placated. The kid was a worrier. Intuitive, too. The last thing Jason wanted was his son lying awake thinking he was going to be part of a single-parent family.

Jason reached to help as Josh managed to get his feet tied up in his duvet, then waited for him to wriggle down under it and tucked it up to his chin. 'Might be an idea to put the glasses away safely, mate.' He nodded towards where they were perched on the edge of his bedside locker. 'Don't want to end up knocking them off and breaking them, do you?'

'Oops.' Josh smiled and plucked them up. He'd hated the things up until a couple of years back. He'd previously had to wear an eye patch to correct his lazy eye, and he hadn't understood why the doctors couldn't correct his short-sightedness, so Jason could hardly blame him for being fed up. He was stuck with the glasses, but at least now he didn't feel so much like a 'goggle-eyed freak' – as some of his shitty little classmates at school had referred to him.

Thank God for Harry Potter, Jason thought, watching as his son inspected the glasses for smears before picking up his box, placing them carefully inside and returning them to his locker. 'Night, tiger,' he said, ruffling his hair as he snuggled back down again. 'Sleep tight.'

'Night, Dad.' His eyes growing heavy already – unsurprisingly, since it was now past one in the morning – Josh yawned widely. 'Kiss Mum for me,' he mumbled.

'I will,' Jason promised, glad that Josh wasn't shying away from showing affection. He doubted Karla would be very receptive to him kissing her though, since she'd turned him down flat when he'd tried to reach out to her. Maybe he should hone up his skills on the dance floor, he mused cynically.

Sighing, he went to check on Holly. After finding her sleeping like an angel, despite his fears that she wouldn't after viewing totally unsuitable horror crap, Jason paused on the landing, wondering how it was that things seemed to be falling so badly apart. Not just his business, but them, their marriage. Did Karla feel the same way? She'd given up her acting degree to be with him. He'd wanted to be with her, more than anything, but… what had happened to the friendship they'd shared? Their determination not to become like their parents: his constantly arguing, hers barely speaking? They'd promised themselves they would never fall into the same traps as other people, that they would stay invested in each other, never become indifferent or contemptuous of each other. They had planned to scale mountains together, literally, both preferring activity holidays to lying around on the beach. Granted, they couldn't have done that when the kids were younger, but they'd intended to once Holly and Josh were older. They'd both wanted the same things, to do the same things. He'd been training as a skydiving instructor when he'd first met her. Karla had wanted to skydive. She never had. She'd wanted to learn how to scuba dive, sail, windsurf and abseil. Yet, they'd made no plans, which was largely down to him, he reminded himself guiltily, because they couldn't afford to.

She'd planned to pick up her acting career, once Holly was born, and then Josh. She'd never done that either. Her father would have forked out her fees; her mother would have had the kids. Yet Karla had turned down both offers. She rarely left the kids with her mother, in fact, which Jason didn't quite get. Diana loved them, and Josh and Holly both adored her.

Jason loved the children. With his bones, he loved them. He hadn't done what he'd wanted to with his life either, but he would never have missed out on fatherhood in exchange for indulging his extreme sports hobbies and business dreams. As long as Josh and Holly were healthy and happy, he told himself it didn't matter, but suddenly, with the company looking more and more likely to fold, it did. Mostly because it was becoming glaringly obvious that Karla wasn't any happier with the way things were between them than he was. She was an incredible mother, always putting the kids' welfare above everything else. Her job was okay, she'd said. She was obviously good at it, getting promoted to office manager and personal assistant to the chief executive, which had brought in some much-needed extra income.

Fundamentally, though, she wasn't fulfilled. She was frustrated, mostly with him. And Jason had no idea what to do about it, other than what Karla had suggested: talk to her father about a business loan. He would probably choke before he got the words out.

Heading downstairs, Jason swallowed back the bitter taste in his mouth. What irked him most about Fenton was that the man held himself up as some paragon of perfection: successful business-man, captain of the golf club, still married to the same woman after thirty-five years. It was bollocks. Fenton was a womaniser and a bully. Someone who would suggest to his daughter that she abort the child he knew she wanted wasn't fit to be a father, as far as Jason was concerned. He'd never understood why he'd been so insistent she shouldn't go through with the pregnancy. Even if Fenton hated his guts, which he obviously did, why would he try so hard to pressurise Karla, a grown woman capable of making her own decisions?

Suppressing his thoughts around that, because it wrenched his gut every time he considered the fact that his own daughter might never have been born, he poured away the hot chocolate he'd promised Josh he would finish and headed to the lounge for something stronger. He shouldn't, but he needed it. He poured a large measure of whisky, knocked it back and poured another. He should have told Fenton what he thought of him when he'd cornered him at the party, and sod the consequences. He'd rather be seen as a failure than a 'self-made man' who thought his millions entitled him to treat people like shit.

Cautioning himself to make it his last, Jason topped up his glass and went back to the kitchen to turn off the lights. He picked up his phone and was heading back to the hall, supposing he should sleep in the spare room, rather than wake Karla, when he was reminded of an earlier text. From Mark, letting him know he'd made some headway on the software glitch they'd been struggling with.

Not there yet, the message read, *but think I might have identified the problem. Working on it over the w/end. Meanwhile, Tinder calls. What do you reckon?*

Jason opened the photo he'd attached, and very nearly choked as a woman who would definitely qualify as a blonde bombshell popped up – or rather, out. Wearing two wisps of lace, she was as underdressed as it was possible to get without being actually naked.

Jesus. Quashing down an undeniable stab of lust, Jason composed himself and texted back: *Ten. Definitely.*

Might be a bit late in tomorrow, Mark replied, including a thumbs-up emoji.

Lucky git. Has she got a sister? Jason typed.

I'll ask.

Jason smiled ruefully. *Fill me in tomorrow*, he texted back. *Cheers for your efforts, mate. I owe you.*

Muting his phone, Jason sighed in frustration and acknowledged he was possibly a touch jealous of his friend's freedom. What he'd give to be that carefree occasionally. Was he truly envious though? His marriage had hit a rough patch, but it could be fixed, given they could relearn how to communicate. He would quite like someone to be listening when he tried to. Judging by the profile photo, though, he doubted if the woman in it would be up for a night's not-so-scintillating verbal intercourse. She might well be a complete nutjob, and probably didn't look anything like her profile. Attempting to console himself with that thought, he climbed the stairs, swallowing back his guilt at even entertaining the idea as he bypassed his kids' bedroom doors.

CHAPTER FIVE

KARLA

As it's Saturday, and Jason was so late to bed after seeing to Josh, I left him to lie in for a while. Hearing him stirring now overhead, I flick the coffee machine on. I make it strong, thinking we could both use it after a stressful night.

'Holly, Josh!' I call, hoping to entice the kids to eat something rather than squabble about CBBC's *The Playlist* and which episode was cool.

'I'm not watching that one.' Holly's voice drifts huffily from the lounge. 'Alessia Cara's playlist is way cooler.'

'Well, go and watch it on your iPad then,' Josh retorts. 'I bagsied the TV first.'

'No, you did not, you little toad. I've been down here ages. *You're* not even dressed yet. And anyway, I'm older than you, so I get to choose.'

'No, you do not. *Geddoff!* Mum, tell her,' Josh cries. 'She's snatching the remote off me again.'

'Telltale,' Holly mutters. 'Weedy little—'

'Holly!' I cut her short, skidding into the hall. 'Kitchen. *Now!* Both of you.' Wearing my no-nonsense face, I wait while my little darlings slope past me – Josh sulkily, Holly mumbling and looking po-faced.

'Stop picking on him, Holly,' I say, behind her. 'Repeating what the other children say at school is not clever.'

'What? I'm not.' Holly splays her hands innocently. 'Anyway, he started it.'

'Did not,' Josh mumbles from the kitchen. '*You* did.'

'Enough, you two,' I warn them, 'or no more TV today and *no* allowance.' Sighing exasperatedly, I follow them, and almost collide with Jason, who's hurrying down the stairs, wearing his work clothes and carrying his laptop bag and mobile, I notice, surprised.

'You're going into the office?' I ask him, trying not to sound peeved that he's working again at the weekend. I feel awful about him sleeping in the spare room. And, judging by the shadows under his eyes, which seem to grow darker every day, he doesn't look as if he's actually slept much. I wish I hadn't turned him down in bed last night. That would have been so humiliating for him, given how dejected he must already have been feeling. He probably assumed I was upset about his refusal to approach my father for financial help. I was, but it was more the things he'd said about Dad that got to me. I just couldn't push them away this time – the memories, the empty loneliness I'd felt after Sarah had gone. My mother hardly ever talks about her, and my father… It's as if he's forgotten she existed. How does a person do that? Forget about their own flesh and blood?

I watched him as a child sometimes, willing him to look at me with some acknowledgement of the unbearable guilt I was carrying. He did occasionally, but his eyes always held a warning. As time went on, I stopped believing his threats that terrible things would happen if I told what had happened on the day Sarah died. But I never did tell, for my Mum's sake. I tried to bury it instead. As I watch my father through adult eyes, though, I wonder, does he realise the psychological damage he's caused me? I don't think I'll ever sleep soundly again. I will always have this knot of anger curled tight inside me. Sometimes, when something reminds me and my mind plays it over, I want to scream, to release the anger – and shut out Sarah's voice, which is always there, constantly whispering in my head. I never do. My acting skills allow me to switch off, to be somewhere else.

Last night at the party, I channelled my emotions into the dance, feeling blissfully carefree for a while. I still can't quite believe Jason was jealous of the toy boy, though I understand why he would have been, having been made to feel useless by my father. I feel bad for him. Yet, when we came home, I turned on him. Or that's how it must have seemed to Jason. I wish he would believe that my loyalties lie with him, that I believe in him. If only he could believe in himself. Yes, I want him to do something that goes against his principles, but only because accepting a loan from my father will allow his business to survive; allow us to move house eventually, and get him out of our lives.

Jason doesn't appear to have heard me speaking to him. Looking preoccupied, he dumps his computer bag and his mobile on the hall table and searches through his pockets. 'Haven't seen my wallet, have you?' he asks, a frown crossing his face.

'On the dressing table,' I supply. 'I found it in the bathroom this morning. You must have left it in there last night.'

'Oh, right. Cheers,' Jason says distractedly, and turns back to the stairs.

'Are you going into the office?' I ask him again, as he bounds up them.

'Yes, sorry,' Jason calls back. 'Mark's made some headway with the software problem. I'm hoping we'll be able to video link with the client later. Are you okay with that?'

'Yes, fine,' I assure him, hiding my disappointment and mentally crossing my fingers for him. 'You did say you would go to the park and play football with the kids, but I'm sure they won't mind me as a substitute.'

'*Damn!*' Jason turns at the top of the stairs. 'I forgot.' He shrugs guiltily. 'Do you mind?'

'No problem.' I smile. I'm determined to make sure Holly and Josh do stuff that doesn't involve looking at a screen: outdoor things, preferably – everything from planting a bulb and watching it grow to flying a kite. Jason will probably be glad to be off the hook. As the park backs onto Mum and Dad's house, I usually drop in whenever we go, and I know Jason would hate every minute.

'Apart from the fact that Mum can't play football,' Holly pipes up from the kitchen.

'Thanks for the vote of confidence, Holly.' I sigh and eye the ceiling. 'I was going to suggest we make an afternoon of it and go to Coffee and Cupcakes, but I'm not sure you deserve cupcakes now.'

'But she's brilliant in goal,' Holly adds hastily.

Shaking his head, Jason laughs. 'Good move, Holly,' he says. 'You're sure?' he asks me. Even from the foot of the stairs, I can see his dark, all-telling eyes are clouded with concern. I'm grateful that, after last night, he still cares. Glad he's still fighting.

'Of course. They are my children, for my sins.' Urging him on, I turn towards the kitchen, aiming to grab him a couple of cereal bars, since he won't have eaten. And then I step back as the landline rings.

'I've got it,' Jason shouts.

Hearing him saying hello to his sister on the phone in the bedroom, I head onwards, only to stop again as his mobile beeps atop the hall table. Mark calling with a progress report, I wonder. My gaze flicking to the stairs, I hesitate for a second and then pick it up to check his messages – and my stomach turns over. Too stunned even to breathe, I stare – confused, at first, and then disbelieving at what I glean is a profile photograph. A sexually explicit photograph: a near-naked, voluptuous woman with her breasts spilling out. On my husband's phone? I almost laugh at the absurdity of it, and then work to control the explosion of bewildered emotion inside me.

It's a mistake, I tell myself. Some random message sent by…
Who? Why? My mouth dry, I check the stairs again, and then brace myself to thumb up through the preceding messages.

Fill me in tomorrow, Jason's last text reads. *Cheers for your efforts, mate. I owe you.*

My hands trembling, my senses reeling, I scroll up to the next.

And my heart stops dead. *Lucky git. Has she got a sister?* Jason had asked.

My blood turns to ice as I realise he's actually *scored* her. Ten out of ten. Nausea churning my stomach, I squeeze my eyes closed. Dimly, I register Jason ending his phone call upstairs.

'I'll drop by next week,' he tells Hannah. 'Sorry I can't stop. I'm due in the office.'

Is he? I swallow back the parched lump in my throat. Is it really his office he's so eager to get to? Where he's been going all these weekends? Is it even his actual sister he's talking to?

It is. I heard him. 'Hi, Hannah,' he'd greeted her. They talk occasionally on the phone but don't see each other often enough. They drifted apart after the family split up. I'm reminded of the fact that Jason's childhood wasn't a good one. That his adoptive parents stayed together until being together became intolerable. That they were both unhappy, his mother desperately so, because his father cheated. My father cheats. Do *all* men fucking well cheat? My fury surfaces, white-hot, rising inside me.

Breathing in hard through my nostrils, I try to dampen it down. I have to stay in control. Inhaling another long breath, I exit his messages and place the phone back.

Attempting some level of outward calm, I fix my smile in place and, though the strength seems to have drained from my body, force myself on to the kitchen. He hasn't done anything, I try to reassure myself, other than indulge in immature chat. *Yet.* My sluggish heartbeat drums a prophetic warning in my chest. He's toying with the idea though, isn't he?

CHAPTER SIX

JASON

His lack of sleep catching up with him, Jason yawned widely, and then almost had heart failure as he realised he hadn't checked for traffic at a roundabout before entering. *Crap!* Pressing his foot down on the accelerator, he drove on, leaving a cacophony of horns blaring behind him. *Christ.* That was a close shave. Swiping a hand shakily over his face, he glimpsed in his rear-view mirror and breathed a considerable sigh of relief when he established that none of the drivers he'd cut up had pursued him. He wouldn't have blamed them.

He'd been miles away, running through the glitch in the computer software and hoping that Mark really had made some headway with it. It was the only way they stood a chance of keeping their key client, and thereby securing referrals. Selling stylish gym wear to fashion-conscious gym-goers, the client's company had revenues in excess of £6 million. Jason needed this deal, but, as much as the client loved the sales package they'd put together for him, he doubted he would maintain his turnover if the site crashed before his customers had hit purchase. He hadn't sounded majorly impressed when they'd last spoken.

Jason had to rescue this. Or else throw in the towel. Wouldn't his father-in-law just love that? No matter what he said, Fenton didn't want him to succeed, but Karla couldn't see it. He wanted him to go under, left with nothing to offer Karla. He wanted him out of her life, regardless of the fact that they'd now been married twelve years and had two children. Children they would never have had if Robert Fenton had had his way.

And whose lives they would ruin if they kept constantly arguing, he thought soberly. Jason had been there, a casualty of parents who chose to stay together for the sake of their children. They'd believed they were providing stability for him and his sister. The reality was that their tangible unhappiness created the very kind of atmosphere that was emotionally toxic to a child.

He needed to turn this around. Somehow. Opening his window, Jason took a gulp of bracing air and tried to concentrate on the road. He could have killed someone back there. Been seriously injured or killed himself, leaving his kids without a father. He pictured Holly, who, for all her sassy eleven-year-old attitude, still wouldn't go to bed without her Pink Cuddles Build-A-Bear; Josh, his skinny, sensitive son, who was trying to act 'cool', while quietly worrying his parents were going to split up, Jason swallowed back a tight lump in his throat.

Karla had been fine that morning, despite their argument last night. Everything was seemingly back to normal. She hadn't seemed to mind him coming in to work on a Saturday – again – even though his efforts were surely doomed to failure without the dubious help of her father. There'd been a troubled look in her eyes though, he'd noticed, when he'd leaned in to kiss her cheek before leaving.

'It is only the office you're going to?' she'd asked him.

Noting her expression, which had been almost guarded, Jason had looked at her, puzzled. 'Yes,' he'd answered. Where else would she think he was going? He'd long since abandoned playing rugby at the weekend, and he barely had time to see the inside of the gym. His life had been all work and not a lot of pleasure lately. 'Why?'

'No reason,' she'd said, searching his face. 'I just wondered.'

'I'll be there all day,' he'd assured her. 'I'll be back as soon as I can. Call me if you need me to pick anything up from the shops.'

Karla had nodded, her gaze flicking briefly down. Jason had felt his chest constrict for a second as she'd looked uncertainly back at him, something akin to fear flitting across her eyes. She'd dismissed it when he'd asked her if she was all right, mustering up a smile and saying she was fine. Jason hadn't been convinced. She was as worried as he was. Obviously she would be, with things the way they were.

Was he being selfish? He pondered it as he parked up and walked towards his office. He desperately didn't want to be beholden to her father; the thought of him being involved in his business, having access to his employees, one of whom was female, young and pretty – exactly the sort Robert Fenton liked to prey on – was intolerable. Then there was the small matter of his pride, which wouldn't allow it. Was he prepared to risk his marriage, though, his family's future, for the sake of his dignity? He had his kids to think about, their education, as did Karla. Didn't she have some say in this, when all was said and done?

Feeling conflicted, as he permanently seemed to lately, Jason let himself through the security door and headed for the main office rather than his own small office, where he found Mark already seated at his PC. Jason was surprised. He'd expected him to come in later, given that he'd hinted his hot date might be an all-nighter.

'How did it go?' he asked him, dropping his laptop on the desk facing Mark's and shrugging out of his jacket.

'Phenomenally.' Mark blinked blearily at his screen, one hand groping for the paracetamol to his side.

Jason smiled wryly as Mark popped two pills and reached for his mug of black coffee. 'That good, hey?'

'A ten, definitely,' Mark said with a wink, and then winced and washed his painkillers down. 'What's more, I have another date.'

'Better stock up on the pills then,' Jason suggested, eyeing his friend amusedly. He doubted whether it would actually get past two dates. Mark had been married once. It had lasted approximately a year, before he'd discovered his wife wasn't fully committed. This much he'd gleaned when he found her in bed with her ex-boyfriend. Mark had decided to play the field after that sobering experience. And he was obviously playing hard.

'I might need to. The little blue variety.' Mark yawned, leaning back in his chair and stretching wearily. 'The woman's insatiable. Sorry, mate – no sister, I'm afraid.'

'More's the pity.' Jason sighed, turned to plug in his laptop and then seated himself in front of it.

Mark eyed him thoughtfully for a second. He'd gathered Jason was having problems, here and at home, but was diplomatic enough not to comment. 'So,' he said, looking back to his screen, 'how did the mother-in-law's party go? Has the self-made man thawed yet?'

Jason's laugh was scornful. 'You must be joking. There's not a snowball in hell's chance of that happening. I "got his daughter pregnant", remember?'

'Twelve-odd years ago,' Mark reminded him. 'That's a long time to bear a grudge.'

'Yeah.' Jason was well aware of that. He doubted the man would warm to him, whatever he did. Turning his company around wouldn't do it. Robert Fenton's grudge went deeper, Jason was sure of it. It was more than him simply being protective of his daughter. Though if protective was what he was trying to be, it was laughable anyway, bearing in mind the man's proclivity to sexually harass women Karla's age and younger. He just wished he knew what the hell his problem was. Maybe he thought no man would ever be good enough for her. Jason definitely wasn't.

He sighed heavily. 'Sometimes, I wonder whether Karla does too,' he admitted. 'Bear a grudge, I mean. Being married to a loser wasn't quite what she had in mind when she walked down the aisle.'

She had been so optimistic, that day. Looking radiant, with her long blonde hair sweeping her bare shoulders, her eyes shining, she'd been positive they were doing the right thing. They were going to get married anyway, she'd told her mother. They were just doing it a little sooner than planned, for the sake of the baby. She'd been positive about their future together, determined that their home together would be a happy one, built on love. At twenty-two, and working part-time while completing his final year in computer science, Jason's income had been a pittance. He hadn't quite worked out how they were going to build this house of love. Enter Robert Fenton, the great benefactor. He'd never let Jason forget that they had a roof over their heads thanks to him. God help him if he found out he'd taken out a mortgage against it to shore up their finances. Karla falling pregnant with Josh not long after having Holly had put paid to her going back to RADA. She'd remained bubbly though, enthusiastic enough for both of them, still determined that they could get through whatever life threw at them, provided they loved each other.

Jason was pondering that when Mark asked, 'Do you still love her?' as if reading his mind.

'She's the mother of my children,' Jason answered. He'd never questioned his love for her. Lately, though, there seemed to be a hell of a lot more anger between them than affection.

'Because if you don't—'

'Shall we take a look at the software package?' Jason changed the subject.

'I'm just saying that if you're as miserable as your face has been telling me lately, maybe you should think about parenting your kids separately.'

So much for diplomacy. Jason was about to tell him the subject was closed when the office phone rang. *Saved by the bell*, he thought, twirling his chair around to answer it.

'Tara might not have a sister, but there are plenty of other women out there looking for what I imagine is lacking in your life,' Mark imparted, as Jason picked up the phone. 'Plenty of other dating apps, too, if you're looking for more than a quick hook-up.'

Unbelievable. Jason shook his head and pressed the phone to his ear. Just what mates were for: to offer you shite advice when your marriage hit a blip.

'Though, personally, I think that would do you the world of good,' Mark trundled on. 'A quick no-strings-attached—'

Jason held up a hand, his look hopefully telling Mark to zip it, as he realised who it was calling.

'Jason, Robert here,' Fenton said. 'Karla said you were working.'

'I am,' Jason confirmed, immediately agitated by the brusque tone.

'Right, well, I'll get straight to the point. Time is money, after all,' Fenton went on, predictably. 'I'm prepared to put a deal on the table.'

A… '*What?*' Jason laughed, incredulous at the man's gall.

'Don't be obtuse, Jason. It's not a good business attribute,' Fenton said, with his usual condescending sigh. 'A deal. A business loan, boy. You're haemorrhaging money currently and making nil profit. Come to my office, two o'clock on Monday, and we'll discuss terms.'

And those terms would be what, Jason wondered. Apart from the fifty per cent share in his business he fully expected Fenton would demand. Karla had clearly discussed it further with him. Once he'd left this morning, presumably, which pretty much summed up her confidence in him. 'Thanks,' he said, his throat tight, 'but I think I'd rather bleed to death.'

CHAPTER SEVEN

KARLA

I was hoping the children would be worn out after an hour spent kicking a football around the park. I should have known better. They're still bounding with energy while I'm flagging. We troop dutifully across the park to my parents' house for our regular Saturday visit, which Jason, understandably, prefers not to accompany us on, usually going off to the supermarket, or else to the office. I find Mum in the kitchen when I let myself in with my key. 'Trainers off, guys,' I instruct Holly and Josh, who need no encouraging. Having had the usual lecture about not treading mud onto the carpet, they're already halfway out of them in anticipation of *Star Wars: Episode II – Attack of the Clones* – the second prequel to the original *Star Wars* trilogy which is showing on Sky, Josh has reliably informed me – and Mum's home-made cake in front of the TV.

I head towards the kitchen as the children skid to the lounge. They're possibly already on a sugar high, I realise guiltily. I was a bit distracted in the park, not quite as 'brilliant in goal' as Holly claimed I was. My mind was on the photo I'd found on Jason's phone, his exchange of messages with Mark. Jason and Mark go back years, right back to their errant youth. I suppose I shouldn't be surprised that they swap boyish messages. I'm more surprised that Jason would comment chauvinistically about a woman's appearance. But then, women do that sort of thing all the time. The gossip about six-packs and who's met who online is rife in the administrative assistants' office at work. As I'm the office manager as well as personal assistant to the chief executive – to whom they imagine I might report back – there's usually a lull in the conversation whenever I go in, but not for long. I'm as up for the juicy details as the rest of them. That Jason hadn't immediately deleted the photograph though, and that he'd scored the undeniably beautiful woman, bothers me. If he'd replied 'not my type' or even 'nice', I might not feel so uneasy, but to have been so impressed, to have actually asked Mark if she had a sister…

I know it's just a turn of phrase, but I can't help thinking that Jason might be tempted elsewhere. That – with the problems between us and the many arguments lately – our marriage might be floundering along with his business. Might Jason be growing tired of the responsibility of having a family? We were so young when we married, after all. Is he fed up of being tied to one woman? A woman who's constantly nagging him and apparently not overjoyed at the prospect of having sex with him?

Icy trepidation prickles my skin, despite my repeated attempts to reassure myself. I so wish I hadn't looked at his messages. With things so unsettled between us, my suspicion seems to have gone into overdrive.

Checking the phone Jason had eventually rushed off without is safe in my bag, I push the kitchen door open and freeze as, out of nowhere, stark memories of my childhood assail me: sheet rain lashing against the window, my mother oblivious to me as she gazes at the windswept trees in the park beyond it. I see them: ethereal, solemn-faced funeral guests, whispering in hushed tones, warily watching my mother as she goes into the lounge. Following behind, I watch her carefully from where I hover uncertainly in the doorway. I see the look in her eyes as she locates my father, who's stoically circulating, despite his grief. My gaze travels between my parents, but I focus on my mother, trying to read the expression on her face, to find some comfort there. I see the confused incomprehension in her crystal-blue eyes, which fleetingly hardens to deep hatred. And I wonder, does she know? Has he told her that Sarah didn't move when she fell, but lay on the path like a porcelain doll?

'Karla!' My mother says delightedly, yanking me back to the here and now, to the smell of home cooking, which is supposed to be comforting, but somehow isn't today. 'How are things, my lovely?' She downs her baking tray, atop which sits her own-recipe cinnamon apple pie, reaches for the dish towel to dust off her hands and comes across to me.

'The same,' I say, with a wan smile. Mum knows that with Jason's business problems on top of the demands of two children, things are not all rosy at home.

She looks at me kindly and then pulls me into our ritual hug. I hang on to her for a second, wishing I could truly go back, to a time before the dark days, and make all the bad things go away.

'He's not managed to get things sorted out then?' she asks, scanning my eyes, her own peppered with concern as she eases away from me.

'No,' I admit, with a disconsolate shake of my head.

Mum nods, a small sympathetic nod, and turns to put the kettle on for a cure-all cup of tea. The way she is, always cooking and cleaning, you would imagine an older woman, a mumsy mum, living a life of dull domesticity. But Mum's not dull or dowdy, always dressing trendily but understatedly and never without a wisp of make-up – just enough to accentuate her high cheekbones and fine features. I'm not sure who I take after, but it's definitely not her, with her natural beauty and elegance. Why does my father cheat on her, I wonder, as I've often done over the years. How is it that she's always seemed so indifferent to the fact that he does?

'And he won't consider talking to your father?' Mum asks.

'No. He's adamant he won't take money from him.' I sigh and wander across to drop my bag on the table and take the weight off my feet. I'm tired. Unfit, obviously. I'm not used to running around, playing football. That's usually Jason's job.

'Oh dear.' Mum sighs in turn and joins me at the table with two mugs of tea. 'It's a self-esteem thing,' she imparts, pushing the biscuit barrel towards me. 'A man's ego is a delicate beast.'

Aware of that, and that I'd badly bruised Jason's last night, I smile sadly and help myself to a biscuit, reminding myself to watch the calories. After giving birth twice, I'm not likely to be able to compete with the perfectly sculpted woman on his phone. Piling on the pounds now, therefore, is possibly not a good idea.

'We'll each have to get ourselves a carefree toy boy,' Mum says, giving me a conspiratorial wink.

I smile half-heartedly. I wish now that I hadn't danced quite so enthusiastically with him. A nice mover, muscular and very well-packaged in a tight white T-shirt and jeans, his attributes would certainly score a ten. I think of the double standard regarding men ogling women and vice versa. Am I being too judgemental of Jason? Paranoid, because of the problems between us? He was jealous. He would hardly have cut in, looking most definitely put out, if he didn't care about me, would he?

But does he love me? Caring is not loving, and he doesn't often say that he does.

'Can I ask you something, Mum?' Furrowing my brow, I reach for my bag.

'As long as it's nothing technical,' Mum says, glancing uncertainly at the phone I pull out.

'It's not,' I assure her, and quickly check over my shoulder. I'd hate one of the children to wander in. 'We argued,' I explain, taking a breath, 'after the party.'

'Not about the toy boy?' Mum's expression is a cross between bemused and amused.

'No,' I say quickly, feeling defensive of Jason. 'Well, sort of. Jason was a bit miffed I was dancing with him, but that wasn't what we argued about.'

'I don't see why he'd be miffed,' Mum says, looking po-faced on my behalf. 'You're an attractive young woman. If he couldn't be bothered to dance with you, then he really shouldn't object to you dancing with someone else.'

'Dad had been on at him,' I say.

Mum's face straightens at that. 'Oh. I see,' she says. She's seen how Dad belittles him sometimes and has reprimanded him for it. She tries to make Jason feel welcome here, but sadly he doesn't. The way Dad treats him, I can't blame him.

'I broached the subject of him approaching Dad for a loan again when we got home,' I go on. 'Stupidly, so late at night. We had a few words, and… The long and short of it is, Jason tried to kiss and make up and I… Well, I just didn't feel like it.' I don't elaborate on why – that the things I try to forget had swamped me, thanks to my father's behaviour at the party, and then Jason reminding me of it, as if he'd needed to.

Mum reaches to squeeze my arm. 'Things are that bad between you then?' she says understandingly.

I nod, feeling close to tears. I'm not sure why I'm so upset. Jason's done nothing terrible really. Looking at a photograph of a woman sent to his phone is hardly evidence of infidelity, is it? He was just—

Window shopping? Sarah pipes up, offering her unwelcome thoughts on the subject.

'We had more words, obviously.' Ignoring her, I rush on. 'Josh heard us and woke up. Jason put him back to bed and then… he slept in the spare room.'

'Definitely not good then?' Mum says, her tone soft.

'No.' I sigh miserably. 'He seemed okay this morning. He was tired, but I thought things were okay between us. And then…'

Bracing myself, I turn my attention to Jason's phone and bring up his messages. 'I saw these.'

Mum takes the phone, glancing curiously from it to me as she realises it's Jason's. She takes a moment, scrolling through the messages, a myriad of expressions crossing her face as she appears to ponder. And then, 'It's just boys being boys, Karla,' she tells me soothingly. 'Just laddish banter.'

I'm relieved she thinks so, too, but... 'He's not a lad though, is he?' I point out, still unable to quiet the suspicion gnawing away at me. 'He's a married man with two children. He scored her, Mum,' I say bewilderedly, 'ten out of ten.'

'And?' Mum says, and waits for me to get to the point.

I glance down and back. 'I can't help thinking he might have sampled the goods, or soon will,' I admit, hot tears of humiliation and frustration finally spilling over.

CHAPTER EIGHT

ROBERT

Seeing Karla's car on the drive as he pulled up, Robert gathered his daughter was visiting. He did hope she wasn't going to give him grief regarding his attempts to talk some sense into her useless husband. She'd already reprimanded him at the party last night for 'talking business', telling him they were supposed to be enjoying themselves.

Diana had certainly been enjoying herself. He'd parted with his hard-earned cash, organising a lavish party with silver service and a live band, which had cost him a small fortune, and she was prancing about with some jumped-up little twerp a third her age on the dance floor, making a complete poppy-show of herself. Robert wondered why he'd bothered. He couldn't do a thing right in his wife's eyes. He'd never quite regained her trust after succumbing to his urges and taking what was obviously on offer from one of her friends, a monumentally stupid thing to do with Diana pregnant and their wedding plans already underway. Robert bitterly regretted the tacky affair, which had cost him dearly, financially as well as emotionally. Julie Ferguson had driven a hard bargain in exchange for her silence – one he'd had no choice but to meet, since she'd been in his employ. Thus his decision to include non-disclosure clauses in contracts in future. The last thing he'd needed, having just received his UK Business Entrepreneur of the Year Award, was for her to run off tittle-tattling to the tabloids, as these women do. Diana's father, town mayor and chairman of the golf club, ergo extremely influential, would not have been impressed.

He would definitely have been unimpressed by the events that followed months after the wedding. No amount of money could bury that unfortunate incident, once it had landed squarely on their doorstep. Fortunately, as their wedding had been featured in several glossy magazines, with a follow-up featuring her as a glowing expectant mother in *Stylish Homes*, Diana had seen the sense of keeping the incident to themselves. Under their own roof, as it were. The timing around her pregnancy had been opportune. Robert had counted his blessings in finding someone as pragmatic and forward-thinking as Diana, who realised that some things were best kept secret in order to preserve his business reputation – and their luxurious lifestyle.

She'd been cool towards him initially, which Robert had understood. Finding herself with two little ones to care for couldn't have been easy, but they'd jogged along. She'd withdrawn from him completely since the episode in their lives he didn't care to dwell on, but which Diana, with her barbed looks and long silences, would never let him forget. She had never openly stated she didn't believe his side of the story – that Sarah had stumbled and fallen that day in the garden – but Robert knew in his heart that she didn't.

He'd felt bad lying to her, but he'd had no choice but to deny everything, particularly being in the girls' room that night, inebriated to the point of unconscious. How was he supposed not to? The police would have been involved. He would have been ruined. They might even have taken Karla away. Karla… He regretted, too, that he'd had to convince her she might end up on her own in care. If she loved them and wanted to stay with them, she couldn't tell tales on him, he'd warned her. It hadn't been his proudest moment.

A deep sadness washed over him as he recalled the watchful, suspicious gaze he'd often seen in Karla's eyes thereafter. Robert tried to consign it to history as he let himself through the front door, out of the rain. He supposed Karla would take the opportunity while she was here to accuse him of being ruthless and controlling where Jason was concerned. He was ruthless, to a degree. He'd had to be. Building a multimillion-pound company up from scratch hadn't allowed him the luxury of indulging his emotions. As for indulging other people's, that was definitely a recipe for failure. Robert simply didn't have the patience for sob stories. He preferred to focus on the practical and move forwards, unlike Jason, who seemed content to idle in the slow lane. The man hadn't got a business bone in his body. God only knew what Karla had seen in him, why she'd become involved with him. Robert dearly wished that she hadn't. He'd tried everything to convince her not to go through with the wedding. Nothing had been able to dissuade her.

Robert hadn't doubted Karla had fancied herself in love with him. He'd very much doubted Jason's motives in marrying her, however. The more he'd tried to talk sense into him, pointing out the idiocy of tying himself down at such a young age, the more he'd appeared to dig his heels in. He'd been determined to go against Robert's wishes. More than determined. A man who's successful in business never mistakes a challenge in another man's eyes.

Assuming it was Karla's family fortune he was attracted to, Robert had made a fundamental mistake, one he'd kicked himself for every day since. He could see the cocky bastard now, his dark eyes narrowed quizzically as he'd handed him the cheque, for a substantial sum of money – his, if he did the sensible thing regarding his own future and got out of Karla's life.

Studying the cheque, Jason had shaken his head and emitted a scornful laugh, as if money meant nothing, and then, 'Go fuck yourself,' he'd said, locking eyes full of contempt levelly on his.

Robert had hardly been able to contain his fury as the impudent bastard calmly tore the cheque up in front of him and tossed it at his feet. He'd sealed his daughter's fate that day. Short of telling her the truth, which would mean losing all that was dear to him, nothing could persuade her not to marry this man who would ruin her life.

So much for his principles: Jason hadn't quibbled too much when Robert paid for their house, rather than allow his daughter and future grandchild to live in a shoebox of a flat on some common estate while her husband fucked about, attempting to start up a company with nil experience. Having spent his own childhood in such a place, Robert had shuddered at that thought. Karla had talked Jason round, Robert suspected. It was a wedding gift, after all, and being the penniless prat that he was, Jason had been in no position to turn it down.

Robert wasn't completely heartless where Jason was concerned; he did have a begrudging respect for his efforts to keep his floundering business afloat without adequate financial backing. He'd agreed to offer him a business loan when Karla had asked. She'd clearly found out what a stubborn son of a bitch he was, when, yet again, he dug his heels in. He would change his mind. Jason Connolly *would* realise he had no choice but to swallow his pride and come to him, and then they would get to the real deal on the table: Robert's silence in exchange for Jason's. It was that simple. If he truly cared about Karla, Jason would realise the truth could never come out and, finally, he would walk away. He could take the money Robert was prepared to offer him to soften the blow, or he could leave it. That was up to him.

Glancing into the lounge, he noted that Holly and Josh were superglued to some alien thing on the TV. He wasn't sure it was suitable viewing for an eleven and ten-year-old, but it was more than he dared do to question Karla's parenting skills. She would jump down his throat in an instant.

She'd been emotionally delicate after Sarah's death, alternating between withdrawal and raging grief in the months afterwards. Robert had been frightened for a while that she might tell the secret he'd made her promise to keep. She'd finally come to her senses when he'd pointed out that it wasn't just her world that had been torn apart. His had too. Her mother's had. Diana wasn't coping with any of it because of her inability to move on, he'd explained to her carefully. *Did she want to lose her mother too?*

They hadn't been as close since then, something that saddened Robert greatly. He'd hoped he might have more time to repair the damage between them, once she qualified at RADA. But then along came Jason Connolly, creating yet more complications. He would be gone soon. Robert consoled himself with that thought.

Deciding to leave greeting his grandchildren until he had their full attention, he shrugged out of his coat, hung it up and carried on towards the kitchen, from wherein wafted the smell of baking. Did the woman ever stop cooking? Robert was sure Diana had developed some sort of obsessive–compulsive disorder. If she wasn't cooking, she was cleaning. It had started just before the funeral, and she hadn't let up since. The only time she stopped being the world's most conscientious housewife – she didn't like being called that, so Robert tried to remember to avoid it – was when she slept. Back then, he'd lived in fear that she might leave him, not sure what he would do without her. He was confident she wouldn't leave him now. She was still a fine-looking woman, but it was a sad fact of life that women of a certain age simply didn't have any options.

He was about to walk into the kitchen, but then he paused, his brow knitted in consternation. Was Karla crying in there? He was sure she was. Because of Connolly? Had to be. What had that bastard done to her? About to march in and demand to know, Robert stopped himself short.

'But why would he keep a photo of a semi-clad woman on his phone?' he heard Karla ask tearfully. 'Why didn't he delete it?

CHAPTER NINE

KARLA

I can't believe that my father, the very last person I want to know about this, would walk into the kitchen at the precise second I'm crying my eyes out. Aware that my father hasn't rated Jason since the day he discovered he'd 'blighted' my life, getting me pregnant – which was nothing to do with me, of course – I feel as if I've just handed him the dynamite with which to blow our marriage apart. He's bound to say something to Jason about this, if only to wind him up. *God, what have I done?*

Mum reaches across the table for my hand as I exhale a deep breath, trying to hold back the tears. 'His friend sent it to him,' she reminds me firmly. 'It's not like he's been browsing these sites himself, for goodness' sake. Don't go rushing in, accusing him of anything without the facts, Karla. You'll only end up arguing again.'

'You've been arguing?' my father asks, arching an eyebrow questioningly as he looks at me, and then down to Jason's phone on the table, on which is the bloody photograph. I dearly wish I hadn't said anything to Mum.

'About my offering to help him out financially, presumably, before his business goes under?' My father looks back at me, unimpressed.

'No,' I lie, in defence of my husband, and then backtrack. 'Not that, exactly. Jason's been worrying. Obviously, he has.' *Not least about what you might want in exchange for this financial help*, I don't say. 'And when we got back from Mum's birthday party, we found the babysitter had allowed Holly to watch unsuitable stuff on Netflix, and... Oh, I don't know.' I sigh, growing agitated and weary with it all – Dad's tiresome crusade to prove Jason isn't 'good enough' for me; Jason's flat refusal to accept the help he clearly needs. This. I would never have spoken to Mum if I'd known my father was right outside the door. I shouldn't have. I should have spoken to Jason first. I should never have gone behind his back and talked to my father about offering him a loan.

But then, Jason's decisions affect my future too, and the children's futures, I'd reasoned. I've supported Jason every step of the way while he's been trying to build up his company, juggling the children and my job. I can't work any harder. And, yes, I pulled away from him in bed last night, but only because I was upset and confused. I love Jason. I used to feel that I'd lost the other half of me. I found it in Jason. Found myself. I've never really gone for all that 'he completes me' stuff, but the truth is, Jason made me whole again. My father treated him contemptibly from the moment he met him, determined I shouldn't marry him. Many other men would have been frightened off – or even paid off; I wouldn't put my father above that. They would have probably thought they'd had a narrow escape. It wasn't just my unplanned pregnancy, after all. It was Jason's, too. His future to consider. Jason had considered. He was equally determined to stay. He loved me, he said. There was nothing my father could ever say or do to change that. He wasn't going anywhere. Jason gave *me* the confidence to stand firm. Perhaps I could have without him. But I was stronger with him. Our love is stronger than this. I can't make myself believe he's cheated on me. He wouldn't. We haven't struggled for twelve years, through thick and thin, and made two beautiful children together, for Jason to throw it all away. He loves his kids without question. He *wouldn't.*

'It was my fault,' I say to Mum, determined now to end the subject and not give my father any more ammunition. 'I shouldn't have brought the subject up at that time of night. I'm just too tired to think straight lately.'

'Exhausted, I shouldn't wonder, what with working almost full-time and two children to look after,' my father says pointedly. 'You'd think, with a wife and children he can barely support, he would have put his pride aside by now.' Shaking his head, he picks up the phone and scrolls through it before I can stop him.

'Dad!' Jumping to my feet, I attempt to take it back. This has nothing to do with him. If he dares mention it…

'Give it back, Robert.' Mum gives him a warning glance. 'It's just a misunderstanding. It doesn't need you interfering.'

My father's expression is scathing as he sweeps his eyes over her. He's not happy being told what to do, having his authority questioned. His employees are loyal because he pays them to be, but none of them ever dare to confront him.

'Do you honestly believe Jason has been browsing these sites, Karla?' Mum turns back to me. 'That he's contemplating doing so?'

'No,' I say, after a second, though part of me still isn't sure.

'Well, there you go then.' Mum glances again at my father, who finally places the phone back on the table. 'Speak to him when he gets back. You'll no doubt find he's full of apologies and devastated that you're upset. Go home, get the children to bed early, crack open a bottle, and cuddle up in front of a film together. And steer clear of anything emotive. You're both too exhausted to see things objectively.'

She's right. I'm getting things out of proportion. I'm so busy trying to avert a crisis, I'm creating one. I drag my hair back from my face. It's a bedraggled mess, desperately in need of a cut and nothing like the soft, glossy curls of the woman I have imagined I'm competing with.

'In fact, why don't you let Holly and Josh stay over?' Mum suggests, getting up to collect the mugs. 'It will give you two some time together.'

'No!' I say quickly, grabbing the phone and my bag, ready to herd the kids up.

Her back to me, Mum stiffens visibly. I've hurt her feelings, but she knows I won't let them stay over. She knows why, but she never speaks about it. It's like it never happened. But it *did*.

My father turns away as I look at him, avoiding eye contact. I don't need to wonder why.

'I'll go and drag them away from the TV. Maybe another time, Mum,' I say brightly. *When Dad's away on one of his business trips*, I don't add.

She turns from the dishwasher, nods and smiles, but there's a sadness in her eyes. How could there not be?

Going into the lounge, I maintain my false cheery demeanour. 'Come on, you two,' I say, clapping my hands to get their attention. 'Time to go. Dad will be back soon.'

'Aw, *Mum…*' Josh looks around from where he's lying on his tummy in front of the TV. 'It's only halfway through.'

'It's recorded,' I remind him, my attention going to Holly, who's curled up in the armchair, riveted to the screen, despite having taunted Josh on the way here, telling him *Star Wars* was for little kids. 'If you both behave and get your skates on, we'll stop off for takeaway on the way.' I'm possibly overdoing the treats today, but cooking for four is not on my agenda tonight. A romantic meal for two and making love with my husband, however, definitely are.

'Yay!' Holly whoops, unfurling herself from the chair in a flash. 'Pizza,' she plumps for. 'Triple pepperoni and cheese, stuffed crust.'

'Epic meat feast.' Josh scrambles up, the film forgotten in favour of his belly.

'I bagsied first,' says Holly.

'You picked last time,' Josh moans. 'It's my turn.'

'No, it's not. Dad picked last time,' Holly informs him. 'And anyway, I'm older than you, so I get to choose.'

'We'll have half and half.' I offer them a compromise, averting the inevitable squabbling as I grab up Josh's abandoned sweater.

Mum comes in behind me to pull the children into a hug. 'Bye, you two. Be good for your mum.' She kisses them in turn, and I feel guilty, yet again. I wish I could let my guard down and let them stay over – I know Mum would love it – but I can't.

I'm reminded why as Dad appears, heading straight for the whisky bottle.

I watch him fill a large tumbler, take a sip and top it up, and my stomach immediately recoils. He'll have several more. If he goes out to his club, several more when he comes back. The bedroom stank of whisky that night. He stank of whisky. Closing my eyes, I see him reeling and stumbling. He wouldn't listen when I tried to tell him Sarah wasn't breathing properly. Beyond a certain point, he couldn't even hear me. The smell of whisky was still there in the morning. No matter what he said, no matter what fictional story I corroborated, Mum must have known.

Downing his glass, my father watches Josh head towards the hall. 'Don't I get a hug?' he asks him, and Josh immediately turns back to launch himself into his arms. 'Bye, trooper.' Squeezing him hard, Dad ruffles his hair before letting him go.

'Bye, Grandad.' Josh waves behind him as he scoots off to retrieve his trainers.

'Holly?' Dad glances after her.

'Come on, Holly. Chop-chop.' I allow my father a brief hug with Holly and then catch her by the arm and steer her to the door. 'I want to get back in plenty of time to cook your dad something special tonight.' I'm toying with the idea of wearing something special, too. The red dress I wore for our anniversary weekend in Paris, possibly. Jason said I looked sensational in it, adding that he couldn't wait to get me out of it. I smile as I remember how mutual urgency overtook us and the location of our lovemaking dictated I keep the dress on.

'Why?' asks Josh, peering up through his Harry Potter specs from where he's sitting cross-legged on the hall floor. Clearly, he's figured out that stuffing his feet into trainers without unlacing them is not conducive to getting them on any quicker.

'Because he's been working very hard,' I supply, shooting my father, who's followed me out, a pointed look over my shoulder.

Mum sees us to the door, where I pause to give her a firm hug. 'See you next week,' I say, smiling and then kissing her cheek.

'Bye, sweetheart,' my father says behind me.

'Bye,' I answer. I know he'll be looking disappointed he doesn't get a hug too. I don't look back.

CHAPTER TEN

JASON

Great! Jason groaned inwardly. First, he rings him – on a Saturday – not asking, but demanding he go to his office. Then he turns up at his house. The man was bloody well haunting him. As he looked at Robert's car, parked in front of his home, Jason wondered whether to turn around and go back to his office, particularly as Fenton had had the gall to block his drive. No doubt there was a not-so-subtle message therein. That being that he was entitled to park where he liked, since he'd paid for the house. *Prick.*

About to park behind the car, a gleaming Mercedes-Benz S-Class Coupe, which would have cost upwards of a hundred grand, Jason reversed sharply, pulling around to park in front of it instead. He was being juvenile, but he was sick to his back teeth of standing in the great Robert Fenton's shadow. Would the man not just stay out of their lives? It was the weekend. Could they never be free of him? Granted, Jason wasn't where he should be – at home with his family – but he would quite like to be now, and that picture most definitely didn't include his sodding father-in-law.

So, what was he doing here? *Stupid question.* After climbing out of his car, Jason slammed the door and headed past Fenton's statement car and along the drive he hadn't been allowed access to. He was obviously in there trying to influence Karla, just like he'd tried so hard to persuade her not to marry him. Jason felt the same repulsion he'd felt back then, when he'd overheard him asking her if she couldn't have found someone more suitable to give her virginity to. He'd been sick to his soul, listening to him trying to manipulate her, coercing her, as he did to so many people: staff too scared to stand up to him; young women who he *sexually harassed*, for Christ's sake. And Karla knew damn well he did. She'd seen him last night with her own eyes. Yet still she refused to discuss it whenever Jason tried to point out he was *not* the kind of man he wanted dealings with of any sort, let alone in his kids' lives. Why the hell had she let him just waltz in tonight? Jason supposed she couldn't have texted him to warn him he was here, since he'd left his phone at home, but surely she must realise that her father was the last person he wanted to see after their argument about him when they'd arrived home from the party? They'd slept in separate rooms. They'd argued about him most of their married life. How plain could Jason make it that he did not *want* him here?

Shoving his key into the lock, he laughed cynically as realisation dawned. He really was being dense, wasn't he? Karla had obviously invited him. Hadn't she approached her father regarding a business loan in the first place, forgetting to mention that she'd done so? Robert must have rung her, telling her he'd refused his 'invitation' to meet at his office, and so Karla had arranged for them to have a nice cosy conversation here. In front of her. And the kids.

Not happening, Karla. No bloody way. Jason resisted slamming the front door, dumped his laptop on the hall table, yanked off his jacket and tried to quash his immense agitation. Holly and Josh were already on to the fact that things were not great between him and Karla. He wasn't going to lose it in front of them. Wouldn't Fenton just love that? It would present him with the perfect opportunity to point out how uncaring of his family he was.

He guessed his anger was pretty apparent, however, by Karla's nervous expression as she stepped from the lounge into the hall.

'Dad's here,' she said, her eyes flitting back to the lounge door.

'Really?' Jason looked at her in mock surprise. 'I would never have known from the *fucking* great status symbol blocking the drive outside.'

'*Jason.*' Karla glanced quickly towards the stairs.

Guessing the kids were up there, Jason tugged in a tight breath and reminded himself to watch his language. 'Are they in bed?' he asked, glancing up after her and then checking his watch.

'They have an hour to read before lights off,' Karla said, reaching to ease the lounge door to. 'Can we talk?' she asked him.

'I don't know, Karla.' Jason looked back at her, his jaw tensing. 'Can we?'

Looking as weary as he felt, Karla sighed heavily and turned towards the kitchen.

Jason followed. He supposed the fact that she wanted to prepare him before pushing him into the lion's den was at least something. She should know, though, that whatever forecasts of doom her loving father had tried to influence her with, he wasn't going to go for it. He would rather walk out now than keep arguing with Karla over this. Which would, of course, be giving Fenton exactly what he wanted. How would the man feel if he actually did that? Jason couldn't help but wonder. Having fought so hard to get him out of Karla's life, he had no doubt he would revel in his victory, but would he have any remorse, any sense of shame at all, that he might have done it at the cost of his daughter's happiness, his grandchildren's? Jason didn't think so. Robert Fenton didn't care whose emotions he trampled on to get what he wanted. He had one aim in life, and that was to win at whatever cost.

Karla waited for him to close the kitchen door, and then, 'I didn't know he was coming,' she said quickly.

'Yeah, right.' Emitting a scornful laugh, Jason shook his head.

'Jason, I didn't.' Karla's voice bordered on desperate.

'Right, so' – Jason glanced back at her, unconvinced – 'he just dropped by for a cosy chat and a cup of tea with his daughter?

In which case, I can go up and take a shower and leave you two to it, can I?'

Sighing, Karla lowered her gaze and pressed her fingers hard to her forehead. 'He was hoping to have a word with you, but—'

'No, Karla,' Jason stated categorically. He wasn't about to go through it all again – the reasons he would never consider accepting any proposition her father had to offer. He'd already said it, time and time again. Even in the wildest scenario – that the man wouldn't try to control their lives – Jason needed to be the one to provide for his family. If his reasons weren't good enough for Karla, then… He didn't know what then, but he'd had enough of this.

'Jason, stop,' Karla said, as he turned back to the door. 'Talk to me, please.'

'About what?' Jason faced her, his temper rising, despite his best efforts not to let it. 'What do you want me to say that hasn't already been said, especially with *him* sitting on the other side of that wall?' He nodded angrily towards the lounge. 'The answer is no, Karla. I can't do it. Could you please just *accept* that and ask him to—'

'Right. Fine,' Karla cut across him. 'Don't then.' She held her hands up, as if in resignation. 'I understand. You don't think I do, but I do. We'll manage on my wage if we have to.'

That hit home. There was no way they would manage for long on Karla's income alone, not now they'd taken out a mortgage on the house. Glancing down, Jason drew in a long breath. 'It won't come to that, Karla,' he said, his gut tightening as he reminded himself he would not only be jobless if his company went under, but also up to his eyes in debt. Karla had a trust fund, due to her when she was forty – Fenton had made sure she wouldn't see a penny before then – but how could Jason ever justify forcing her to use that money to pay their way because of his pride?

'It might well,' Karla reminded him soberly. 'And I'll stand by you, you know I will. I always have. But on one condition, Jason.'

Wondering where this might be leading, Jason looked curiously back at her.

'You have to stop this ludicrous battle of wills with my father,' Karla announced.

'I have to?' Jason laughed, amazed.

'Yes, you,' Karla said forcefully. 'He is what he is – I don't need to be constantly reminded of that. But, whatever he is, he's the only person you're likely to get the financial help you need from. If you won't accept that help, then you have to sell the business. It's either that or end up in the bankruptcy court, and then you really will have messed up our future.'

'I see.' Nodding slowly, Jason digested. *Great move, Karla.* So, it's either give up and sell up or sell my soul to your father?'

'Yes.' Karla held his gaze. 'You're giving him exactly what he wants by refusing. He won't need to work at destroying our marriage if we go on like this. We're doing it for him by arguing all the time. Can't you see?' She searched his face, her expression imploring. 'Because if you can't, our children can. They're aware of what's going on. You must know they are. Can you not just stop this? Accept defeat? If not for me, then for them?'

Feeling that like a low body blow, Jason drew in a long breath. 'Right,' he said, breathing out slowly. 'Message understood.' Or rather ultimatum, one undoubtedly suggested by her delightful father. 'Do you mind if I go, now you've delivered it?'

'Oh, I give up. Just… do what you like. You probably will anyway.' Looking him over disappointedly, Karla turned away, going across to the oven to pull it open and start dragging out dishes.

Which meant what? Exasperated, Jason watched as she carried the dishes across to the work surface. Banging them down, she retrieved the tin foil from the drawer underneath and set about covering them.

His gaze went to the dining table at the far end of the kitchen, which was set for two, he noticed, and with two candles which had obviously been recently snuffed out, judging by the smell of candle wax and smoke. He looked back to Karla. She was wearing make-up, or had been. She was wiping most of it from her face now, along with her tears. She was also wearing the dress he loved her in. A clingy, short red dress. She'd worn it in Paris last year. It had been the first romantic break they'd had in a very long time, when his sister, Hannah, had offered to have the kids so they could do something special for their anniversary. Fitting in all the right places and showing off her long legs to maximum advantage, the dress had turned him on. It had turned the waiter who was serving them on. Karla had looked hot that night. Jason had been desperate to get her out of the restaurant, back to the hotel and out of the dress to make slow, sensual love to her. His plans hadn't quite worked out.

They'd strolled along the Promenade Plantée, which had been bursting with cherry trees, wildflowers and spring aromas. They'd wanted to take in the alternative views of Paris: tucked-away rooftops and balconies. They'd smelled the flowers, but they hadn't actually enjoyed much of the views. Karla had kept the dress on while they'd made love with the lust-fuelled urgency that doing it al fresco brings.

She was wearing the dress tonight for him. She'd got the kids up to bed early and had been cooking a special meal for him. She hadn't known her father was coming.

Jason felt like the worst kind of hypocrite ever, assuring himself he cared more about her than her phony father ever could, that he was taking a belligerent stance in order to somehow protect her from being at the man's beck and call. It was bullshit. He just couldn't accept failure. He had been refusing to consider the cost of putting his ego above the real needs of his family. *Christ.* What the hell was wrong with him? 'Karla…' He stepped towards her, wanting to apologise, to try to make things right.

'Oh, you might want this.' Karla stopped him, moving away as he attempted to thread an arm around her waist. 'Nice profile photograph, by the way.' Picking up his phone from the work surface, she handed it to him.

'Profile...?' Jason's confused gaze shot from his phone to her.

Karla said nothing, eyeing him meaningfully instead, before turning away to walk across to the dining table and pour herself a large glass of wine.

Jason flicked to the messages he and Mark had exchanged late last night, the attachment Mark had sent, and his heart flipped over. *Shit.* 'Mark sent it,' he said quickly. 'He's on Tinder.'

'Looking to hook up,' Karla said. 'I gathered. So, *does* she have a sister?' Taking a large gulp of her wine, she picked up the bottle and came back towards him.

Jesus. Jason scrunched his eyes closed. 'I was joking.' He scrambled for a plausible way to explain. 'It was just... something to say. Look, Karla, I'm sorry. I can see how this might look. I shouldn't have—'

'Fancied a foursome, did you?' Karla stopped in front of him, the look in her eyes one of soul-crushing humiliation.

'*What?*' Astonished, Jason searched her face. Surely she didn't think...? 'Come on, Karla.' He reached for her hand. 'You don't seriously imagine I...'

'Sounds like fun,' Karla said, her wounded gaze never leaving his. 'Maybe I should try it sometime. I wouldn't want to be seen as sexually unadventurous, after all, would I?'

'Karla...' Realising how hurt she was, Jason's heart dropped like a stone. 'Please don't. I forgot to delete it, that's all. I promise you there is no way I—'

He stopped as there was a tap on the kitchen door.

Karla retracted her hand, moving away from him, as Robert stepped in. Jason ran his hand over his neck in frustration. He felt utterly powerless. She must have imagined all sorts, which might explain why she'd gone to so much effort tonight. And what did he do? Her reliable husband, who appeared to be keeping dubious images on his phone? Storm in and accuse *her* of being disloyal. She'd been reaching out to him. She'd been trying to fix things. She was always trying to fix things, rescue bad situations that he'd created. She was always there for him. And all he could do in return was mess things up. Was he really going to mess up the rest of her life out of sheer bloody-mindedness? Mess up his kids' lives? Karla was right. He needed to stop thinking about himself and start thinking about his family.

'Not interrupting anything, am I?' Robert asked, looking interestedly between them. 'I thought I'd get off, Karla,' he went on. 'I can see Jason's too distracted to have any kind of sensible conversation tonight.'

Sarcastic git. Jason's gaze went to Karla, who said nothing. She didn't have to. She was busying herself at the sink in order to hide the fact that she was upset from her father, which pretty much said it all.

'Robert, wait.' Jason stopped him as he turned to the hall.

Robert turned back, his eyebrows raised enquiringly.

Feeling sick to his gut, Jason steeled himself to do what he'd sworn he never would. 'I'll call you,' he said, though the words almost stuck in his throat. 'About the proposition you mentioned.'

Robert's eyes widened momentarily, as if he was taken aback. Then, 'Not before time,' he said, a smile Jason couldn't quite work out curving his mouth. 'I'll look forward to our discussions. No need to call. Just turn up on Monday. Two o'clock. Make sure to be punctual, though, Jason. I have a tight schedule.'

'Hold on, Dad, I'll see you out.' Karla turned from the sink, as, having set the tone for their dealings together, Robert continued on up the hall. 'Thank you,' she mouthed to Jason, immense relief obvious in her eyes as she hurried past him.

'No need,' Robert called back, followed by, '*Damn*. Silly place to leave a computer, Jason, if you don't mind my saying. I almost fell over it.'

Robert made a great show of untangling the strap of the computer bag from his feet. Karla hurried to relieve him of it, and placed it on the hall table.

'Thanks, Dad,' she said, squeezing his arm as she showed him out of the door.

Jason so wished *he* could show him out of the door. Permanently.

CHAPTER ELEVEN

JASON

Waking up in his own bed, rather than the spare bed, Jason was disorientated for a second. He'd slept badly, despite the fact that they were at least avoiding spending the night in separate rooms. The immense frustration he'd been feeling when they'd come to bed – after a strained Sunday, avoiding discussion of anything emotive around the kids – hadn't been helped when he'd found himself incapable of making love to his wife.

Karla had turned to him, wanted to make love with him. And he'd wanted to. After so long lying together, barely touching, with their problems hanging ominously between them, he'd been desperate to close the gap, to feel the kind of closeness that making meaningful love brings, but he hadn't been able to. Karla had been understanding, snuggling up to him, whispering that it didn't matter, that it was perfectly understandable, given the stress he was under. Jason had seen the fleeting uncertainty when he'd looked into her eyes though. Her insecurity, just for a second. Insecurity which had undoubtedly been planted there by him and that damn stupid photograph on his phone.

Sighing in despair, he ran a hand over his face and stared up at the ceiling. He would make it up to her. Organise a romantic evening out – the theatre or a dance club, maybe – and a luxury hotel room for the night. At least now he might be able to afford to. Hopefully, caving in and agreeing to take the loan from her father would go some way towards showing her that he did want to make things up to her. That he cared about her and really wasn't looking for cheap sexual kicks ogling other women.

He still wasn't convinced that accepting financial help from Fenton wouldn't invite more problems than it would solve, but the reality was that his business would fold without it. And at least this way, even if it meant he would have to swallow every ounce of his pride, Karla would have some peace of mind. Things were never going to be right between them while they were both constantly worrying about money; he could see that now. Jason just hoped he didn't live to regret it. He had a feeling he would, but if it meant Karla's and the kids' futures were safe, it had to be the right thing to do.

Propping himself up on his elbow, he studied his wife in the early light of dawn. She was beautiful. Even with all they'd been struggling with, she tried to be upbeat and positive. Supportive – she'd always been that.

Picking up a strand of her long, blonde hair, he ran his thumb and forefinger along the length of it. He loved her hair. He hoped she never cut it, as she sometimes threatened to when she claimed it looked like straw. Jason never thought it looked anything but glorious – more so when it was messy, like it was now. He loved her, he thought determinedly. After so many arguments between them lately, which had come close to breaking them, he needed to prove that to her.

He saw her eyelashes flutter slightly as she stirred. She hadn't slept well either. She hardly ever did, always seeming to wake in the night. He often woke, sure he could hear her quietly crying. Sometimes, she would jolt awake, which scared him half to death. She would talk in her sleep, calling out her sister's name. She never talked to him about what was haunting her, which completely gutted him. Jason had never learned the details of Sarah's death, other than that it was something to do with a bang on the head. The whole thing seemed to be cloaked in secrecy for some reason. Diana had said that Karla found it too painful to talk about. Judging by the nightmares, Jason had to accept that that must be the case, even now. He wished she would trust him enough to confide in him though. Sometimes, when she was upset, she seemed to go into herself, to switch off almost, rather than reach out. He wished she wouldn't, that she would realise he was there for her. Always would be.

Brushing her hair gently aside, he pressed a soft kiss to her bare shoulder, at which Karla wriggled onto her back. 'Sorry,' he whispered. 'I didn't mean to disturb you.'

'You didn't,' she assured him, stretching languidly. 'I was awake, sort of.'

'Have I ever mentioned how beautiful you are?' he asked, his gaze sweeping her face.

'Yes.' She reached to trail her hand delicately across his unshaven chin. 'But then, you're an excellent bullshitter.'

Jason laughed. 'It's not bull,' he assured her, wondering why she never seemed to realise how attractive she was. 'You're beautiful. I'm not interested in other women, Karla. I know you must have been upset, seeing that photo on my phone. I should have deleted it immediately. Please believe me.'

Karla studied him, giving him a long, searching look, and then reached to trace his lips with her fingers.

'She couldn't hold a candle to you anyway.' Jason smiled and kissed each of her fingers in turn.

Karla rolled her eyes amusedly. 'Now you're definitely bullshitting.'

'Never.' Jason leaned to brush her lips with his. 'Those sharp blue eyes of yours would see through me in an instant.'

'You'd better believe it,' Karla said. 'And then I would be forced to do unspeakable things to you.'

'Promise?' Jason's smile widened. He tasted her lips again and then, thinking he could possibly live up to expectations, closed his mouth over hers, kissing her softly, before working his way slowly down her slim neck.

'Oh God.' Karla arched her back as he moved to her breasts, and then, 'Oh God!' she cried, and almost shoved him off the bed.

Not quite the reaction he'd hoped for. Confused, Jason rolled over as she shot up.

'It's gone eight.' Karla flew to the door to grab her dressing gown, stuffed her arms into it and yanked the door open. 'Holly, Josh – up!' she yelled, attempting to rouse the kids, who'd obviously also overslept. 'Now, please. We're late!'

Groaning, Jason threw the duvet back and blinked at the clock. They'd slept through the alarm? No, they hadn't. They'd forgotten to set it. *Crap!*

Bathroom or kitchen, he debated, pulling himself off the bed. Karla would need some help downstairs. On the other hand, he was seeing her father later today, and he needed to be ready for whatever knots Robert Fenton would no doubt try to tie him in. He needed to go through the company accounts. Liaise with Mark as to where they were with the software glitch.

Heading for the landing to make sure Karla would be okay coping with the pandemonium that was bound to ensue downstairs, he met Holly coming out of her room. She'd obviously gone to bed in an experimental hairdo. 'What time is it?' she asked blearily.

'Late,' Jason supplied, straightening the lopsided bun thing on her head. 'You have about fifteen minutes and counting.'

'Fifteen minutes?' Holly's sleepy eyes shot wide. 'God, I'm never going to get my make-up done in that time.'

Make-up? Jason squinted after her as she twirled around to hurry back to her bedroom. Since when did eleven-year-olds go to school wearing make-up? He sincerely hoped she didn't emerge wearing the red lipstick she'd been playing with the other day. That would definitely ensure pandemonium before they left.

'Josh?' Deciding he might do well to leave the battle of the make-up to Karla, he knocked on his son's door and then peered around it.

'What? I *know*,' Josh said, looking stressed as he stared at him from where he stood in the middle of his room, wearing not a lot. 'I'm coming. I've got my underpants on back to front.'

'Oh.' Jason hid a smile in favour of a suitably serious look. 'Might be a good idea to put them on the right way around then.'

'Obviously,' Josh retorted, pushing his glasses up his nose. 'I'll be struggling to pee otherwise, won't I?'

'No flies on you, are there, tiger?' Jason replied smartly.

'Funny. You should do stand-up. Not.' Josh's response was smarter still.

Jason couldn't help but laugh at his son's flat expression. 'Thirteen minutes,' he warned him.

'And counting. I know. *Go.*' Walking across to him, Josh shooed him out. At ten years old, and still to hit the growing phase, Josh didn't have a lot to be shy about, but Jason got it, and dutifully closed his door to allow him some privacy.

'All right if I go in the shower, Karla?' he called downstairs. 'I…' He stopped as she appeared in the hall, cling film in one hand, presumably with which to wrap the children's lunches, and a coffee in the other. 'I have my meeting with your father to prepare for,' he finished, trying not to look too depressed at the prospect.

'I know. I've rung work, told them I have an urgent dental appointment, so you go ahead,' Karla said, mounting the stairs to hand him the coffee and then dashing down again.

'Cheers.' Jason had no idea how she'd made it so quickly, but he grabbed it gratefully. He had a feeling he might need plenty of caffeine today, and possibly something a lot stronger later.

'Oh, in case I forget to say before you go,' Karla shouted from the kitchen, as Jason headed back to the bedroom, 'I love you, Jason Connolly.'

'Me too,' Jason shouted back. He couldn't help wondering, though: would her love have wavered if he hadn't been prepared to go through with this, which was undoubtedly going to be as humiliating as Fenton could make it?

Twenty minutes later, Jason cursed silently as he tried to get his collar to sit right. He loosened his tie and was halfway through re-knotting it when he stopped, surveying himself in despair in the mirror. *I can't believe I'm doing this.* He was dressing as if he were going to an interview, about to be scrutinised for his first job. Obviously, he would be scrutinised by Fenton – when had he ever not been? – but more for his unsuitability than his ability. In Robert Fenton's eyes, he was sadly lacking. Pulling the tie loose again, he yanked it off and tossed it on the chair. Should he even wear a suit? He would wear one if he were about to see his bank manager, but Fenton was his father-in-law. He shouldn't have to dress up as if he were meeting royalty.

'Bye,' Karla called from downstairs, as he started unbuttoning his shirt. He never wore a suit in the office unless he had clients coming in, and he was feeling uncomfortable enough as it was. 'Don't forget to ring me. Good luck!'

'Good luck, Daddy! Give my love to Grandad,' Holly shouted.

And Jason's gut constricted. 'Will do.' He forced the words out and tried very hard to oust the image that immediately sprang to mind: his baby girl's image on the monitor, her heart beating sure and strong. A heart Fenton had never wanted to beat, a child he'd never wanted to come into being. He would have expunged her life. He would have had Karla abort her. And now he was supposed to pass on that child's love to the man?

Jesus Christ. He couldn't do this. He would never be able to live with it, would never get his head around it. How the hell did Fenton live with himself?

Hearing the front door close, Jason dragged in a ragged breath and held it. So, what could he do? Exhaling slowly, he studied himself hard in the mirror. Bail out now? Or save his marriage and give that child, both of his children, a chance of a decent future?

It wasn't really open for debate any more, he realised. He cared about Karla and his kids, while Fenton never had and never would.

Determined to go through with it, whatever it cost him personally, Jason rebuttoned his shirt – and reached for his tie.

CHAPTER TWELVE

KARLA

Skidding into my office terribly late, I make it my first priority to send Jason a quick good luck message, praying that the meeting with my father goes well for him, and then settle down to do some actual work. My presence has obviously been missed. Noting the mountain of post that should have been sorted departmentally and distributed by one of the admin assistants, I make a start on it, and then glance up as there's a tap on the adjoining door.

'Morning, Karla,' says John, the chief executive, coming through from his office.

'Morning.' I smile brightly. That's who I am when I come here: bright and bubbly me. It's not an act, though I've had to force it a bit lately. I'm much happier with this side of me, which has been eclipsed recently by the problems at home. Problems I hope we can put behind us now that Jason has finally agreed to accept my father's help. I know how humiliating it is for him, that it goes against all of his principles, and it makes me love him all the more. He's doing it for me, for his children. Because his business is failing, he sees himself as a failure, but I am so proud of him. I always have been. He's tried so hard to turn his company's finances around, while always trying to be the best father a man can be to his children. Children we might never have had if Jason had allowed my father to bully him when we'd first met. To bully me.

My stomach clenches involuntarily, as it always does when I recall my father's absolute adamance that I was about to ruin my life, his expression: a combination of ill-concealed fury and disappointment when he'd learned I was pregnant. What terrifies me is that, had he succeeded in driving Jason away, I might not have stood up to him. Thank God, Jason was there for me, equally adamant that there was nothing my father could do to make him stop loving me. I don't tell him often enough how much I love him. I make a mental note to address that, starting tonight.

'All sorted?' John asks me.

'Sorry?' My mind has shifted gear. After the mad rush this morning, I'm now worrying about whether I remembered to put yoghurts in the kids' lunchboxes.

John indicates his cheek. 'The toothache.'

'Oh.' I quickly tone down the smile. 'Yes, thanks. Sorry about having to dash to the dentist. I would have booked it for later in the week, but I didn't get a wink's sleep all night.' That's actually not far from the truth. Instead of worrying about our finances or dreaming about Sarah, her voice popping into my head, forcing me awake, I was concerned about Jason. I do believe that he simply forgot to delete the photograph on his phone and that he has no inclination to ogle other women, but after what happened in bed last night – or rather, what didn't happen – I couldn't help worrying that he didn't fancy me any more. But then, he'd been so gutted, with such a tortured, remorseful look in his eyes – because he was assuming I would think the worst, I suspect – which only goes to show how much he does care. My concern now is more for him than myself. I can't bear the thought of him feeling more humiliated than he must already.

'No problem. You needn't have rushed in, apart from the fact that the place might grind to a halt without you, that is,' John says, bringing my mind back to work, rather than where it is at present: wondering what might have happened this morning. He'd kissed me so tenderly, said such sweet things to me…

Dismissing my thoughts, which are not entirely appropriate for the office, I smile up at John. 'I'm fine,' I assure him. 'Still a little bit sore, but it's nothing a painkiller won't fix.'

'Well, slip off early if you do find you're suffering. You have plenty of overtime owed to you, and I'm sure we can keep the ship afloat for a few hours.' John gives me a friendly wink.

'I will.' I nod and quietly pray that, with my father's help, Jason can keep the ship afloat. He will. My father is a wily businessman, but when he's made up his mind to invest in something, he will plough as much cash into it as is needed. I'm half hoping he and Jason might get on a little better if they have a business interest in common. It's a bit of a forlorn hope. My father seems to go all out to antagonise Jason sometimes.

'Sorry about those.' John indicates the several files on my desk, atop which are audio tapes, which will need distributing for typing up. 'The development department has hit some problems with the snagging report on the new-build site, and the community services department rota's gone to pot again. People off sick with the bug that's going about, I'm afraid.'

'I'll get it sorted,' I assure him. I'm not quite sure how, conjuring trained staff out of the ether not being one of my skills. I usually manage it though, with a bit of rejiggling and sweet-talking.

'Thanks, Karla. I really don't know what this place would do without you.' John smiles, relieved. 'I'll get us a coffee, and then I'll get on with that report for the board meeting tonight. We're discussing funding. It's going to be a long one.'

'Black, no sugar,' I call after him, as he heads out. 'I'm on a diet.' *Again.* I sigh inwardly and then renew my resolve. No more half-hearted attempts, I tell myself firmly. I am reassured, after the compliments he paid me, that Jason does still find me attractive, but I really can't use the fact that I've given birth twice as an excuse for carrying extra pounds any more.

'You don't need to diet,' John shouts back, which does my ego no harm.

Smiling, I go back to my pile of post. John is all right. I would much rather be doing what I'd had my heart set on what seems like a lifetime ago now – learning my lines for some magical stage play – but if I have to work in an office, there are much worse places.

Twenty minutes later, the post sorted and delivered to the various departments, I collect the files and tapes and head to the admin assistants' office, knocking before going in, which I've learned earns the women's respect.

'Right,' I say, wearing my stern look, which they can see straight through, 'whoever forgot to do the post this morning gets to make the coffee today.'

'That will be Lucy.' Our senior assistant, Zoe, nods across to Lucy with a grin. 'She's a bit distracted. New boyfriend,' she mouths conspiratorially in my direction.

'Ah.' Glancing knowingly in Lucy's direction, I head over to Zoe's desk with the files. 'I remember it well,' I say, smiling indulgently.

'Ooh.' Yasmin makes wide eyes at me from across the room. 'Come on, give us the goss. That husband of yours is hot.'

'Most definitely,' I concur. With his dark, moody good looks, Jason definitely qualifies as hot. I don't give them the goss, obviously, just enough carefully embroidered detail to assure them all is right in our marriage. Aware that Jason and I have had some problems – I've shared on occasion, empathising perhaps when someone has been struggling with a relationship – the girls are pleased for me. We're not all besties – the age gap and the fact that I'm their superior doesn't allow it – but we are friends, and I value that. It's nice to be able to chat about things other than work. Plus, having a good relationship with the women makes my job so much easier.

Back in my office, I manage to reschedule the community services rota, which is miraculous but essential, with a young single mum who has a boy with severe physical disability relying on us for assistance. Well into my lunchtime, I'm actually thinking about having some lunch when my mobile rings. My dad, I realise, noting his number. Strange that he would call now, when he's seeing Jason in half an hour.

'Hi, Dad,' I say, curious.

'Karla. I imagine you'll be busy, and I'm in a meeting myself, so I won't keep you,' Dad says with his usual officiousness. 'I was wondering, have you checked his laptop?'

'Sorry?' I furrow my brow.

'I thought I'd mention it. It's just that, after our conversation on Saturday about the – shall we say – *undesirable* content on Jason's phone, and then my almost falling over his computer in your hall, it occurred to me that you should check it.'

It wasn't 'our' conversation, I think, peeved already with his interference. It was a private conversation with Mum which he eavesdropped on. I would never have dreamed of confiding in Mum if I'd thought there was the slightest danger of my father overhearing. And hang on a minute. What does he mean, 'check it'? Does Dad think he damaged the laptop?

But I know what he means. The implication lands like a cold stone in my chest.

CHAPTER THIRTEEN

JASON

Fenton's receptionist, Abbie – whom Jason had met once before, and whom he'd gathered didn't rate her boss highly, unsurprisingly – smiled apologetically when he arrived at Fenton's premises. 'He's in a sales meeting,' she said, nodding towards the glass-sided conference room.

'Right.' Jason sighed, immediately irked, since he'd made sure to be there bang on time, as instructed.

'He shouldn't be too long. Why don't I grab you a coffee, while you wait?' she suggested, nodding him towards the waiting area.

'No, I'm good, thanks, Abbie.' Hiding his agitation, which he would have to do if he was going to get through this, Jason smiled back and took a seat. He had no doubt that Fenton was going to keep him waiting, indicating the shape of things to come.

After several minutes, Fenton acknowledged him with the briefest glance and then carried on pontificating, pointing at his whiteboard, his gestures animated, demonstrating what a great businessman he was.

Jason sighed in despair, and then suppressed an almost overwhelming desire to leave as he watched the man plant his fists on the long conference table, leaning forwards to mouth off at some poor guy sitting at the other end who was clearly under attack and looked as if he would quite like to crawl under the table. He wasn't sure how he stayed put when, after walking around the table, his hands laced behind his back like a sergeant major, Robert paused behind a young female employee who was now addressing the meeting. It was apparent from where Jason was sitting, directly opposite them, that the man was paying more attention to how she looked than what she was saying.

What he did next was unbelievable – or totally believable, depending on how well you knew the man. Staggered, Jason watched as Fenton leaned over her, placing an arm around her shoulders, ostensibly to peer down at her figures. Yeah, right. It wasn't her numerical figures he was studying, that was for sure. Did people like him really still get away with that sort of shit?

Disgusted, Jason debated whether to walk away from the whole thing now. His own marketing manager, Rachel, would probably clock the bastard one, and with Jason's blessing. She wouldn't want to be within a million miles of someone like Fenton, let alone involved in business with him.

'Still as charming as ever, isn't he?' Abbie commented.

Jason shook his head contemptuously. 'Delightful,' he said. 'Why does she put up with it?' He had to ask, though he guessed it was because she didn't have a lot of choice.

Abbie glanced nervously towards the meeting room and then back to him. 'Because she'll be "let go" if she complains,' she supplied. 'She's a single mum with two children. She's looking for alternative employment, but she'll need a decent reference, so…'

And therein lay the problem. Jason wondered at the workings of a world that allowed men like Robert Fenton to thrive. If anyone deserved to be put out of business, it was a misogynist and bully like him. But then, money talked, didn't it, as his father-in-law was fond of telling him. And with non-disclosure agreements no doubt signed as part of their contracts, his employees couldn't say a word. Did he ever consider that his daughter worked in an office environment? Or wonder how Karla would feel at the hands of some chauvinistic, sexist prick like him? Jason laughed scornfully. Even if he did consider it, he probably wouldn't give a damn, imagining it was part of what women got paid for. Jason's jaw tightened. If he had any hint that Karla was subjected to anything like this, he doubted he would be able to stop himself fighting that battle for her, whether she wanted him to or not.

'I can't believe he's your father-in-law.' Abbie's expression was a mixture of appalled and sympathetic.

'Me either,' Jason said, feeling deeply embarrassed. Fenton had been up to his usual tricks when he'd seen him that first time in Abbie's company. He'd called to collect Karla, who'd been out to a birthday lunch with Fenton. She was in the toilets when he arrived. Fenton was in reception, standing way too close to Abbie, his eyes everywhere but on her screen as he'd supposedly been checking his appointments. Jason had felt like apologising for the man that day.

'And you're going to be involved in some kind of business merger with him?' she asked, her expression surprised.

'Not a merger exactly, no.' Kneading his temples, Jason sighed tiredly and wondered how he'd managed to find himself manipulated into a corner by Fenton. He'd tried to convince himself he was doing the right thing. The immediate benefit of Robert's investment would be that he could inject more cash into the software issue they were struggling with, meaning he could save the contract with his major client, which would undoubtedly secure business with other interested parties. Karla had begged him to do this, though she knew he'd been determined not to. Sacrificing his principles and finally agreeing had certainly improved things on the home front. Despite the fact that things hadn't worked out in bed last night, he and Karla had been more relaxed with each other this morning. Jason was regretting his decision now though. Coming here had reminded him why he'd wanted nothing to do with the man. But how the hell did he backtrack without telling Karla they would be basically living hand-to-mouth while he filed for bankruptcy?

'Good luck with that. I'm glad he's not my father-in-law,' Abbie said, then looked sharply up, plastering a smile in place as Fenton marched out of the meeting room, leaving the female employee he'd been harassing throwing murderous glances after him.

'Afternoon, Jason,' he said, with a short smile. 'Sorry about that. Sales team needed a sharp reminder of what their jobs are.'

Yeah, and you need a sharp reminder of what an obnoxious prat you are, Jason wanted to say. But he simply nodded.

'Bring some coffee in, Abbie, would you?' Fenton addressed her rudely. 'And pass me Jason's company file. It's in the cabinet, under…' he paused, pondering demonstratively. 'What's the name of your company again, Jason?'

Jason looked at him with a combination of disbelief and disdain. 'Upwards Online,' he supplied, as if Fenton didn't know.

'Ah, yes. More downwards currently, I believe.' Fenton held his gaze for a second before looking away. 'Bottom drawer, Abbie, please.'

His anger bubbling up like mercury inside him, Jason gritted his teeth hard, watching Abbie struggle to extract the file from a filing cabinet behind her without giving Fenton a bird's-eye view of anything he fancied helping himself to.

'Right. Shall we?' Fenton said, without even a glance in Abbie's direction as she handed him the file.

Half an hour. Jason sucked in a breath, braced himself and walked after Robert as he sailed off down the corridor. Thirty minutes – less, if possible – and he would be out of there. All he had to do was bow and scrape to a complete bastard and his business would be safe. His family's future would be safe.

Fenton answered a call as he strode off ahead, much to Jason's further irritation. He followed a little way behind as Fenton barged into his office and sat behind his desk – the solid mahogany executive variety. 'Well, *find out* where the missing funds are,' he said sharply. 'Balancing my books is your *job*, Edward.'

His accountant, Jason gathered. Obviously not quite so on the ball as Fenton had claimed he was.

'Right, Jason, grab a seat.' Banging the phone down with an agitated sigh, Fenton nodded to a chair. 'I won't keep you long. I'm sure your schedule is as busy as mine.'

Jason was torn between telling him he'd rather stand and about-facing altogether. Cursing inwardly, he took the seat instead. Fenton knew how he felt. To react would be to do exactly what the man wanted him to.

Fenton skimmed perfunctorily through the file, closed it and then, finally, looked up at him. 'I've been through the figures with my accountant, Jason, as you would expect me to,' he said, 'and, as mentioned, I am prepared to extend you the financial backing you need.'

That's very gracious of you. Jason curtailed the contempt already rising inside him, offering Abbie a small smile instead as she came in with the coffee.

'Given certain stipulations.' Fenton gave Abbie a cursory nod, pushed the file aside to allow her to place the tray on his desk and leaned back in his chair, not bothering to thank her as she slipped back out of the room.

'Which would be?' Jason tried to read his expression. He'd expected to find the same challenging look he'd seen when he'd tried to buy him out of Karla's life with an obscene amount of money twelve long years ago, but, strangely, Fenton looked away.

After an unnerving minute, Fenton got to his feet and walked across to the window, where, hands thrust into his pockets, he gazed out for another interminably long minute before turning back to him. 'I have something to tell you, Jason,' he said, his expression pensive. 'There's no easy way to say it, so I'm going to say it as it is.'

Apprehension creeping through him, Jason narrowed his eyes. If he was aiming to put him on the back foot here, it was working.

'I'm not asking you this time, Jason. I'm telling you,' Fenton went on, his face holding a warning as he studied him carefully. 'You have to get out of Karla's life.'

'Right.' Shaking his head, Jason laughed scathingly and got to his feet.

He was halfway to the door when Fenton froze him to the spot. 'You're related,' he said.

CHAPTER FOURTEEN

KARLA

Standing outside Jason's office, I hesitate, wondering again what I'm doing here; what it is I hope to find. I felt shocked after my father's phone call. John commented that I looked pale as I sat dumbfounded at my desk. I couldn't quite believe it: that my father would stoop to this. The idea that Jason has been actively searching for women online is ludicrous.

Is it though, really? I know that Mark sent him that damn profile photograph. The question burning inside me, now, is why? Why were he and Jason discussing online dating sites and near naked women, Jason indicating he liked what he saw, unless they did it regularly? Why would they exchange messages about her? Is it likely it's just a one-off? And why in God's name had Jason asked if she had a sister? If it was joke, just 'laddish banter', it wasn't a very funny one, was it, since *I'd* seen it.

My heart almost folds up inside me as I acknowledge that he might have been asking seriously. The cold reality is that we haven't been intimate in weeks, if not months. And last night, Jason couldn't. Gullible me put it down to stress. Could it be that he's actually having sex elsewhere? Regularly. Meeting another woman – other *women* – he's contacting online?

It's preposterous. I know it is. Yet still, sick with nerves and uncertainty, I feel I have to go through with this. If I don't see with my own eyes, won't I always be wondering? Much as I'd like to think I could ignore it, I know that I can't. This will be yet another thing that will haunt me at night.

Will Mark talk to me, I wonder? I toy with the idea of surreptitiously trying to extract information from him, or even openly asking him, and then abandon the idea. Jason and Mark go back years. Mark would never tell me anything that might betray their friendship.

Bracing myself, I check my watch. I know exactly where Jason is right now. He's doing what I begged him to do: 'selling his soul' to my father. He doesn't want to do it. He'll be feeling utterly humiliated, thinking he's lived up to my father's low expectations of him, perceiving himself as having failed in his fundamental obligation as a husband and father to provide for his family. And I'm about to do this.

Swallowing my deep sense of shame, I close my eyes. I have to do it. I have to know. I can't carry this around, and I can't confront Jason with accusations fuelled by my father. I just can't.

Attempting to still the nausea churning inside me, I key in the security code, take the stairs and swing into the tiny foyer of Upwards Online. I need to act naturally, be the bubbly me, not this uncertain, wretched creature I suddenly feel I'm becoming.

'Hi, Rachel,' I smile cheerily at Jason's marketing manager, who works many more hours than she should, as she comes out of the main office to head for the loo. She's very young – early to mid-twenties, I guess – and extremely pretty, I notice afresh, and immediately wonder why she pours so many unpaid hours into a company she has no vested interest in.

Taking a deep breath, I try to shut it out, this suspicion that seems to be blooming into some hideous thing inside me, but I can't. I am so wound up I can actually feel my heart thrashing against my chest.

'Hi, Karla.' Rachel smiles easily back. 'Jase is out, I'm afraid.'

I notice the familiarity, too. I'm bound to, because of my bloody, *bloody* father, a man who's never rated my husband, who's looked for ways to pull us apart ever since the day he met Jason. Why in God's name am I listening to him? Because I can't live with this doubt. As I admit that to myself, I realise part of me believes that my father might be right.

'I know.' Answering Rachel, I push determinedly on. 'I'm not after him. I'm after the use of his computer. Job application.' I offer the most plausible explanation I've been able to think of for using Jason's office. If she or Mark mentions my being here, I can bluff my way through it; tell Jason it's a better paid job at a rival housing association or something, thus the need for secrecy. I'd rather that than try to bluff my way out of why I would be checking his laptop while he was sleeping.

'Ah, got you.' Rachel goes for it, assuming I wouldn't want to apply for other jobs from my work computer, as I'd hoped she would. 'Good luck,' she says, behind her.

'Thanks, Rachel.' The first hurdle over, I push on into the main office, where Mark is seated in front of his computer.

'Hi, Mark,' I say, my cheery smile still in place. 'How's the internet dating going?' I decide to broach the subject, thinking that, if he has anything to hide on Jason's behalf, he might hesitate or look slightly sheepish.

Mark does neither. 'Interesting,' he answers straight off, 'depending on how riveted you are by your date regaling you with tales of her ex-husband's assignations with other women while weeping into her wine.'

'Oh dear.' I laugh as he glances despairingly at the ceiling.

'The latest one seems promising though. We've got past first base at least.'

'Brilliant.' I widen my eyes and try to look pleased for him, though my stomach is now churning like a washing machine on full spin. 'We'll have to have a meal out together sometime.'

'Yeah, nice idea. Jase isn't here,' Mark says, as I head towards the small office Jason uses to entertain clients who might need a little extra 'chatting up', as he calls it – *and maybe more*, whispers Sarah's mistrustful voice in my head.

I ignore it. I wondered why he needed the extra office space when he first started up, but when I thought about it, it made sense. Some clients will need the reassurance of a certain level of successfulness, I reasoned. And Jason had thought he could afford it then.

'I know.' I repeat what I said to Rachel: 'I've snuck out of work to send off a job application. Hope that's okay with you?'

'No problem.' Mark stands, stretches and picks up his mug. 'I'll grab you a coffee.'

'I'm okay, Mark, thanks. I've not long had one,' I lie. My mouth is dry, my throat parched. I let myself through to the office, close the door, lean back against it and try to do the simplest thing in life and just breathe.

Jason's laptop is there, wired up and open on his desk. I wasn't sure whether he would take it with him, but as he'd said he wanted to consider whatever deal my father might offer him before going through any of the company software with him, I'd hoped he wouldn't. I would have used the desktop computer, otherwise, or pretended to, whilst going through the paperwork in his drawers.

I can't believe I'm doing this. Jason has given me no reason to.

But he has, whispers Sarah.

And I realise she's right. Dad might not like him, but it wasn't he who first planted these seeds in my head. It was Jason.

Stop. Steeling my resolve, I pull myself from the door and go straight across to fire up the laptop. I know his passwords. Jason's never had any reason to hide them from me. If he has now, then won't my suspicions be as good as confirmed?

CHAPTER FIFTEEN

JASON

His emotions colliding violently inside him, Jason made it out of Fenton's Bespoke Plumbing and Bathroom Services before he leaned over to retch, bringing up the contents of his stomach. Robert Fenton had to be totally fucking insane. Was he really so consumed with hatred for him that he would resort to *this*? It was bullshit. It *had* to be bullshit. Straightening up, he loosened his collar, wiped the back of his hand over his mouth, leaned against the outside wall of the building and slid to his haunches.

Jesus… Gulping back the bile rising like acid in his throat, he looked skywards and prayed. *Please don't let it be true.*

'Jason?' someone called, as he tried to still his racing heart and get his chaotic thoughts in some sort of order.

Disorientated, feeling as if he might actually pass out, Jason glanced sideways to see Abbie hurrying towards him.

'Are you all right?' she asked him worriedly.

Jason answered with a tight nod and attempted to lever himself to a standing position.

'Stay. Give yourself a minute,' she said, passing him the glass of water she was holding.

His hand shaking, Jason accepted it gratefully, his teeth chinking against the glass as he gulped it back.

'Did he turn you down?' Abbie asked, after a second. 'I don't mean to pry, but I—'

Jason laughed cynically. 'No,' he said, his voice hoarse. 'He didn't turn me down. He's willing to give me all the financial backing I need.'

Relieving him of the glass, Abbie looked at him quizzically.

'On one condition,' Jason added.

'Which is?' Abbie asked warily.

'Oh, nothing much.' Pushing himself from the wall, Jason heaved himself to his feet. 'I just have to walk out of my marriage.'

'*What?*' Abbie's look was one of shock. 'But…' She shook her head, bewildered. 'Why would he…?'

'Because he's a complete bastard.' Jason shrugged, offering her a semblance of a smile for the kindness she'd shown him. He actually felt like breaking down and weeping. But he wouldn't do that. Not here. 'You might do well to start looking for another job, Abbie,' he suggested. 'The man's toxic.'

'I am,' she called after him, as he turned to go. 'And as soon as I do…'

She would hopefully shop the fucker for sexual harassment, Jason thought, fury smouldering like white-hot lava inside him as he walked towards the car park.

But it occurred to him, as he climbed into his car, that it wasn't Fenton who was the bastard, was it. Apparently. Starting the engine, Jason laughed again, sucked in a tight breath, pinched the bridge of his nose hard, then dropped his head to the steering wheel and stifled a cry that came from his soul.

Go. Desperate for Fenton not to witness any of this, his total and utter humiliation, he pulled himself up sharp, crunched the car into gear, rammed his foot down and screeched away from the premises.

He drove to his own company almost on auto. He didn't even realise he'd cut a red light until he was blasted by a horn from the side. His driving was erratic. He was losing his grip – on his life, on his mind. He was losing his family. Fenton had finally won. He'd thrown down the gauntlet years ago, when he'd tried to entice him to walk away. To convince Karla to abort their child: Holly, his beautiful daughter. And Jason had fought. He'd fought hard. He just didn't have the will to keep fighting him any more, fighting for survival. He couldn't fight this. He had nothing to fight it with.

What in God's name was he going to do? Wiping the back of his hand across his eyes, Jason tried to control the fresh wave of nausea rising inside him. What could he do but what Fenton had always wanted? No way. He couldn't walk away from them. He would *not* walk away from his children.

Parked in the car park outside Upwards Online, he braced his hands against the steering wheel and tried to contain his spiralling emotions. Resting his head against the headrest, he stared, unseeing, at the roof upholstery for a long, agonising minute. He'd never contemplated suicide, not in his darkest moments – and there had been some, when he'd wondered as a small child whether anyone could truly love him – but the thought was going through his head now. It was possibly the only way he could leave Karla with *her* pride intact. Leave his family provided for, via the proceeds of his life insurance. But it would haunt them forever. That reality hit him full on. He had no life any more, but no way out of it either. Robert Fenton really had stuffed him. He'd always aimed to take away what mattered most to him: his family. He'd succeeded. Had it occurred to him, anywhere along the line, that he would be taking away his daughter's family too? She would be losing her husband, the father of her children. If she found out the truth, she would also be losing her own father. She could never forgive him for this.

Diana? Did she know about any of this? Jason hoped she didn't. Prayed, for Karla's sake, that she didn't. Because if she did, if she'd kept this information from her, Karla would want nothing to do with her either. And without her mother, she would have no one.

He needed to go inside. Jason glanced towards his office, where he'd once hoped to build a business that would thrive. He'd never wanted to compete with Robert Fenton as a businessman. It had been Fenton who'd made that part of the war between them. He'd simply wanted to support his family, and have something to hand down to his son, who showed an interest in computer technology. He'd failed. It was abundantly clear that he had. He would need to let Mark and Rachel know the outcome of his meeting – there would be no injection of cash. It was amusing, really, that Fenton actually thought he could buy his way out of this, throw money at him in exchange for his silence. Jason would keep his secret, for now, because he had to, until he'd worked out what to do. He wouldn't be bought though. Because whoever he was, he was nothing like the man who prioritised the accumulation of wealth above the people he was supposed to love and care for.

He suspected Mark and Rachel would insist on sticking with him and continuing to try to keep the company afloat, but he couldn't allow that. He had no idea how he was going to pay them their salaries beyond another month – two at most. He would have to be honest with them about that aspect of things, tell them to jump ship now before they went down with him.

Feeling jaded to his very bones, he dragged a hand over his neck and climbed out of his car, reaching for his ringing mobile as he did. It was the major client he'd been hoping to hang on to – had thought he would be able to hang on to, with some funding behind him. He debated briefly and then steeled himself to take the call.

'Jason, hi. Paul Edwards here,' the guy said, his tone cautious.

'Hi, Paul.' Jason tried not to sound as desperate as he felt. So, did he tell him that the customer-fronting software he'd promised to deliver within the week wouldn't be ready? Or did he try to stall – again? The latter, he decided. His children were still his children. He still had to provide for them. He wouldn't accept defeat until he had to. It would mean working 24/7, but he could at least give it one last shot. 'Look, Paul, I'm going to be honest, we're making some headway, but we need a little more time. There are just a few minor problems we need to iron out. Can I call you back on Friday?' he asked him. 'I should be able to give you a definite timing by then.'

Jason heard the man's long intake of breath, which didn't bode well. 'No need, Jason,' Paul said eventually. 'The thing is…'

Apprehension knotting his stomach, Jason stopped walking.

'There's been a development,' Paul went on, sounding apologetic.

'As in?' Guessing he was about to hear his company's death knell, Jason held his breath.

'Logic Solutions,' Paul supplied awkwardly.

One of his competitors? Jason wondered if he was hearing him right. But they were smaller than he was. Paul had approached them before coming to him. He'd liked their ideas, he'd said, but suspected they hadn't got the funds to back them up.

'They have a benefactor, apparently,' Paul enlightened him, as Jason struggled to get his head around it. 'Someone who's invested in the company, thereby allowing them to get their program up and running. I'm sorry, Jason, but I can't afford to delay any longer.'

Jason felt his gut constrict. 'Who?' he asked.

Again, Paul hesitated. 'I don't think the information's public knowledge yet, Jason. I'm not sure I should—'

'No. Right. No problem.' Biting back his anger, Jason cut him short. 'I understand, Paul. Thanks for letting me know.'

Feeling as if the express train that had slammed into him had reversed to roll over him again, Jason ended the call. He didn't need confirmation. He already knew who it was: Robert Fenton. And his motive: to make sure that Jason knew he could either walk away with something, as long as he kept his mouth shut, or with nothing.

CHAPTER SIXTEEN

JASON

Rachel stood from her desk as Jason pushed through the door into the main office. 'Hi, Jase. Do you think I could grab you for—?'

'Can you give me five minutes, Rachel,' Jason said shortly, and then pulled himself up. The fact that he'd just been crucified by Robert Fenton wasn't her fault. 'Sorry. I, er…' Smiling apologetically, he attempted to get his emotions in some sort of order. 'Five minutes.'

Mark looked up from his laptop as Jason walked past his desk. 'Oh,' he said warily, obviously noting his dour expression. 'I take it the meeting didn't go too well?'

Answering with a sharp shake of his head, Jason banged through the door into the small office – and then stopped dead.

Confused as to what she was doing there, and why he hadn't known she would be, he looked from his laptop to Karla, who'd just shot up from the seat behind his desk as if ejected from it.

'Jason.' She smiled nervously, obviously alarmed by his arrival, 'I didn't expect you back yet.'

'Clearly,' he said, his gaze going back to his laptop.

'I was just typing up some job applications.' Her face flushing with embarrassment, Karla moved back towards it.

But Jason was quicker. His gut told him that, whatever she was doing, it wasn't filling in job applications. He was across the room in two strides, twisting the laptop around to face him.

Studying the screen, it took him a second to comprehend fully, and then he laughed in sheer disbelief. 'Find anything interesting?' he asked, narrowing his eyes as he looked at her.

Karla appeared not to know how to answer.

'What are you doing, Karla?' Jason asked, now working very hard not to lose his temper.

'I was just' – Karla dropped her gaze to the floor – 'looking,' she finished, with an awkward shrug.

'I can see that!' Jason lost it. 'What the bloody hell were you looking *for?*'

Taken aback, Karla snapped her attention back to him. 'Nothing,' she said quickly.

'Right.' Jason held her gaze. 'So you were just browsing my internet history out of idle curiosity?'

'Yes. I…' Karla trailed hopelessly off.

Fuck it! Jason dragged in a terse breath. He wasn't sure what she was looking for, but he thought he knew why. Fenton suspected he wouldn't go quietly. If the man knew nothing else about him, he knew he would never abandon his children. Not ever. He hadn't yet fully considered the consequences of staying in their lives. The consequences of just up and leaving, though, that he had considered. Jason knew from experience how that might affect them. And he wasn't about to do it. No matter what.

'Did your father put you up to this?' he asked, heading around the desk towards her.

'No!' Karla took a step back. 'Why would he?'

Jason scanned her face, his anger mounting. '*Why?*' he repeated, incredulous. '*Christ…* You really don't get it, do you, Karla?'

'No, I don't!' Karla swiped at a tear spilling down her cheek. 'I don't get why you're so angry just because I'm looking at your bloody laptop! Unless there's something you don't want me to see?'

'Like *what*?' Jason raked a hand furiously through his hair. 'For fu— There's nothing *to* see! Why the hell would you think there was?'

'I'm leaving,' Karla said tearfully, walking around him.

Jason went after her. 'All this because you found a photograph on my phone that someone *sent* to me? Were you looking for other evidence of my supposed… what? Browsing the internet for other women? Cheating on you? Is that it? Prompted by your loving father, no doubt, who would just love it if—'

'Yes!' Karla whirled back around, her sharp blue eyes blazing. 'And I found it! You bastard!'

Jason stared at her, incredulous, for a second. Then, 'Where?' he asked, feeling suddenly way off kilter.

'Right there.' Karla nodded at his laptop, her expression one of utter contempt. 'Scroll further back, Jason. The "evidence" is there, just as I thought it might be. Me!' She banged a hand against her chest. 'Not my father. Actually, I'm lying – I didn't think I would find anything. I imagined that, being such a computer wizard, you would have deleted it.'

Ignoring the facetiousness of that comment, Jason attempted to pull his scrambled thoughts together. 'It wasn't me,' he said eventually, denying it outright. 'I haven't… I wouldn't—'

'*Liar!*' Karla screamed. 'Do *not* compound what you've done with bullshit, Jason. I am not stupid! Are you going to tell me you haven't been trawling dating sites? Your online *activities* are right there!'

'I haven't been near any bloody dating sites!' Jason yelled back. 'This is absolute bollocks. No way—' He stopped, as the only explanation there was occurred to him. 'Your father,' he said, trying to recall. 'My laptop was in the hall. He said he'd fallen over it. He couldn't have. It was on the hall table, not—'

'For God's sake!' Karla came back towards him and slammed the laptop lid shut. 'Just stop! This is pathetic. You're pathetic, trying to blame my father for this! Is he responsible for everything that's gone wrong in your life?'

Jason was torn between laughing out loud, given the bombshell the bastard had just dropped, and smashing his fist through the nearest window.

'Your bad business decisions?' Karla went on, as he struggled with the urge to just spit out what the man had told him and be done with it. 'Marrying *me*?' She searched his face, her eyes full of incomprehension. 'If you wanted out, Jason, all you had to do was—'

'*Whoa!*' Mark intervened from the door. 'Cool it, you two.'

'Ah, here he is. Our very own dating site Casanova,' Karla's tone was thick with sarcasm.

'Not quite,' Mark said, with a rueful smile. 'It was me, Karla. Not Jason.'

Folding her arms, Karla tipped her head to one side, her expression somewhere between amusement and complete disdain.

'I used Jason's machine while mine was running a software check. I should have said.' He glanced cautiously at Jason. 'It was me browsing those sites, Karla, not Jason.'

CHAPTER SEVENTEEN

KARLA

The damp, grey drizzle of the mid-February afternoon seems to be seeping through my coat and into my bones as I stand outside the school, waiting for Holly and Josh to come out. I feel so empty, so cold and lonely. A combination of nerves and nausea grips my stomach, as I recall the look on Jason's face when he walked quietly from his office. He was no longer furious at having found me there, snooping on him. He didn't say a word, he simply looked at me, his eyes frighteningly void of any emotion. It was as if the shutters had come down. And then he turned and walked away.

Unsure what to do, I followed him, called out to him. Begged him to stay and talk to me. He wouldn't even meet my gaze. As he climbed into his car without a word, his body language was that of a defeated man. It was as if all the fight had gone out of him. And that's down to me. I should never have pushed my father's proposal. I should have stood by the side of the man I am in love with, have always been in love with, the man I chose to be with, whatever our financial circumstances. Instead, in Jason's eyes, I have taken my father's side, against him. My heart plummets icily as I recall how I ranted at him like some demented thing – in front of his employees, for God's sake. He must have felt so crushed. So alone.

Did Mark use Jason's laptop? It's possible. The truth is, I have no idea what to believe. My heart wants to believe my husband, but my head… Has he been accessing these sites? Have I driven him to look outside our marriage for whatever it is he needs?

I pull my phone from my pocket and check my messages, hoping Jason will have replied to the one in which I apologised and suggested we go out together to talk properly. There's nothing.

He won't be licking his wounds. Jason's not like that. I know him. He's quiet sometimes – when he's pondering his business problems, mostly – but he doesn't sit around blaming the world for them. My heart sinks further as I remember that I accused him of doing just that: blaming other people for what's wrong in his life. Jason doesn't do that. He blames himself. He takes action to try to fix things. He's not a sulker. He never gives me the silent treatment. That's how I know his silence now is significant. And it frightens me.

Dropping my gaze, I will him to message me, if only to tell me he's all right. I desperately want to speak to him, to tell him I trust him. I have to, despite my uncertainty. And he has to be able to trust me. I hope he can, after today. Without trust, our marriage will be over anyway.

'Karla, hi,' someone calls across the playground. 'Long time no see.'

I snap my gaze up to see a mother I know waving at me from under her brolly.

'Holly and Josh are still inside,' she yells, and hurries on through the rain to the gates.

I haven't noticed that the drizzle has turned to heavy rain. I haven't noticed, either, that the exodus of children from the school has dwindled to a straggle. 'Thanks, Mel,' I shout back, and hurry in the direction of the building, wondering what's keeping them.

Pushing through the doors, I almost walk into Holly's teacher, who greets me with a flustered smile. 'Hi, Mrs Connolly,' she says. 'Holly said you were picking them up. I was just coming out to find you. We've had a bit of an incident, I'm afraid.'

'Incident?' I repeat, a tingle of apprehension running through me as I follow her down the corridor.

Miss Thompson stops as we round the corner to the headmistress's office. Josh is sitting on a chair, his head down and his hands tucked under his thighs. 'We've had a little bit of bullying in class,' she says, with a sigh. 'It's not something we tolerate, obviously, so we're speaking to the parents of the boy responsible, but…'

But what? Alarmed, I look away from my vulnerable boy and back to her.

'Holly hit him,' Miss Thompson informs me, her expression one of correct disapproval, though I see a smidgeon of admiration in her eyes. 'She was sticking up for her brother, but you'll understand that we can't condone it. Could you have a word, do you think?'

'Of course,' I assure her, swallowing back my heart, which is wedged somewhere in my throat. 'Can I?' I nod towards Josh, my emotions in turmoil. I'm angry and mortified for my boy, who's one of the smallest in his class and seems to get picked on, but also quietly proud of my daughter, who I never imagined would stick up for her little brother like this.

'He's fine.' Miss Thompson nods me on. 'No damage, apart from his glasses.'

I'm horrified as I realise the implication. 'His glasses?'

Miss Thompson clearly understands my panic. 'Oh no, he wasn't in an actual fight,' she reassures me quickly. 'The boy was calling him names. Josh got upset. He took his glasses off to wipe them and dropped them, and… he stood on them, I'm afraid.'

Oh God. It had taken ages to get Josh to accept wearing glasses. He'd only fallen in love with them when we'd splashed out for some Harry Potter specs. Now, he would be devastated. My heart aching for him, I go to him, ruffle his hair and crouch down in front of him.

Josh wipes his arm under his nose and blinks at me through his lopsided glasses. 'Sorry, Mum,' he mumbles. 'I know you're short of money.'

Realising my children are much more intuitive and sensitive than I give them credit for, I swallow hard and take hold of his hands. 'Not that short,' I assure him. 'In any case, I reckon the optician will easily be able to fix them.'

Josh brightens at that. 'You reckon?'

'I reckon.' I'm sure can feel my boy's heartbeat next to mine as he stands to give me a firm hug – something he rarely does anywhere near school now that he's 'growing up' – and I squeeze him a little bit closer before he wriggles away.

'Holly was ace,' he says enthusiastically. 'She smacked Nathan Miller right in the mouth.' Josh quickly stops talking as the headmistress's door opens and his sister appears.

Holly's wearing a scowl. The headmistress is frowning behind her.

'I've had a word with Holly about speaking to her teacher or coming to see me before she gives in to the inclination to hit people, Mrs Connolly,' she says. 'Do you think you could reinforce that at home?'

'I most certainly will.' I match her stern frown with one of my own, then take hold of Holly's hand and offer Josh my other one. 'I imagine her father will have something to say, too.'

Holly's shoulders drop dejectedly at that. She drags her feet all the way back to the exit. 'Are you going to tell Dad?' she asks worriedly, once we're outside.

'Not sure.' I glance sideways at her. 'For the record, though, while I don't want you doing that again – ever – I'm quite proud of you.'

'You are?' Holly's eyes spring wide with surprise.

'I am. Make sure to go to your teacher next time, or text me, but yes, I'm proud of you for sticking up for Josh. In fact, I think we'll pop by Nan's for a little apple pie and ice cream,' I say, feeling inspired by Holly's attitude. 'It's not a reward,' I make sure to add. 'Just a bit of a treat after a bad day. What do you think?'

'Cool,' the kids say in unison, and I feel marginally better that they're healthy and happy, despite the problems between Jason and me.

Thus my unscheduled visit to Mum's. I need to talk to her. I really need to talk to my father. I can't punch him in the mouth for his constant bullying of Jason, but it's time I start sticking up for my husband.

I just hope to God I still have one.

CHAPTER EIGHTEEN

KARLA

'Good Lord, you're absolutely drenched.' Mum looks me over, her eyebrows raised in concern as I let myself through the front door, herding Holly and Josh in before me. 'What have you been doing, trying to drown yourself?'

'It's a thought.' I smile wanly.

'Karla? Everything all right, sweetheart?' Mum asks worriedly.

'Holly thumped Nathan Miller in the mouth,' Josh supplies excitedly.

'Did she indeed?' Mum gives him an unimpressed look.

'But only because he was picking on me,' Josh adds gravely.

Mum arches an eyebrow in Holly's direction. 'Is this true, Holly?'

Holly nods, and shrugs guiltily. 'He made him break his glasses, so…'

'She smacked him in the gob,' Josh finishes, clearly still awe-struck. 'Pow! She was totally awesome. The headmistress told her off though, so Mum brought us here for some apple pie as a treat.'

'Not a treat, twit!' Holly rolls her eyes in despair, and then turns her best beguiling gaze towards Mum. 'Because we've had a really bad day.'

'Ah, I see,' Mum says, as I stand there, dripping rain all over the carpet and willing myself not to cry in front of the children.

'In which case, you shall have some. But upstairs first. Grab some towels from the airing cupboard and give your hair a good rub. Both of you – go on. And then into the lounge and watch some TV while I talk to your mum.'

Ushering them in the direction of the stairs, she turns back to me. 'I take it it's not Holly hitting some little bully you're looking devastated about?' she asks shrewdly.

Breathing in hard, I shake my head, pull my phone from my pocket, select my texts and hand it to her.

A frown crossing her face, Mum reads the cryptic text Jason eventually sent in response to mine: *Need some space. Don't wait up for me. About the financial backing, by the way, it's not happening. Your father way exceeded my expectations.*

That was it. No further contact, and his phone's been going to voicemail since. I have no idea where he is. How he is. What happened between him and my father. I can only assume he went through Jason's accounts and turned him down.

Mum's frown deepens. 'Oh no.' She closes her eyes, a swallow sliding down her throat, then, 'That *bloody* man,' she seethes. 'What on earth is he up to now?'

Her eyes are fraught with worry as she looks back at me. 'I take it you two have argued again?'

'Worse than.' I avert my gaze, fixing it hard on ceiling, but as hard as I try to stop them, still the tears come. 'I think he hates me.'

'Nonsense. Jason couldn't hate you if he tried,' Mum says, discernible agitation in her voice as she tries to reassure me. 'You're overreacting.'

That's exactly what I've done. My father is the one full of hatred, for Jason, for reasons I will never understand. He hinted that there might be evidence of my husband cheating on me on his laptop and I leapt on it. Evidence that might even have been planted there by him. I don't know whether my father would sink that low, but I'm not sure I believe Mark's claim to have been using Jason's laptop either. Isn't it more likely that, realising Jason needed help getting out of a hole, he was covering his friend's back? Regardless, I can't believe Jason would do such a thing. Yet I hurled accusations at him, loudly, in front of his staff. And all this after he'd come from a meeting with my father that had clearly been soul-destroying. Jason should hate me, but he could never hate me as much as I hate myself right now.

'He found me in his office,' I confide miserably, as Mum wraps an arm around me and steers me firmly towards the kitchen. 'He came back from seeing Dad to find me checking his internet history.'

'His internet history?' Mum's step falters. 'But... Why?'

'Because of Dad,' I say, as she stares at me, astonished. 'Why is he doing this, Mum? What does he have against him? I don't understand.' The tears come in earnest then. 'Please... make him stop.'

CHAPTER NINETEEN

DIANA

Hearing Robert's key in the lock, Diana placed the last of her grand-children's dinner dishes in the dishwasher and braced herself to go and speak to him. She rarely talked to him about anything meaningful, mainly because, being the opinionated person that he was, Robert rarely listened. But she needed to now. She had to establish what had gone on between him and Jason earlier that day. Karla was worried to death, and she couldn't believe Robert was so oblivious to that fact that he would continue these ridiculous attempts to drive Jason from her life. He and Karla were together, married with two children, for goodness' sake. It was time Robert damn well accepted it.

'Evening,' he called shortly from the hall.

Diana didn't answer. That would be far too happy-couple-ish. They hadn't been that in a very long time. They rubbed along, he doing his thing, she doing hers, but that was all. She was content to do so. If he rocked the boat, though… She had assets now, and wouldn't hesitate to leave him clinging to the wreckage on his own.

She waited a moment while Robert flicked through his mail before going to the lounge for his pre-dinner drink – he was a creature of habit, and she was wise to it, though little did he know it – and then followed him in.

His glass half full of whisky, Robert arched an eyebrow as she walked through the door. He would be surprised, she supposed.

She normally retired to the orangery to read, leaving him to microwave his meal once he'd had his aperitif – often more than one. As Robert rarely read, and was therefore disinclined to join her, it was the only place she really felt able to relax.

'Want one?' Robert pointed his glass in her direction.

Diana shook her head. 'Not yet, no.' She would have one later, when Robert was out, which she had no doubt he would be, and she was free to talk to Michael without fear of him overhearing.

'Good day?' he asked her, taking a large gulp of his own drink and turning away.

'Average,' Diana answered. 'You?' she asked him, out of civility.

'The usual. Firefighting, thanks to incompetent staff.' Robert sighed, tipping his glass back again. 'Dealing with morons.'

Diana watched him loosen his tie, looking suitably harassed and work-worn – for her benefit, she'd no doubt. He never failed to remind her that he worked his fingers to the bone day after day to provide her a luxurious lifestyle. A lifestyle she wouldn't have if she wasn't with him, as he'd also reminded her over the years. Little did he know that, in the absence of any funds from him other than those he deemed necessary, Diana had made provision of her own.

'I gather you had a meeting with Jason today?' she asked him. 'Karla mentioned it,' she supplied, when he glanced enquiringly in her direction.

'I did,' he said, with another discernible sigh. 'Complete waste of time.'

'I see,' Diana said. 'Why do you hate him so much, Robert?' she asked him, wanting to catch him off guard.

She had, clearly. Turning back to her, Robert searched her face warily. 'I don't hate him,' he refuted. 'I don't rate him, but I don't hate him.'

'You disliked him from the moment you set eyes on him,' Diana reminded him scornfully.

'He got our daughter pregnant, Diana. Is your memory that short?'

'No, Robert, it's not,' Diana replied, pointedly holding his gaze. She remembered very well the events of twelve years ago: Robert's shock and outrage to the news that Karla was pregnant, his determination to try to persuade her not to have the child. Diana often wondered whether, on seeing Holly grow from a tiny baby into the beautiful young girl she was, he might have any regrets about such a suggestion. She very much doubted it. Robert never had regrets. His philosophy in life was to look to the future. He never looked back, possibly for fear of seeing the casualties he'd left in his wake. Herself being one of them. Her dear friend another.

Upon learning exactly what kind of man Robert was, in the early days of their marriage, she'd thought that perhaps they deserved each other. She'd made her bed, and so she would lie in it. The 'luxurious lifestyle' made it tolerable.

She should have left him after losing Sarah. She would have, but for the fact that she hadn't been emotionally strong. After suffering a double bereavement – her mother had also passed away – just getting through a single day had seemed an unsurmountable task. She'd functioned, but she hadn't felt anything very much. She felt now though.

It had taken a while for her anger to surface after Sarah died. When it had, she'd subdued it, deciding to stay until Karla built a life of her own. And then she'd fallen into a routine, she supposed, once the grandchildren had come along. Seeing Robert's continual attempts to destroy Karla's marriage, though, had rekindled her simmering hatred for this bully of a man who would lie about his child's death. The thing Diana could least forgive was that he'd simply carried on, doing exactly as he'd always done, running his business, controlling people. Still, he continued to think he was untouchable. But one day his past was going to catch up with him. The pity was, Diana wouldn't be around to see his downfall.

'So, what did she say?' Robert asked as Diana studied him, looking for the usual signs of his lies. Was he aware, she wondered, that she could see his mind ticking over. The way he smoothed his hand along the drinks table or the coffee table, examining it for non-existent dust, or his tendency to fiddle with a shirt cuff or his watch strap – those were the little things he did when the cogs were going around, formulating explanations to account for his contemptible actions.

'Nothing much. She was too upset,' Diana supplied. 'I gather you've refused to back his business. Why, Robert? Jason didn't come to you easily. Karla had to practically beg him. Why would you arrange a meeting with him and then turn him down?'

Robert's expression was one of surprise. Was it genuine? Diana thought it actually was. 'I did no such thing,' he blustered, walking back to the drinks table to slosh a considerable measure of whisky into his glass. 'What did he tell her?'

'I'm not entirely sure.' Diana continued to study him as he took another hefty gulp. He was agitated, but knowing Karla would find out, she didn't think he would lie about something like this. 'Karla thought it was something to do with his accounts.'

'That's absolute rubbish.' Robert was adamant. 'I offered him the loan. A considerable amount, in fact.' Shaking his head, he drained his glass. 'I told Karla from outset, the man's a loser, hanging on in there, determined to make his business succeed even though he knows it's doomed to failure without the right backing behind it.'

'Determination is no bad trait though, is it?' Diana suggested. 'He's a lot like you in some ways.'

Robert's gaze shot to hers. 'He's *nothing* like me,' he replied sharply.

CHAPTER TWENTY

JASON

Jason guessed he'd be here at some point this evening. Contempt thick in his throat, he waited while his father-in-law drove into the car park of the golf club. Counselling himself not to do what he very much wanted to, he stayed put in his own car until he had parked in his designated space, and then climbed out.

Fenton got the shock of his life when he climbed out of his car and turned around to find Jason standing behind it. 'Jason,' he said, collecting himself and offering him that short, derisory smile of his. 'Am I to assume you've reconsidered the offer I made you? Because, if so, this isn't quite the place to—'

'Don't,' Jason warned him, his throat tight, his gut twisting with a mixture of burning anger and sheer disbelief.

Fenton clearly got the message, appraising him silently for a second, and then looking away to close his car door. 'I'm not sure what this is about,' he said, his gaze coming back to his, 'but you should know there are security cameras overlooking the car park.'

'Fortunately for you,' Jason said, fighting back the temptation to floor the bastard anyway. To hurt him badly. It would be worth doing time for.

Sighing demonstrably, Fenton shook his head and walked towards him.

Jason made no move to let him pass by, causing his step to falter.

Fenton kneaded his forehead agitatedly, glanced down and then back at him. 'What is it you want, Jason?' he asked him, his expression one of impatience. The man was scared though. Jason noted the nervousness in his eyes as they pivoted towards the building. It gave him no satisfaction. Seeing the man beg for his life just might.

'Apart from to break your neck…' he said, and paused, and watched as a slow swallow slid down Fenton's throat, 'from you, nothing, Fenton, other than to substantiate the bullshit you've been spouting – which is all you really have, isn't it, at the end of the day: nothing?'

'I'm going inside,' Fenton muttered, attempting to push past him.

Jason didn't budge. 'A DNA test, is all,' he said. 'There isn't anything else I want from you, Robert, trust me.'

Fenton looked at him in bemusement, and then spat out a derisory laugh. 'Do you honestly think I wouldn't have already taken steps to establish whether this nightmare was true?' he asked him. 'I've done the *test*,' he went on, with another despairing shake of his head. 'As soon as I learned Karla was pregnant, I did the test.'

When Karla was…? Jason felt as if someone had just punched him. Winded, physically, he stared incredulously at him, trying to understand what would drive someone to do the despicable things he did. Failing. 'Why the fucking hell didn't you *say* something?' he yelled.

'Say what?' Fenton growled back. '*When*, precisely? I tried everything to dissuade her from having the baby. I begged her. She was adamant she was going to go through with it. Was I supposed to tell her after she'd given birth? When the child reached her first birthday? *When?*

The child? Anger kicking ferociously inside him, Jason almost reeled where he stood.

'She claimed she loved you. What in God's name was I supposed to do?' Fenton continued, actually imagining his actions were *defensible?* The man was inhuman. Jason squinted hard at him.

'Of course, assuming you had any traits that were worthwhile, I considered you might at least provide for the child.' Fenton's laugh this time was a derogatory sneer. 'You soon dispelled that hope, didn't you?'

'You're talking about your *grandchild*,' Jason could barely get the words out. 'Your *daughter*.'

Fenton said nothing, merely held his gaze for a long, cold moment. Then, 'I have the paperwork. I'll email you a copy,' he said, adjusting his shirt cuffs, and then continuing on past him.

Jason didn't try to stop him. He didn't dare touch him. If he did, he would kill him.

'Oh.' Fenton turned back from a safe distance off. 'Note I said, 'loved'. Not present tense, Jason.' He smiled again, a gloating smile. 'I couldn't help overhearing Karla and her mother talking in the kitchen one evening. Karla was upset, as she often is lately. It was most telling, I thought, that when Diana asked her if she loved you, Karla said, she did… once.'

Pulling his gaze away, he walked on. 'They were discussing the merits of the young man Karla was dancing with at Diana's party versus yours afterwards,' he imparted, over his shoulder. 'I didn't interrupt. Girl-talk. More than I dare do.'

Swallowing back the bile rising in his throat, Jason watched him swagger on towards the golf club entrance. Tried to assimilate. Breathing hard, he stayed where he was for several seconds, acrid grief crashing through him as he felt his world crumbling around him.

He felt hollow inside as he walked back to his car, numb from the inside out. He barely flinched as his passenger wing hit one of the bollards at the exit as he trod on the accelerator and screeched out of the car park.

Arriving at his office a couple of hours later, Jason placed the bottle of whisky he'd purchased on the desk, plunged his hands into his pockets and stared down at his laptop. It was still in the same position as when he'd walked out, yanked around to face the doorway. It was strange how, despite his whole life being turned upside down, his innards being ripped out, everything looked exactly the same as it had yesterday and the day before that. He felt almost as if he could simply push the hands of the clock back and make all the shit go away. But he couldn't, could he? It just kept on coming.

He'd always wondered about his roots. And now he knew. He'd been spawned by an abomination of a man. Born to a woman he could only suppose had been on the receiving end of Fenton's abusive behaviour. He should never have happened. Karla and him, they should never have happened.

His kids…

Jesus. Swaying slightly on his feet, Jason pressed a hand against the back of his neck and glanced up at the ceiling. No point looking up there, he supposed. He must have done something beyond abhorrent in another life. He looked back to the whisky. After downing several beers with whisky chasers at the pub, he'd splashed out and bought a bottle of the good stuff: 18 year old Glenfiddich. If he was going to drink himself to death, he was going to do it in style.

Might as well live up to his reputation, he'd decided, and be the loser he obviously was – a cheating, lying failure and obviously a complete bastard. He hadn't needed Karla to confirm that. Smiling cynically, Jason picked up the bottle, twirled his computer around, negotiated his way unsteadily to his chair and dropped heavily down into it.

So, what sites had he been browsing, he wondered? And had he found anyone worth dating? Maybe he had. Unscrewing the cap, he tipped his head back and drank straight from the bottle. Maybe he'd been sleep-dating, fucking any and all available women he could find, which was obviously why he didn't remember doing it.

Perhaps he should remind himself? He took another large gulp of whisky and swallowed it back, getting no comfort from it as it burned its way down his oesophagus. *Why not go out with a bang, hey?* He had nothing to lose, after all.

Wiping the back of his hand against his mouth, he fired up the laptop and… voila! Up came his internet history, as accessed by Karla behind his back. He had no doubt her father had put her up to that. And he was sure that Robert had accessed his laptop while he and Karla had been in the kitchen. Why, Jason had no clue. Because he'd still been debating the wisdom of delivering the news he had, and this was his fallback plan? Because he'd wanted to make sure Karla would want nothing to do with him, whether or not he delivered the news? Whatever his reasoning, he'd succeeded in his aim. As far as Fenton was concerned, it was mission accomplished.

Karla had clearly already grown disillusioned with him. According to Fenton, he reminded himself. Did he believe it? Had he really been mistaking what he thought he saw in Karla's eyes? Jason wasn't sure. It didn't much matter whether she loved him or not now, though, did it, he also reminded himself.

His heart feeling as if it was turning inside out inside him, he reached for his keyboard and scrolled down through the history. 'Shit.' He drew in a breath as he noted the sites listed there: Match.com, Zoosk, Flirt, FlirtEasy, QuickFlirt and more. It was no wonder Karla had been so upset. Taking another slug of his whisky, he nearly choked when he came to the BeNaughty and LocalNaughties sites. Sobering up, briefly, he almost closed his laptop down – and then thought, stuff it. If he was going to be accused of the deed, he might as well take a look. After all, he was going to have to stop thinking of himself as a married man now, wasn't he? Although, actually, it probably hadn't ever been legal anyway.

Swallowing back an overwhelming sense of loss, Jason opened up one of the sites. He wasn't certain how good an idea it was when he read the overview, which stated that everyone on the site had the same goal: to find people with similar interests who were looking for casual and erotic relationships. He wasn't sure that fit his preferred criteria. He would need either a lot less whisky or a hell of a lot more to go there, no matter how frustrated and lonely he was feeling.

The next site offered much the same: casual dating and hook-ups. Jason supposed 'hook-ups' were what he had in mind. But then again, maybe not. Though he definitely wasn't looking for what some of the other sites claimed he would find: a relationship or his 'special someone'. He'd already found her. He was probably more up for something in between a one-night stand and a relationship, conversation definitely being one of his 'search criteria'.

Christ, he needed someone to talk to.

Sipping steadily from his bottle, he browsed a few more sites, finally clicking on one that made him want to continue reading – or rather squinting at. It offered email and IM chatting, and also had a facility to switch between searching for 'love' or 'flirting', which might allow him to tread the middle ground.

Did he want to tread the middle ground? Jason had no idea… Right now, he felt as if the ground had dropped from underneath him, leaving him freefalling into a very dark pit. Hesitating, he took another long drink and continued on to the sign-up page. The site promised the application process took only minutes – basic details, a username, password and email address being all that was needed before he was 'in and free to browse'.

It lived up to its promise. After entering the information and scribbling down his password – 'Megaidiot1', which he thought appropriate – Jason was indeed in, and clueless about what to do next. Fill in his profile, he guessed, which presented him with an immediate problem. Did he tick single or married? Separated, he opted for, and then he hit his next snag. He wasn't much into selfies. The only photos he had, therefore, were of him and Karla together, or with the kids, which was even worse. He couldn't bring himself to crop any of those. A quick search of his laptop produced a security ID photo he'd had taken in order to access a high-tech computer meeting. He didn't look very happy in it, but then, he wasn't exactly feeling ecstatic. It would do.

So, criteria? His lips poised on the bottle, he debated, swilled back another mouthful of whisky and then completed a few categories. And then went back and hit delete. He was narrowing his search down to Karla, he realised, his chest constricting painfully.

Swiping a hand over his face, Jason blinked hard. Don't go there, he warned himself, and then started afresh, this time making sure his 'preferences' were as unlike Karla as he could get. Hair, eye colour – all different. Once he was finished, he took another fortifying drink and hit search. He skimmed through them, skipping most, but clicking on two he liked. And then he buried his head in his hands. What the hell was he doing?

His heart like a lead weight in his chest, his head swimming, he massaged his temples with his thumbs and stayed where he was. The keyboard was out of focus, and the room began to spin as he closed his eyes. He needed to lie down, but he doubted the nausea now churning his gut would allow him to sleep. Folding his arms on the desk, he was about to rest his head when he heard a distinctive ping, followed by another.

Closing one eye, Jason glanced blearily up. *Jackpot*, he thought, congratulating himself on the fact that somebody out there liked him.

One of the women he'd clicked on had messaged him. *Hi. Are you feeling lonely?*

Bloody lonely, Jason replied.

CHAPTER TWENTY-ONE

KARLA

Jason still hasn't come home and with each call I make I grow more desperate. I've tried his mobile a thousand times. I've sent him texts, left umpteen messages. I've texted Mark, who has no idea where he is. I've even rung his sister, Hannah, who hasn't seen Jason for two weeks, and who confided in me that she's been concerned about him seeming so exhausted and worried lately. Aware of what frame of mind he's in, that hasn't helped one little bit.

My mind now running through all sorts of scenarios – I can almost see him lying in some hospital bed somewhere, unconscious – I try his office number again. Again, it rings out. I can't imagine he's there, deliberately not picking up. Unless, of course, he simply doesn't want to speak to me. He was so furious at finding me there, that it was so blindingly obvious I didn't trust him, that I would believe my father's word over his. It scared me. He's scaring me now. My heart drums erratically and then leaps in my chest as I hear the alert of an incoming text. Hastily, I check it.

On my way, Mum has sent. *Five minutes.*

Relief on some level sweeps through me, while I scramble frantically for what to do next. Of course – his car will be there. Why didn't I think of that before? If he is in the office, his car will be in the car park. Already, I am reaching for the address book for the security guard's direct line. Mercifully, he answers the call and

I gabble out that Jason doesn't have his mobile with him, that his office phone seems to be permanently engaged – a small lie – and ask him to check the car park.

The wait is interminable while he does. 'Yep, it's there,' he says, coming back on the line. 'Sorry, I must have been doing my rounds when he arrived. I can give him a message, if you—'

'No, no. Thanks,' I say over him. 'I just wanted to drop his mobile off. I'll drive over now.'

Headlights sweep the hall walls as I hang up. Mum has arrived. Knowing I would never ask her to babysit so late and at such short notice unless it was urgent, she agreed to come immediately when I spoke to her.

'Anything?' she asks, her expression worried as I pull the front door open.

'He's at the office.' Tears of frustration and fear prick my eyes as I grab up my car keys. 'Holly and Josh are in bed. They—'

'Go,' Mum says, stepping in and urging me past her to the door. 'Ring me,' she calls, as I race down the drive and climb into my car.

Acknowledging her with a nod, I reverse haphazardly off the drive, now feeling truly desperate. I have no idea what happened at Jason's meeting with my father, other than that the offer of financial backing wasn't forthcoming. I don't know whether the two of them argued. I do know that Jason went straight from that meeting into his own office, only to end up having to defend himself to his wife, the one person he should be able to depend on. He'd been crushed by the awful things I'd said to him. I swear I could feel his heart breaking as he walked away from me. I have to find him. Talk to him. Convince him that I love him and that I am there for him. That even if his damn business does go under, it won't be the end of the world. I will always be there for him, no matter what.

Nearing his car, my stomach tightens. It's parked askew. Not just clumsily, but carelessly, diagonally straddling two bays. The front wheels are wrenched hard right, it's as if he's driven at speed, pulled up and simply abandoned it. This is not Jason. He's a careful driver. Becoming a father made him a better driver, he says.

Oh God, no. Pulling up alongside the car, my heart misses a beat as I realise the passenger side is damaged, the wing badly dented. He's had an accident. Hit something. Praying that no one has been injured, above all, that Jason hasn't, I curse my *bloody* father, who I suspect cares about no one. Why did I insist on Jason borrowing money from him, when my father thinks so little of him? I must have been completely insane.

I climb out of my car and tentatively try Jason's car doors. They're open. A cold chill of trepidation runs through me. Jason would never not lock his doors. His tie is thrown on the passenger seat, as if torn angrily off. The interior is filled with the pungent smell of cigar smoke. But Jason doesn't smoke. He stopped years ago. Or at least I thought he did. It's not that that bothers me most, though. It's the unmistakable smell of whisky, which tells me my husband has been drinking and driving. This is *not* Jason.

Not the Jason you know. Sarah, worming her way into my head, reminds me of the one thing I'm overwhelmingly good at: letting down those I love when they most need me.

Quieting her, I turn away from the glove compartment. I don't want to search Jason's car. I don't need to. I need to find him. I slam the door shut and head towards the office, giving the security guard a wave as I go. He's emerging from the side of the building to do his rounds.

'Looks like someone had some pressing business,' he shouts, nodding towards Jason's car.

'Is he inside?' I shout back.

'His lights are on,' he says.

Thank God. Relieved, I give him another wave and quickly punch the code into the security door.

There are no lights on in the main office, but I see a glimmer of light emerging from under Jason's door. Attempting to still the nerves twisting inside me, I push on, and then pause with my hand poised on the door handle. There's no noise from inside. I press my ear to the door. No sound at all. 'Jason?' I call.

He doesn't answer.

'Jason?' Goosebumps prickle my skin and I pray again that he's all right. That he hasn't been injured or done anything awful. I have no reason to imagine he would, but there's this hard knot of fear in my chest that just won't go away.

Taking a breath, I squeak the door open, my gaze going immediately to his desk. Seeing no sign of him, I step inside and then start as I realise where he is. Slumped in the leather club chair to the side of the door is my husband. Arms crossed over his chest, a bottle nestled in the crook of his elbow, Jason appears to be fast asleep. Close to unconsciousness possibly. My heart skitters against my ribcage as I crouch beside him and realise the bottle is empty. He chose to come here, not answering his phone, drinking himself into a stupor, rather than go home.

Oh, Jason… Moving closer, I check to make sure he's breathing. His eyelids flicker as I study his face, tracing my fingers lightly over his high cheekbones and strong jawline. He's in need of a shave, not that I've ever minded his unshaven chin grazing my skin. Dearly, I wish I hadn't been so quick to judge him without establishing the facts. I've hurt him. I'd do anything now to undo it. To be home with him lying next to me, safe and sober. Then I would show him how much I love him. That I could never contemplate a life without him.

I press my lips lightly to his. 'Jason,' I whisper. He doesn't stir and panic grips me afresh. I have no idea what to do. Should I call an ambulance? Try to get him home? But how? Easing myself to my feet, I pull out my phone, hoping to enlist the security guard's help with getting Jason into my car. But… should I let him sleep it off for a while?

Uncertain, I decide to call my mum before moving him. My body feels heavy, weary with the weight of too much worry. I walk to Jason's desk and sink into his chair.

My eyes fall on a Post-it note next to his laptop. I don't really register what's written there at first, and then a single word leaps out at me: 'FlirtEasy'. My breath dies in my throat, my mind reeling as I read what's beneath it: 'Password – Megaidiot1'. Jason's handwriting. My eyes confirm this, but my head refuses to believe it. My gaze shoots to the laptop and I reach towards it as if it might bite me.

Tentatively, I stroke a finger over the mouse, and the screen comes to life. I stare, stupefied, at it for a second. And then my heart lurches violently. He's signed out, but it's quite obvious which site he was signed into. Feeling sick to my stomach, I place my phone down and type in the password. Apart from the tears sliding down my cheeks, I am quite still as I read the profiles of the women who have responded to Jason almost blindly. There are several.

It's Jason's response to a message, though, that I can't tear my gaze away from. *Are you feeling lonely?*

Bloody lonely, Jason answered.

Mega idiot. That would be me. My heart folds up inside me.

He was right. The raw ache in my chest turns to a hard kernel of anger. My father was right. I laugh, disbelieving.

But he's a liar! Sarah shoots back.

He was right! The evidence is right there before my eyes. I heave out a gasp, feeling as if my lungs are turning inside out. Is this what he wants? These women, desperate for a man? Trembling with rage, I study the profile photographs – women as far from me as it's possible to get. Fake faces caked in make-up, fake hair, fake photographs. False personas.

I can do fake. I can do false. I'm a fucking actress! An anguished moan escapes me.

I can do desperate.

I am desperate.

CHAPTER TWENTY-TWO

KARLA

'You've decided to come home then?' Working to keep any facetiousness from my voice, to stay in control while the cement that holds the foundations of my life together is crumbling to dust, I turn from the sink as Jason walks quietly from the front door to the kitchen.

Two days he's been gone. Two whole days without even a word. Does he really care so little about me? Disillusioned, utterly, I simply stare at him. I know I will need to call upon all of my acting skills in order to detach from the crushing pain where my heart should be and carry on; to pretend I don't know that he's been doing what he so vehemently denied. I am so furious that he could do this, not just to me, but to our children, I have to force myself not to walk across the kitchen and punch him. Part of me is filled with hatred for him. There is part of me, though, the part that's not bleeding inside, that still loves him, that truly is desperate to keep him, whatever it takes.

I have no idea how my legs are still holding me. They threatened to buckle beneath me when I saw him standing so uncertainly in the doorway: my husband, the man I gave everything to and imagined I would be spending the rest of my life with. I want to give in to it, to drop to the floor right here and weep like a baby, but I won't. I don't want his sympathy. I don't want him to feel sorry for me. I want him to love me. But I want the impossible, because if he's doing this, then in his heart, he has already left me.

Jason looks towards me. His expression is apprehensive. 'I needed some time,' he offers. A lame explanation. He knows it.

Looking him over, I nod. He looks dreadful. He's still wearing the clothes he had on when I left him deep in inebriated sleep in his office. He hasn't shaved, and the dark shadows under his eyes, growing ever darker, indicate he hasn't slept. *Welcome to the club*, I feel like saying. The dreams that have haunted me all my life have been relentless these last two nights, snatching me from fitful sleep whenever I manage to doze off. As I look at my husband, who I sense is leaving me as surely as my sister did, I feel it all over again: the empty loneliness of losing someone who is a fundamental part of you.

And then I am back there, living my nightmare, standing over the slim body that lies so still and cold. And I am inside, looking out. Silently, I ask myself, why did you lie for him? No breath escapes her blue-tinged lips, yet she breathes. Inside me, she breathes. We were independent, but one, inseparable. My father took her away from me, and I allowed him to. I allowed him to get away with the horrendous thing he'd done.

Jason and I are individuals. But we *were* one: a couple, a unit, a family. Now broken. I can't allow the person who chipped relentlessly away at our marriage, who mercilessly destroyed two more lives, to escape the consequences. Not this time. When Sarah died, I was too frightened of our father to tell.

I lied for him. I lied to myself. I tried to convince myself that our father would never do such a thing. But he did. I tried to convince myself Jason would never cheat. But he has. The life I lived after she was gone was a lie. My marriage is a lie. Should I feel guilty, then, for continuing the lies, for pretending to be a person I'm not in order to open my husband's eyes? Jason did love me – that is a truth I am sure of. He could still. If only he remembered all the pieces of me that make the whole. I can't lose him.

'You've cut your hair,' Jason says, breaking the silence that hangs heavy between us.

Instinctively, my hand goes to my bare neck. I sense disbelief in his voice, rather than disapproval. I couldn't believe it either, as I'd stared into the mirror, watching the hair Jason always claimed he loved fall to the floor. Little pieces of me. I won't miss them.

'It's nice,' he says. 'Suits you.'

I don't pursue it. I'm not after false compliments either.

'Where were you?' I ask him. I assume he won't tell me the truth, but I wonder obliquely whether he cares that I haven't tried to contact him either. I, too, needed some time. Time to process my feelings, to decide what to do – whether I should pack his bags and leave them outside or pray he came home and that, for now, he would stay. Whatever I do, I don't want to initiate an argument he will then claim drove him away. He will take responsibility for the decisions he makes – perhaps already has made. I made a horrendous mistake; I accept that. Insisting he ingratiate himself with my father was wrong. Jason didn't want to be beholden to him. But I won't let him lay the blame for destroying our family at my feet.

'I stayed at my sister's,' he says, with an awkward shrug. Is he telling the truth? I can't tell. I have yet to learn the body language of my husband's lies. 'After that last argument we had, I thought we could both use a little space,' he goes on, his expression wary, his eyes meeting mine briefly.

So he is blaming me then? I hide a disappointed smile. I can't quite believe he would actually imply that my 'snooping' on him, accusing him of doing what I now *know* he's been doing, is reason enough for him to disappear for two days without even having the courtesy to let me know he was alive.

I squash my growing anger. I'm determined not to fall into the tit-for-tat trap. 'It must have been a bit cramped there,' I say, aware that, with two children under five in a two-bedroomed house, his sister barely has room to swing a cat.

'I slept on the sofa.' He runs a hand tiredly over his neck. 'Where are the kids?' he asks, glancing around as if Holly and Josh might spring out from one of the kitchen cupboards.

'At school,' I supply. Perhaps he's forgotten it's a school day. It must be disorientating for him, I think cynically, having forgotten so completely that we existed. 'Coffee?' I ask him, turning away. I can't look at him for fear I will see the deceit in his eyes. If I do, I will lose control and become the demented woman I was in his office; the woman that I don't like.

'No, I, er... No, thanks,' he answers hesitantly. 'You're not at work today then?' he asks, as if surprised I would take a day off while my world falls apart. I suppose he might be. Knowing I need time stored up for when my children are sick, I rarely take a day off.

'No.' I make myself a coffee, willing myself not to give in to the tears that are now perpetually close to the surface. 'I didn't feel too well, strangely. I have a pain... in my chest.' My voice catches. I inhale sharply.

He doesn't speak for a second. Then, 'I'm sorry, Karla,' he says quietly.

Breathing shakily out, I face him. 'For?'

Jason scans my face and then drops his gaze to the floor. 'Everything,' he says, his tone ragged. 'This. I can't do this any more, Karla. I'm so sorry.'

An icy dagger pierces my heart. 'Do what?' I ask, because I have to. I have to hear the words spill from his mouth before I can process the enormity of what he is telling me.

'Us.' He looks up, his expression anguished. 'It's not working, Karla. Things have become... too complicated. I think we should take some time. Take a step away from each other.' He pulls in a tight breath and waits, as if for the onslaught.

Take a step away? How far a step, Jason? How huge a step away from me is fucking other women? My anger simmers dangerously. I stare at him, too shocked by his calm announcement that he's about to end our marriage, destroy my life and our children's lives, to respond.

'Complicated,' I repeat eventually, my voice choked. 'I see.' I stifle a ridiculous urge to laugh.

Jason says nothing. His eyes fixed to the floor, he pinches the bridge of his nose instead.

'Are you seeing someone?' I force the words past the shard of glass in my throat.

'No.' Jason looks quickly up. 'I wouldn't do that, Karla. I…' Averting his gaze again, he trails hopelessly off, as if realising the absurdity of that statement.

Liar!

I stamp down the furious voice in my head, nodding instead as I assimilate, struggling against the urge to fly at him, to hit him, to keep hitting him until my strength fails me. 'So' – I take another deep breath in and try to contain the emotions warring inside me – 'are you leaving?'

I see his reluctance, his hesitancy, and I know what his answer will be. 'Because if you are, it might be an idea to discuss how we're going to explain to your children that they're about to become *fatherless* suddenly.' Holding his gaze, I short-circuit him, as he makes my worst nightmare a living reality.

Jason closes his eyes. 'I… don't know.' Emitting a heavy sigh, he moves away from the door at last, where no doubt he remained poised for flight should things turn ugly. 'Do you want me to go?' he asks, stepping towards me.

He looks tentatively at me, and I realise this ball is in my court, for now. 'You will eventually.' I swallow hard, force the tears back.

He nods, runs a hand over his face. 'The kids,' he says. 'I just want to do what's best for them. I don't want to upset them.'

Ha! Now I really want to laugh, until I break down and cry. But I *won't*. I will do something at which I am well practised. I will detach from the emotion – from this, the most painful moment of my life. I will focus my energies on the fight, because I will fight for my marriage. Even though the battle might already be lost, I won't give in easily. I will *make* him want me.

'Stay,' I say impassively. 'For now.'

I feel my husband's surprised gaze following me as I walk calmly past him to the hall. 'It's different, Jason,' I call back, as I mount the stairs to cry my tears in private. 'As birthday surprises go, it's definitely different.'

CHAPTER TWENTY-THREE

JASON

Jason watched the display on the clock clicking over the hours before he finally fell asleep. He slept heavily, dark and dream-filled, until he woke with a start. Sure he'd heard a crash in the kitchen below, he scrambled out of bed and headed downstairs. He was aware that the reception he would get from Karla would be cool. She'd barely spoken to him in the week he'd been home. She wasn't likely to want to speak to him, given the circumstances, but he was concerned – for her, for the effect all this would have on their children.

Going into the kitchen, he found things were far from the usual organised chaos of a school morning. Karla was still in her dressing gown, picking up pieces of what appeared to be a broken plate from the floor, and Holly looked far from happy, slumped disgruntledly at the breakfast table.

'I don't even like honey,' she moaned, curling a lip as she leaned in to pluck the spoon from the jar and watch the golden gloop drip from it.

'*Ugh*, looks like snot.' Josh, who was also still in his nightwear, looked up from his iPad to observe.

'Holly…' Sighing, Karla straightened up and pressed a hand to her forehead. 'Just eat your toast, sweetheart, will you?'

Holly flopped heavily back in her chair. 'I don't like toast,' she scowled. 'It's burnt. Why can't we have porridge? We always have porridge in the—'

'Because there's no milk!' Karla snapped, and then, remorse flooding her face, she turned quickly away. 'Eat your breakfast, please,' she said, her voice strained, as she pushed the broken pieces of crockery into the bin.

She was struggling not to cry, Jason realised. Guilt weighed heavily inside him. He watched hopelessly as, her belligerence deflating, Holly's eyes also filled up. She wasn't upset about the breakfast offerings, he was well aware. She was upset because Karla was upset, acting out of character. They both were. The kids could sense that things were far from right between them. How could they not?

Knowing he was the cause of all this, and wary of making things worse, he walked hesitantly across to where Holly was now fiddling with the toast on her plate. It had been cremated and then scraped. She wasn't going to eat it. 'Go and grab a couple of biscuits and an apple, sweetheart,' he said. 'I'll make sure to get some milk in for tomorrow.'

'Dad to the rescue.' Karla smiled shortly, brushing past him to get to the table. Jason didn't miss the sarcasm in her voice. Nor, it seemed, did Holly. She watched her mum guardedly as she climbed off her chair and went to the biscuit barrel. Jason felt his heart drop. Now he'd announced that he wanted out of their marriage, he ought to just go – his being here wasn't helping the situation – but he was growing more and more worried, which Karla would find laughable. He didn't want to leave her like this. He didn't actually have anywhere to go either. And, God help him, he didn't want to. But there was no way he could stay. He'd agonised over whether to tell Karla about the news her loving father had delivered and had decided he just couldn't. Certainly not without knowing whether her mother had any idea.

'Josh?' He walked around to ruffle his son's hair, trying for some kind of normalcy; there'd been none since he'd walked back in to blow their lives apart. 'Go and get some clothes on, tiger.' He offered him a reassuring smile. 'And then I'll drive you to school.'

Josh blinked up at him. 'Can I take my iPad?' he asked.

'I don't see why not.' Jason glanced questioningly across to Karla.

'In the car, yes. Into school, no,' Karla said, her despairing look communicating that he was countermanding an already laid-down rule. Jason made a mental note. Clearly Josh was pushing the boundaries too.

'It's not fair. Everyone else does.' Nudging his glasses up his nose, Josh sighed and slid off his chair.

'Everyone else doesn't, Josh, as you very well know,' Karla pointed out, collecting up plates from the table. 'Now hurry up and get dressed, please. And don't forget to brush your teeth.'

'I *won't*. You don't have to keep flipping reminding me,' Josh replied, his tone exasperated as he trudged into the hall.

'And *you* need to learn a little respect, Josh Connolly,' Karla warned him, which prompted a moody glare from Holly as she followed her brother out.

Running his hand over his neck, Jason decided that not commenting might be prudent. 'Are their lunches in the fridge?' he asked instead.

Karla stopped loading up the dishwasher and walked across to open the fridge. 'Oh?' she said, a puzzled look on her face as she gazed inside it. 'The paid staff are slacking, obviously.' She banged the door shut. 'I'd sack them, if I were you. I mean, we wouldn't want the *lodger* having to lift a finger to help out with the domestic chores, would we?'

He'd asked for that, Jason supposed. 'I'll grab something on the way,' he said quietly.

'Good idea.' Karla went back to the dishwasher. 'You can grab something for dinner as well. I won't be here.'

'No problem.' Jason furrowed his brow. 'Are you out tonight then?' he asked tentatively.

'As it happens, yes,' Karla said. She didn't look at him. She hadn't looked at him full on since he'd come back to casually break her heart. 'I'm going into work this afternoon and then out straight after, so I won't have time to cook,' she informed him. 'But it's actually none of your business any more, what I do, is it?'

She was right. She had no obligation to share anything with him any more. Jason swallowed back a deep sense of grief.

'God, now the dishwasher's not working.' Running her hands through her newly cropped hair, Karla fixed her gaze on the ceiling. '*Why?*' she asked, her voice tight. 'Why is this happening? What did I do – apart from fall in love with *you* – that was so *wrong?*'

Her eyes were full of crushing hurt as they came back to his, and Jason knew he wasn't wrong. Whatever Fenton had said – attempting to drive the last nail into the coffin – she hadn't just stopped loving him. Had she?

He watched a slow tear slide down her cheek, and his heart almost cracked inside him. 'Karla, don't.' He wanted to reach out to her but stopped himself. 'None of this is your fault.'

'No?' Karla did look at him then, her sharp blue eyes a kaleidoscope of bewildered emotion. 'But it's not your fault, is it, Jason?' The facetious tone was back, along with bitter disillusionment. 'I mean, you're just such an all-round great guy. You would never do anything that might risk your marriage, would you? Risk ruining your children's lives?'

Dragging her gaze away from him, she turned to walk out of the kitchen, leaving Jason feeling like the worst hypocrite that ever walked the earth.

CHAPTER TWENTY-FOUR

JASON

Jason had been relieved when Karla said she was going into work. She'd already taken most of the week off and, given how late it was this morning, and how pale she'd looked, he'd wondered whether she would. She needed to be able to function without him. *He* needed her to be able to function without him. Selfish it might be, but he had to know she would find the strength to fight back.

'Got your bags, kids?' he asked, glancing at them in the rear-view mirror as he pulled up outside the school.

'Yeah,' Holly said, sounding less than enthusiastic as she retrieved her rucksack from the footwell.

'Josh?' He turned to his son, whose attention was glued to his iPad. 'You need to move it or you'll be late.'

'Yeah, coming.' Jabbing at his game a few more times, Josh sighed and then reached half-heartedly for his seat belt.

Neither of them was in the best of moods. Guessing he couldn't blame them, Jason climbed out to hurry them on. 'Tablet, Josh,' he reminded him, as Josh slid from the car, still clutching it.

'Aw, Dad.' Josh's shoulders slumped as he handed it reluctantly over. 'Will you bring it when you come and collect us?'

'I'll bring it.' Jason smiled tolerantly. He would quite like to have some conversation with him while they drove, but he supposed that Josh probably wouldn't be very receptive anyway. 'See you later.'

Giving him a quick hug and ruffling his hair, he straightened his collar and then bent to kiss Holly. His heart skipped a beat, though, as she stepped away.

'Holly?' He eyed her questioningly.

Looking uncomfortable, Holly glanced down and then nervously back at him. 'Are you and Mum not friends any more?' she asked, her expression a mixture of wariness and mistrust.

Caught off guard, Jason had no idea how to answer. Realising that he and Karla wouldn't easily be friends again was almost breaking him. Where would that leave their kids?

'Your mum's a bit upset with me,' he said, knowing that much was pretty obvious but offering the only explanation he could. 'It's my fault, not hers. Give her a little time, Holly,' he said, appealing to the adult in her, ludicrously. 'It's not you she's angry with, I promise you.'

'Did you do something really bad?' Josh asked, his expression as uncertain as Holly's.

Jason took a breath and nodded. 'Really bad,' he admitted.

Josh studied him, his forehead creasing into a worried frown. 'Can you fix it?' he asked him.

If only. Jason felt his heart plummet. There was no way to fix it. 'I'm trying,' he said. It was all he had.

'You should buy her some flowers,' Josh decided, after a thoughtful second, which had Jason emitting a strangled laugh. He wanted to cry.

'Maybe you could go out for a romantic meal,' Holly suggested. 'I promise not to stay up and watch crap stuff on Netflix if Megan comes and babysits.'

'It's a thought,' Jason said, his throat tight. 'I'll ask her. So, do I get a hug?' He shrugged hopefully. 'Or…'

He'd been about to ask if he was in her bad books, too, which wouldn't have been fair, when Holly launched herself at him, giving him a very firm hug, which he badly needed.

After watching until they were safely inside the school doors, he climbed back in his car and debated what to do as he headed for his office. Should he stay and cause Karla more pain, or should he go, which might allow her to interact somewhere near normally with the kids? Him not being there might also give the kids the opportunity to interact normally with her, it occurred to him. As things were, it seemed even Holly and Josh were walking on eggshells.

As he pulled into the car park of Upwards Online, he was no nearer to knowing what to do for the best. He'd lost everything – his wife, his home. If he went, he would be losing touch with his children. He wasn't sure he could bear that. He was also about to lose this, the company he'd struggled so hard to keep afloat. That much was certain.

After parking up, Jason kneaded his eyes, then climbed out to head wearily for his office. He hadn't been in there since the day of his meeting with Fenton, other than to drink himself paralytic. Mark and Rachel, who'd both been working 24/7 to try to fix the glitch in their program, would be wondering where the bloody hell he was and what he proposed to do. Jason had gone over it and over it, and the only conclusion he could come to was that there was no obvious solution. He wouldn't be able to pay them for much longer, or meet his bank loan payments. He was stuffed. He needed to let Mark and Rachel know, and tell them to use the facilities to look for alternative employment.

'Jase?' Mark got to his feet as Jason walked into the main office, which was remarkable. Usually, a crowbar was all but required to prise him from in front of his computer. 'Where the *hell* have you been?' he asked him, sounding not too impressed.

'We've been worried about you,' Rachel picked up, from where she'd wheeled her office chair away from her PC.

'Sorry.' Jason offered her a small smile. 'I had some things to sort out.'

'Are you all right?' Rachel stood up and walked across to him, her expression concerned. 'You look like shit.'

'Cheers, Rach.' Jason laughed. 'You do wonders for a man's ego. I'm okay,' he assured her, noting that she actually looked extremely concerned. He should have spoken to them sooner. He couldn't have. He'd been incapable of thinking coherently, let alone communicating.

'Could've fooled me,' Mark said, narrowing his eyes as he looked him over. 'That place stank like a bloody distillery after the last time you were in.' He nodded towards Jason's office.

'Yeah. I, er… Drowning my sorrows.' Jason shrugged an apology. He wasn't about to share why he'd consumed enough whisky to risk alcohol poisoning – not all of it anyway. He needed to convey the outcome of his meeting with Robert Fenton though. He'd been going to do that straightaway, but then he and Karla had ended up having a blazing row in front of them. He just hadn't had the heart since, for anything. 'I need to have a word,' he started reluctantly. 'About the financial backing I was hoping to secure.'

'We know,' Mark said, before he could continue. 'Paul Edwards called.'

The key client who'd gone elsewhere? Jason looked at him curiously.

'He was also worried about you,' Rachel supplied.

'Decent of him.' Jason tried not to, but he couldn't help but feel the tiniest bit cynical. An extra week was all they'd needed to get the customer-fronting software right, he'd been sure of it. He'd asked Edwards to give him a few days. The guy had turned him down. But then, that was business, he guessed. 'And?' Sighing, he pulled up a chair. Exhaustion was catching up with him. If he didn't sit down, he was sure he'd fall over.

'He told us, confidentially, that your delightful father-in-law had backed Logic Solutions,' Mark went on, his expression now bordering on contempt.

Jason flinched inwardly at the mention of the man as his father-in-law. 'Right.' He tugged in a breath. 'So you know we're stuffed then? That is, I am,' he clarified. 'You two need to be looking around. Use whatever you need to here, and if something comes up, grab it. You don't need to work any notice. That goes without saying.'

Feeling emotional, Jason stopped. Mark had turned down the offer of a well-paid position to work with him. Rachel and Mark had always given more than one hundred per cent. Jason felt as if he was stuffing them both.

'Finished?' Mark asked, pushing his hands into his pockets.

Jason smiled ruefully. 'It definitely looks that way.'

'Not quite,' Mark said, walking across to perch himself on the edge of the desk. 'How would you feel about me buying the business?'

It took a second for that to register, then, 'What?' Jason squinted at him.

'Delirious, obviously.' Mark clearly noted his incredulity.

'I'm…' Jason shook his head. 'I'm confused. I mean, *how?*' Mark didn't have the finances. With a divorce behind him, the only asset he had was his flat.

'I've spoken to my bank manager. She's willing to consider a percentage of the amount required, provided I can meet the rest.'

Jason stared at him. 'And you propose to do this by selling your soul, presumably?'

'My flat, actually. I don't think my soul is worth anything.' Mark's mouth twitched into a regretful smile. 'And before you answer, I already have an offer. It's being sold as a buy-to-let. I'm going to rent it back.'

Jason balked, trying hard to keep up with him.

'Turns out my red-hot Tinder date is an estate agent,' Mark went on, with a wink, 'so she's pulling a few strings. I can turn this around, Jason, given time. I know I can. Well, I'm pretty sure I can,' he added, with a shrug. 'Obviously, you'll need time to think about it though. I'll give you a minute and go grab us a coffee.'

After going through Mark's vision for the future of Upwards Online, which took them through lunchtime, Jason was in his own office, having said yes. He'd offered Mark a lower price for the saleable assets, not that they were worth a great deal. The business was in the clients, and Mark and Rachel had clearly been working their guts out on ideas and marketing. They wanted to do this. And he… Mark had suggested he continue working with him, but Jason wanted out of it. He wasn't sure it had ever been an area he'd wanted to be in. He would have to look for a job himself, find a way of supporting his kids, but this seemed like as good a way forward as any, considering he really would have cut his throat rather than touch any of Fenton's money.

Jason sat at his desk, feeling bemused by the fast turn of events. He needed to tie up loose ends and formulate a plan, given that suicide wasn't an option, something he was ashamed he'd considered even when he wasn't getting as drunk as it was possible to get. Getting drunk and chatting to women online, he reminded himself, though he couldn't remember what had been said.

Jesus, he was a mess. He needed to delete the sites – wished he could delete parts of his life. Flicking on his laptop, wondering whether he might actually owe anyone he'd 'chatted to' an apology, he called up the site he'd been browsing. Guilt twisted inside him. He'd been angry. Furious. Figured that, as his marriage was over, he had nothing to lose. Would this really have helped anything though, 'hooking up,' or whatever one did, with complete strangers? He'd obviously been inebriated, to the point of senselessness.

Despairing of himself, he was about to exit the site when he received another 'like'. Jason's gaze strayed to her photograph, and he found himself taken aback. The woman was stunning, her hair, glossy brunette, tumbling over her shoulders, her skin lightly tanned and dotted with cute freckles. Her eyes were dark, rich

Not the world's greatest online conversationalist, are you? she messaged, before he could think of anything else to say.

No. Sorry. Jason answered honestly, and wondered again what in God's name he was doing exactly. If he needed someone to talk to, he should talk to his sister, or possibly Mark. Except, with her husband out of work, Hannah had a shedload of her own problems right now, and Mark… Jason was pretty sure what his advice would be: *Go get yourself laid and take your mind off your problems.* If only it were that easy.

Aw, don't be, Jessie sent back. *I like it that you're shy. Like your profile too. Sporty = good. Pic = good. No six-pack on show = not a douchey shirtless Casanova.*

Glad you approve. You have a nice smile.

My best feature. Fancy talking properly?

Again, Jason wavered. This was nuts. He had a family. Except… he didn't, did he? In fact, he'd never felt more alone in his life. His marriage had ended. That was an inescapable fact. He wanted to hold on to it, desperately wanted to do that, but he couldn't. His business was finished. His life was crumbling. Was this really risking anything, then? He was talking to her, that was all. With the distance between them, it wasn't likely to lead to anything more.

Jason took a breath, typed *Love to*, and hit send.

CHAPTER TWENTY-FIVE

KARLA

I took this morning off, on top of the time I've already taken off 'sick', but I slip into my office just before lunchtime in order to do some necessary private online browsing. John, the chief executive, has his weekly meeting with the housing association's development department manager this afternoon, so I'm confident I can steal a little more time. It's gone two when I check the clock, and I calculate that John will be tied up for at least another hour, so I set about creating my Tinder profile, which according to information I've googled about this particular site needs to be kick-ass in order to stand out and get noticed by the right guys, for the right reasons. I'm not sure what my reasons are, who the right guys are. All I know is that the man I considered to be my Mr Right, my soulmate for life, isn't. I don't know what I want from these sites, other than to feel wanted, desired – to feel something other than the almost debilitating emptiness I now feel. Do I care if Jason knows I'm also playing the dating game? 'Hooking up' with other men? Sleeping with other men, which I know is the end game here?

Yes, of course I do. I'm not sure I'll actually have the courage to sleep with another man. I don't want to. I'm not sure I would know how to. But I do want Jason to feel as crushed as I do. I want him to question everything he ever was to me; to feel as insignificant to my life as I clearly am to his. To feel jealous. I thought, at first, when I discovered he'd been browsing dating sites, that it was some kind of angry reaction to me having pushed him to approach my father for the business loan. I tried to convince myself it was an act of rebellion, that he'd felt somehow emasculated, that it was something he was doing to get back at me. My stomach clenches painfully as I recall how furious he was that I would accuse him of doing this, his vehement denial, when the evidence was there, right in front of my eyes. His lies. It's been more than browsing, more than the odd flirt to reaffirm his manhood, I would bet my life on it. How long he's wanted out of our marriage, I have no way of knowing.

He won't be jealous, Sarah sighs, and my heart, which has been sinking steadily since I accessed his internet history, settles like ice in my chest. He's moved on. He's not likely to be distraught if I seek the company of other men. Even so, as pathetic as I realise it is, there's an ember of hope still burning faintly inside me that he might wake up to the fact that it's me he wants. That he might realise he loves me when he knows he's lost me.

If he doesn't, what will I have lost that was worth anything in the first place?

Ignoring the phone ringing constantly to my side, I concentrate on compiling a list of enticing things about me that I can include on my profile. Tinder is populated by the dating-app generation, after all. If I don't want to be hastily swiped left by men as desperate as my husband to move on to something more exciting, I have to be able to compete with tempting young things. I need to get in touch with the real me, the person I used to be, who felt she could climb a mountain, touch the sky or swim an ocean. She didn't die the day she got married. She got side-lined, that was all. She's still here inside, waiting to unfurl her wings.

Work hard, play hard, I begin. I figure I might as well go for it. *Dance till I drop. Embrace love and life and all the*

world has to offer. Love thrills + excitement. Wind in my hair,
sunshine, sand dunes, cocktails + rollercoaster rides. Seeking
– Man who can dance w/me, not afraid to catch me + lols.
Introduce yourself!

Mentally running through the new clothes I'll need to purchase in order to dare venture into nightclubs, I upload the selfies I've taken, in which I actually look quite acceptable – sexy, even – with my fake tan, fake hair and face. Fake me, I think. It's not really so hard to reinvent oneself. But I'm not trying to do that. I'm trying to find myself. I'm reassembling myself. Repackaging and presenting myself as a more attractive option than a boring wife and mother. Isn't that what men want? What Jason is looking for? Obviously, I have to embellish a little. And when it comes to meeting men in the flesh? I'm an actress. It's time I put my skills to the test.

I'm uploading the last photograph when John walks through my office door, almost giving me heart failure.

'Karla…' Trailing curious eyes over me, John looks surprised. 'You look well.'

Hell. I cringe inside, realising it's probably not a good idea to still be wearing the fake tan and false eyelashes when I'm supposed to have crawled here from my sickbed. 'I thought I'd make a bit of an effort,' I tell him, with a stoic smile. 'If you look better, you feel better, that's my motto.'

He nods, now looking taken aback, possibly because that last came out a little over-brightly and with no hint of the croaky voice I'd phoned in with yesterday. 'It appears to be working,' he says, smiling uncertainly. 'Sorry to interrupt, but do you think we could have the post distributed any time soon? It's just that I'm expecting tenders in for the maintenance contracts on the new-build site.'

'Has it not been distributed?' I glance around my office, where there is no sign of the post.

'I don't think it's been brought up from the post room yet,' he suggests hesitantly.

I look at him, flabbergasted. I know he's the CE, but surely he could have fetched it himself, or organised someone else to. 'Couldn't someone have asked one of the admin assistants to go and collect it?' I enquire, pushing my chair huffily back from my desk.

'I left a note on Zoe's desk.' His response is almost apologetic. 'I suspect she might have missed it.'

'Right.' I plaster a smile in place and heave myself to my feet. 'Well, I suppose I'd better go and sort it out then,' I say, heading for the door. As per usual. What is it with this place? Does everyone have an 'it's not my job' attitude? If I'd had that over the years I've worked here, the bloody wheels would have dropped off long ago.

'While you're at it, do you think you could check to see where we are with the minutes of the board meeting I need typed up?' John ventures. 'I'd quite like to get those sent out today, if at all possible.'

Yes, of course, why not? And I'll make the tea and sweep the floor on the way, I think, peeved – and then stop. I don't remember having had the audio tape for the minutes, let alone distributing that one specifically to be typed up. But I must have done. Though I was distracted, that being the day my father had called suggesting I check Jason's laptop, I distinctly remember gathering up the various files and audio tapes from my out tray and dropping them off before I left.

Was that one there? The truth is, I can't concentrate on anything but the hurt gnawing away at me. I can't think straight. Closing my eyes, I take a breath, gather myself and push through the admin assistants' office door, where there is an immediate lull in the conversation as three surprised faces look up from PCs to me. I haven't knocked, I realise, which I always normally do out of respect. *Tough*. I'm the office manager. I'm here to make sure the housing association runs efficiently, not pussyfoot around, being careful of people's feelings. 'Did it not occur to anyone to collect the post?' I demand, my expression hopefully communicating how unimpressed I am.

Now there are definitely surprised faces. They're not used to me actually exerting my authority.

'No.' Zoe, the senior secretary, speaks up. 'We've all got piles to do. If someone had asked us, we'd have—'

'You shouldn't need asking, Zoe. If I'm not here, then it should have occurred to you. Using your initiative is a requirement of the job,' I snap, unfamiliar anger rising inside me. I don't get angry with the girls. A little despairing, sometimes, when there's more gossiping going on than work, but never murderously angry, like this.

'Well, excuse *me*,' Zoe says indignantly. 'I didn't realise we were supposed to cover everyone else's—'

'And being disrespectful to your superiors is *not*,' I point out.

Zoe and Yasmin exchange disgruntled glances. I can almost feel the daggers going in, as I march further into the room. 'Who's typing up the minutes from the board meeting?' I ask, unable to quash the agitation I'm feeling, despite my conscience tugging at me.

Zoe furrows her brow. 'What minutes? I don't remember seeing any.'

'I put the audio tape in Lucy's in tray when I was last in,' I say, and wait while more glances are exchanged – worried glances, this time.

'I didn't see it.' Lucy looks flustered and stands up to go through her tray.

'I see,' I say, as she then searches her desk, growing more flustered by the second. 'Perhaps you should consider tidying your desk, Lucy,' I suggest, a cattiness to my voice I don't like. 'Your organisational skills are clearly somewhat lacking.'

'I'll help you look,' Yasmin says, rising from her desk to walk across to Lucy's, casting me a disdainful glance as she goes.

'Let me know when you find it,' I say, marching back to the door before I'm tempted to say more. I'm two steps away from my own office along the corridor when Lucy flies past me towards the ladies' loo.

She's in tears, I realise, my anger immediately evaporating to give way to immense guilt.

'Nice going, Karla. She's just split up with her boyfriend,' Zoe says hostilely, moving past me. 'Nice make-up, too, by the way,' she throws over her shoulder. 'I'm not sure what your problem is, but if this is the new you, you might want to tone it down a bit.'

My guilt intensifies, wedging itself like a cannonball in my chest. I'm doing exactly what my father does, I realise, aghast, bullying people, caring nothing for their feelings, what they might have going on in their lives. 'I'm sorry,' I say weakly, but there's no one to hear me. Zoe has disappeared into the toilets after Lucy.

In one fell swoop I have soured my relationships with three people. Broken the trust of the people I work with. They will hate me now, with good reason. Who is this vile person I seem to have become?

Swallowing hard, I go into my office, close the door behind me and lean against it. Is this something that Jason sees in me? This nastiness I didn't even know I was capable of? Why am I doing it? Lashing out. Hurting people because I'm hurting. My colleagues. My children. Holly, my beautiful baby girl. I'm hurting her. Josh, my puzzled, scrawny, sensitive little boy – he's hurting. Jason – he's obviously been hurting for a long time. It has emanated palpably from him at times, when my father has so denigrated him. Yet still, I wouldn't accept that he wanted nothing to do with him. I bullied him, despite hating that trait in my father. Perhaps the blame for the breakdown of my marriage is all mine? Would anyone want to stay in a relationship where they felt they didn't have choices? A voice? Jason told me, over and over, he didn't want to be beholden to my father. I wasn't listening.

Do I really believe that though? Wasn't I only trying to find a way that Jason wouldn't see himself as a failure? To support him? I don't *know*. I gulp in a breath, try to suppress the tears, but they come anyway, hot and salty, tears of bewilderment, guilt and grief streaming down my cheeks. *I'm sorry.* Feeling as if the hard lump in my throat might choke me, I repeat it silently. I'm not even sure who I'm saying sorry to any more. Sarah, the constant reminder of my disloyalty? My children? Jason?

I glance at the ceiling. I don't think I can bear it. My heart is so raw, I feel as if it's tearing apart inside me. Everything that was solid in my life, the very ground beneath my feet, is slipping away from me. I'm falling. And there is no one to catch me.

CHAPTER TWENTY-SIX

DIANA

Recognising the ringtone she'd set to play when Karla called, Diana abandoned her task of cleaning the fridge to take the call. Karla had been in a terrible state after discovering what Jason had been doing in his office, rather than going home to her. Diana was glad she'd been there, babysitting Holly and Josh, when her daughter had arrived back home. She'd been able to persuade her to take a breath and a step back. Screaming at him and demanding explanations, she'd managed to convince her, would only make him defensive, possibly driving something that might actually have no traction.

Diana prayed it didn't. She was still struggling to believe it. Jason seemed to care so deeply for Karla. It had been clear to Diana how much he'd loved her from outset. There was no mistaking a man's love for a woman, and Jason's feelings for Karla had been obvious. He'd fought so hard for her, despite Robert's determination to split them up, which Diana had never condoned. As far as Diana was concerned, fate had brought them together. They'd created a child. After all Karla had already lost, how cruel would it have been for her to lose the man she loved too? It was possible that Jason had grown weary with the battle, she supposed, this constant war between him and Robert, the arguments he and Karla were having, more and more lately, and his fight to save his failing business. Even so, for him to have made the decision to cheat on Karla in such a cold, calculating way… That was more Robert's domain than Jason's.

'*Damn.*' Missing the call as she struggled to remove her rubber gloves, Diana cursed her obsessive need to always be busy while Robert was off doing what she knew very well he was, and then selected Karla's number and called her straight back.

'Mum?' Karla jumped on the call, her voice small and tearful. 'I wondered where you were.'

Diana frowned in concern. 'Here,' she assured her. 'Where I always am.' That was to say, cleaning the house so thoroughly you could perform open heart surgery on the kitchen floor without risk of infection, driving herself more insane than Robert had already driven her and biding her time until she could leave her husband to stew in his own mess, but Karla didn't need to know any of that. 'What's happened, lovely?' she asked her gently.

Hearing a long intake of breath, Diana waited. And then, 'Do you think I'm like Dad, Mum?' Karla blurted.

Well, that was something she absolutely didn't have to tear herself up about, Diana thought angrily. 'If you mean do you run roughshod over people's feelings, then no, Karla, I don't,' she told her firmly. 'You've always been caring towards other people. Too caring sometimes. Why on earth would you imagine you're not?'

'Because I don't think I'm a very nice person,' Karla said, sounding so uncertain that Diana found herself cursing Jason, despite her gut feeling that he would never trample over other people's feelings either.

'That's utter nonsense, Karla,' she scolded her. 'You're looking for reasons for Jason to be doing what he appears to be doing – and I emphasise the word *appears* – and you're wrong. You're nothing like Robert.'

'But I *am*,' Karla insisted. 'I've been vile to the people I work with today, bullying one of them to the point of tears. I did the same to Jason, pushing him, insisting he accept financial help from Dad when he desperately didn't want to. It's no wonder he—'

'Karla, stop,' Diana interjected forcefully. 'If you've snapped at anyone at work, it's perfectly understandable, given your personal circumstances, and you pushed Jason because you were trying to support him. I would have done the same thing in your shoes. It was obvious it was breaking your heart to watch him struggle.'

Karla went quiet, but the tell-tale sniffles told Diana she was quietly crying. 'Have there been any developments?' she prompted her, softening her tone.

Karla took a moment to answer, then, 'No, not really,' she said shakily. 'He went out after I got back tonight. Something to do with making sure everything was in order for the sale of his business to go smoothly, he said, which is rubbish. I know very well he's been chatting to his new woman online.'

'You don't know he's doing anything of the sort, Karla. Now he knows you know, I doubt he—'

'But I *do*,' Karla cut in, with a cynical laugh. 'Of course he is, Mum. Why on earth would you of all people defend him?'

'I'm not. I'm just trying to give him the benefit of the doubt.' Diana sighed, conceding that she was actually harbouring a forlorn hope that somehow her daughter's marriage could be saved. Even if Karla didn't have proof he'd done anything more than browse, it would be naive to imagine he hadn't intended to.

'He's not just looking out of idle curiosity, Mum, trust me,' Karla went on, sounding more angry now than dejected, which was no bad thing. If they were headed for the divorce courts, her daughter would need to stand up and fight, not sit in the corner, licking her wounds. 'I can't believe he was actually jealous,' she said, emitting another short laugh, this time one of disdain. 'When I danced with that young guy at your birthday party, do you remember?'

Diana did remember. She'd been quite enamoured with the young man herself.

'He was so furious, I was shocked. You know, that he would suddenly be so macho and proprietorial when we've been together for…' Karla stopped. She was holding her breath – holding the tears back, Diana guessed. 'He wasn't jealous though, was he?' She finally allowed herself a shuddery breath out. 'His pride was wounded, that was all. He was looking to use that as an excuse to blame me for looking elsewhere.'

The dejection was back, Diana sensed, but at least Karla seemed to be shifting the blame from herself now, which she needed to do. She'd carried too much blame in her life – convincing herself that she was somehow responsible for Sarah's death, which was ludicrous. The blame lay squarely on the shoulders of Robert, a man with no conscience who'd bullied and lied his way out of culpability.

'I don't think he was doing that, darling,' she said carefully. 'From where I was standing, he looked genuinely put out to me.'

'Put out, yes,' Karla agreed, a fatalistic edge now to her voice, 'because I was making a fool of myself, therefore making a fool out of him. Embarrassing him, clearly.'

'Karla…' Diana felt her heart bleed for her. 'You dance with your soul. There were many men's eyes on you that night. Many women's, too. They were green with envy. Some of them would give an arm to look like you do. Please stop doubting yourself, darling. You're a beautiful, talented young woman.'

'Ha,' Karla answered, with a self-deprecating laugh this time. 'Would that my husband thought so.'

Oh, Karla. 'Would you like me to come over?' Diana asked. 'We could watch a film, or just have a good girl talk? It might help.'

'No,' Karla answered tiredly. 'I mean, I'd love it, but it's getting a bit late now, and the children are in bed. I'll be fine, Mum, I promise. I just wanted someone to tell me I'm beautiful.' She laughed again, albeit sadly.

'You are,' Diana assured her. 'Are you sure though? I can be there in half an hour.'

'I'm sure. I'm going to try on some clothes I went shopping for after work. And then have a bath – with lots of bath oil and a large glass of wine on the side, obviously.'

'New clothes, hey?' Diana was relieved to hear she'd opted for retail therapy rather than retreating into herself, as she tended to do.

'I'm reinventing myself.' Karla attempted to sound positive. For her sake, Diana guessed. 'Out with the old and in with the new, more confident me.'

'I'm pleased to hear it,' Diana said, feeling slightly more assured herself. 'Enjoy. But don't get too sozzled. You'll only regret it. And remember, Karla, I'm here if you do need to talk.'

'I will. Thanks, Mum. Love you. Night night.'

'Love you too, sweetheart. Night night.'

Diana placed her phone back down on the work surface and studied it for a second, tempted to ring Jason herself. But then, that might only exacerbate their problems. Having an interfering mother-in-law meddling in his affairs wouldn't help Jason's mood any.

She would speak to him, but not yet. She turned back to the fridge to pour herself a large glass of wine while she pondered. She didn't believe that Jason had just decided one day that he'd had enough and started trawling these sites out of bitterness. If she knew Jason at all, he simply wasn't made that way. There was more to this, Diana was sure of it. Jason wouldn't just throw in the towel because Robert had refused him financial backing. He wouldn't throw away his marriage, thereby giving Robert exactly what he'd always wanted. There was always the possibility he was no longer in love with Karla, but Diana's instinct told her that wasn't the case. Which left one other option: Jason must truly believe he had no other choice.

Diana fervently hope that wasn't the case. Because if it was, then Robert had definitely gone too far. He'd stolen Sarah's life. She couldn't allow him to ruin Karla's. Somehow, Diana had to find out what had gone on in Robert's office. She had to find a way to prevent four people's lives from being destroyed. If that meant bringing forward her plans, then so be it. It would have repercussions for her, but Diana had long lived with the knowledge that the actions she'd taken years ago might catch up with her. She was ready now to live with the consequences, painful though they would be.

CHAPTER TWENTY-SEVEN

JASON

As he pulled up outside the house, Jason looked towards the windows and sighed heavily. He'd never thought there would come a day that he wouldn't look forward to going home after work. Right now, though, with him and Karla only speaking to communicate about the kids over the last few days, he would rather be anywhere else. He had no choice, he reminded himself. His reason for being there was the kids. His reason for being at all.

Which was feeling sorry for himself, obviously. He pulled himself up. Karla was the real victim in all of this. She was changing, moving away from him, building her own life, she'd said, which basically meant she was going out at night, staying out. He needed to be here.

Taking a breath, he grabbed his phone and reached for the car door, then paused as he realised he had a message. He was surprised to see it was from Jessie. They'd chatted for a while when they first messaged. She'd told him about her nursing job at Carlow general hospital, making him smile with a few hair-raising tales of embarrassing accident and emergency situations. She'd also told him about her last boyfriend, who turned out to be a 'lying shite' – married, she'd discovered, and had promptly dumped him. Jason had been vague, avoiding saying anything about his personal circumstances, other than that he was recently separated – and he'd felt he was betraying Karla by saying that much. As he'd heard nothing from Jessie since, he'd assumed she'd shied away from the 'recently separated' scenario. Not sure he knew how to handle it, whether he should just accept being on his own rather than go down this impulsive route, Jason had half hoped she wouldn't follow it up. Wondering now whether to answer, he pulled up the message, and then smiled when he read it.

So, are we still talking? Or did you find me about as scintillating as watching paint dry?

Ouch, he thought. Another woman whose feelings he'd hurt. She'd probably assumed he would contact her. Glancing towards the house, Jason hesitated and then keyed in a reply.

If you were paint, you would be sunshine yellow in colour. You brightened my day. It was corny, but he really didn't want to leave another woman questioning her confidence because of him.

Full marks on the flattery. Keep it up. She sent back, with a winking emoji.

Jason's smile widened. She could have sent a rolling-eyes one, he supposed.

So, you're sporty. Athletically toned then? she asked him. *You look like you are – unless your photo is ten years old?*

It's not, Jason assured her. *Not doing much sport at the moment though.*

What's your fave? Tennis or squash, I bet, so you can sneak off at lunchtimes?

Into more physical sport. Jason didn't mention the extreme sports, fancying that would make him sound as if he was trying to come across as some kind of macho man.

Hmm? Interesting, she sent back.

Jason laughed. *You?*

Outdoors girl: walking, cycling, swimming. Indoors: weightlifting.

Jason raised an eyebrow. *Weightlifting?*

Lager girl. Pint glass. So, do you want to elaborate on the 'recently separated'? Or have I just turned a boring shade of brown?

Jason wavered. He was messing her about. He had to stop this, be honest with her. But then, albeit they were only messaging, she seemed easy to talk to. He so badly needed that: someone to just talk to, someone who might actually be listening, where Karla had simply stopped.

Glancing again towards the house, he debated, then typed. *Can we talk later? I'm in the car.* He pressed send.

Can do. Get back when you can. X

Will do, Jason replied. Would he? Again, he prevaricated, guilt doing battle with the aching loneliness he felt inside. He'd never imagined you could actually feel your heart breaking, but he felt it now. Did he really want to break Karla's heart further by doing this?

Still undecided, wondering now whether he should send a message explaining instead, which would be crass and insensitive, he'd no doubt, Jason climbed out of his car and walked wearily to the front door. Josh was heading from the lounge to the stairs as he let himself in. He noted he was already in his pyjamas, which was unheard of for Josh, who liked to push bedtimes to the limit. 'All right, tiger?' he asked him. 'Going up already?'

Josh shrugged and nodded unenthusiastically. 'Mum's going out,' he said, his eyes downcast. 'I can't stand Megan. All she ever does is talk girl stuff with Holly.'

'Right.' Jason glanced warily up the stairs, to where he assumed Karla would be getting ready to go out for the third time that week – 'With friends,' she'd told him vaguely, when he'd asked. He dearly wished she wouldn't do this, but he was in no position to try to appeal to her. He just prayed she was safe – she was clearly drinking to excess, coming home at all hours, and he was desperately worried that one night she might not.

He also had a problem with Megan, the babysitter, which is why he was making sure he was here. He and Karla had both been majorly unimpressed with her the last time she'd babysat. What would he do about her imminent arrival? Pay her, he supposed – something for her trouble, anyway – and tell her they didn't need her tonight after all.

'Do you need anything, Josh?' he called as his son trudged up the stairs, looking as if he was carrying the weight of the world on his small shoulders. Jason felt something crack inside him as he thought of the angst Holly and Josh still had to come. 'Hot chocolate? Warm milk?'

'No.' Josh shook his head. 'Going to play *Lego Star Wars* for a bit, and then go to sleep.'

'Not for too long, Josh,' Jason reminded him. 'Blue light before bed won't help you sleep – you know that, right?'

'Yeah, I know,' Josh said, with an elongated sigh. 'You tell me that about seven times a week.'

Hating that he couldn't make this right for his kids, make their world safe again, Jason sighed heavily in turn and then shrugged out of his jacket and went straight to the lounge. Holly wasn't in there, which meant that she was ensconced in her bedroom. She and Josh had both taken to hiding away lately, no doubt to avoid the hostile atmosphere.

Kneading his temples in weary frustration, Jason headed to the kitchen to grab a coffee. He hadn't thought about what he would eat. He had no appetite. He flicked the kettle on and was reaching for the coffee when his gaze snagged on a pack of pills on the work surface. Curious, he picked up the box, his heart plummeting as he realised what they were: diazepam, Karla's. Prescribed three days ago. *Jesus.* With nightmares constantly waking her, she hadn't been sleeping well before this. She probably wasn't sleeping at all now. Had she started them? Because if so, he was pretty sure she shouldn't be drinking alcohol. Opening the box and seeing that she had, Jason pulled out the information leaflet. He was halfway through the side effects and warnings when Karla came in from the hall.

'Mine, I think,' she said, walking swiftly across to relieve him of them.

'Karla…' Jason blew out a sigh, as she about-faced and headed back out. 'Look, I know you'll think it's none of my business, but should you be drinking while taking those things?'

'You're right. It's not,' Karla informed him, heading back through the hall to pick up her holdall, in which she stowed her 'going-out gear'. She never got made-up and dressed to go out here, preferring to do it at her friend's house, she said, rather than be scrutinised by a man who obviously hadn't found her attractive in a long time. That couldn't be further from the truth. Jason had always found her attractive, but there was no way to convince her of that. Not now.

'Karla, don't,' he said, his voice tight. 'Please don't take those things and drink at the same time.'

'I'll do what I choose, Jason,' she replied bluntly. 'That seems to be the general attitude around here.'

'For *God's*…' Jason's jaw clenched with frustration. 'You're not supposed to take them with alcohol. It's bloody dangerous! If you're not worried about yourself, think of the kids. They'd be devastated if—'

Karla whirled back around. '*Me* think of the kids?' She stared at him with a mixture of disbelief and fury and then laughed derisively. 'Just piss off, Jason,' she hissed, walking to the front door. 'Do what you like with who you like. As I've no doubt you already are.'

Tugging in a breath, Jason bit hard on his tongue. *I just might*, he thought furiously. 'What time will you be back?' he asked, as calmly as he could.

Karla's answer was to walk out of the front door, allowing Megan access as she went.

Great. What was the bloody point? Nodding a half-hearted greeting at Megan, Jason raked a hand agitatedly through his hair.

What did he do now? He had no idea where she was going, what the hell she was doing.

'Shall I go through?' Megan asked him, hovering awkwardly in the hall.

Jason was about to say no, but... 'The kids are in bed,' he said on impulse. Stepping past her, he grabbed his car keys from the hall table. 'No unsuitable Netflix,' he warned, giving Karla a second to set off and then heading out after her.

'When do you need me till?' Megan called from the door.

'I'll text you,' Jason called back, climbing hurriedly into his car.

Pulling off the drive, he turned in the direction Karla had taken, heading towards the dual carriageway. Was she going into town to meet friends there, he wondered, as he picked up her car and followed her at a safe distance.

Fifteen minutes later, he had his answer, and wished to God that he didn't, because there was only one reason Karla would be checking in to a Travelodge. Her story of 'staying over at a girlfriend's' was bullshit.

His heart beating unsteadily in a combination of anger and jealousy, Jason parked discreetly on the opposite side of the car park. Praying he didn't see anyone arrive and follow her in –anyone male, that was – he settled down to wait until he saw her come out.

His gut twisted as he took in the clothes she was wearing: a short, tight black dress that accentuated her figure and thigh-high leather boots that made her legs look as if they went on forever. She got into a taxi and he trailed her to a trendy wine bar. He waited five minutes and then followed her in, feeling sick to his soul. She was at the bar, with one hand pressed to the chest of some smooth-looking bastard who was wasting no time in trailing his hand down her back to the base of her spine, and lower. Who was he? Someone she was seeing? Her hook-up for the night? Jason laughed sardonically. The hotel room was already conveniently booked. *Fuck!*

CHAPTER TWENTY-EIGHT

KARLA

I am immensely relieved he looks like a regular guy. Standing three or four inches taller than me, he's wearing black boots and black chinos, with a white T-shirt over a tidy torso. As in his photos, he has a hint of a beard, dark hair. I smile my approval. He seems nice enough. Normal.

I couldn't go through with it the first time. My stomach had been a tight ball of nerves, my heart banging against my chest and my head screaming at me to run. In the end, with enough wine consumed to numb my emotions and free my inhibitions, I'd simply closed my eyes and tried to go with the flow, hoping it would allow me to escape from the pain of my husband's infidelity. It hadn't. The pain was still there, pressing down on my chest as heavily as the stranger on top of me. Mercifully, he'd been understanding. He might not have been. I'm aware of the danger.

My 'date' pulls me closer, indicating he's interested in more than the dance. For now, in this moment, he wants me. I am desired, needed, if only for one night. And when the night is over, we will go our separate ways. He will move on, another piece of me will be gone and I will go home to my children.

I try to detach from my emotions, to lose myself on the dance floor, where I can be anyone I want to be. Anyone but me. But as I raise my arms in the air, desperate for the enticing rhythm of the music to transport me to another place, I am seized by a crushing sense of anxiety. The thud of the bass coming through the huge sound system grows too loud, each thump causing my heart to pump manically, my blood to whoosh through my temples. The strobes are too bright. Searing white light. The overabundance of beer and perfume too cloying.

With my heart feeling as if it might burst from my chest, I push myself away from the man opposite me and squeeze through the throng of bodies now gyrating as one. My legs are like butter beneath me. One hand against the wall, I squint, trying to gain some equilibrium as I make my way to the toilets. Rough hands grab me, righting me as I reel. Someone laughs, a loud, raucous laugh, right next to my ear. He shouts something unintelligible. I can't hear anything now but the *boom, boom* inside me, can't feel anything but the panic that claws its way up my throat. I can't breathe.

Focus. I plead with my body not to fail me as I stumble on. My foot goes over; a sharp pain shoots through my ankle. Stupid boots. Thigh-high boots. Mutton undressed. I shouldn't be here. I should be at home with my children. My chest twists painfully as I recall my little boy's closed body language as I tried to say goodbye to him before I left. His eyes fixed to his iPad, he refused even to look at me. Holly, my precious little girl – I see her expression, the unbridled accusation in her eyes as she stared mutely at me. For a second, she looked at me just the way Sarah did, as if I was a traitor. I am. No matter how much I try to deny it, I was the catalyst that set this ball rolling. Constantly badgering Jason to take money from my father belittled him as much as my father himself had. He wanted to destroy our marriage. But it was me who lit the fuse that blew it all apart.

And now I'm losing my husband.

I am sweating, profusely, perspiration wetting my forehead, face and chest, wet polyester plastered to my back like snakeskin. But

I'm not writhing and wriggling. I'm not dancing. I am clutching the sink for support in the toilets, and I don't want to be here. I want to be at home, lying in the arms of a man I know I'll be safe with. Would have been, once, if only I'd been there for him.

CHAPTER TWENTY-NINE

JASON

Jason paid Megan and thanked her, just managing a smile as he closed the door behind her, gulping back the tears he felt like weeping. He couldn't do that, not here, with his children so close. He glanced up at the ceiling, blinking hard, willing himself to stay in control. He needed to check on Holly, make sure she was sleeping. He hadn't even said hello to her when he'd come home earlier. He moved along the hall and swung up the stairs. She knew what was going on, that their marriage was irretrievably broken. They both did.

After tapping on her door and getting no answer, he eased it open, and his heart sank to a whole new level. Holly was asleep, or else feigning sleep. She had her pink Build-A-Bear tucked under her arm. Swallowing hard, Jason closed the door quietly. Realising his little girl needed comforting, and that he couldn't offer her that comfort – tell her everything was going to be all right, which would be an out-and-out lie – he stayed where he was for a second, cursing himself, and then headed for the stairs, where he finally gave in to his urge to cry.

He was trying to resist the urge to get so drunk he would be incapable of thinking the dark thoughts going around in his head – primarily of ripping Robert Fenton's cold heart from his chest – when he decided to message Jessie. Talking to someone, about anything, might just save his sanity. Whether it was right or wrong to be talking to her really wasn't an issue any more, was it, he thought, his gut wrenching afresh as he pictured his wife, and what she might now be doing with another man.

Is this a good time for you? he typed. He hesitated briefly and then hit send.

She didn't reply immediately, causing his heart to plummet, and then – *Can do*.

Jason was relieved. At that time of night, he'd wondered whether she would answer. *Fancy talking properly on the phone?* he asked her.

There was another short pause, then, *OK*, she sent, *but I have a thick Irish brogue. Born in Cork, worked in Donegal for a while. Am told accent sexy but hard to understand. Also, night off so out with the girls. Birthday bash. Teensy bit inebriated, therefore.*

I'll listen carefully, Jason sent back.

Send me your number. I'll find a quiet spot. Call you in five, Jessie replied.

Jason keyed in his number and went to the conservatory, lest the kids wander down and overhear. He hoped she did call. He couldn't reveal details or tell her the insane nature of the personal issues he was dealing with, but he needed to be as straight with her as he could. He hoped that, after that, she would want to keep in contact. He had no idea whether it had a future, or even what he wanted from this other than a friend he could talk to outside of the complete disaster that was his life.

Five minutes later, his phone rang. 'Jason Connolly,' he answered cautiously.

'Hey, Jason Connolly,' a female voice said cheerily. 'So, what're you up to, apart from waiting for phone calls from strange women?' It was her, judging by the light lyrical accent, which was definitely sexy and also definitely had a slight slur to it.

'Nothing earth-shattering,' Jason said, wondering what to tell her. The truth, he reminded himself. There could be no future based on lies. He'd learned that only too well. 'I've just been upstairs, checking on my kids.'

'Ahh,' Jessie said, a wary edge to her voice. 'Kids, as in… how many?'

'Two,' Jason said, already bracing himself for her to say goodbye. 'A girl and a boy, aged eleven and ten.'

Jessie took a second. 'And they live with you?' she asked, her tone indicating she'd guessed that wasn't the case.

'No.' Jason faltered and then pushed on. 'That is… I'm still living in the marital home.'

'Right,' she said, followed by another short silence. 'You're not separated then?'

'We are,' Jason assured her. 'Very much so. It's just…'

'Complex?' Jessie supplied, diplomatically avoiding the 'it's complicated' cliché.

'Extremely,' he said, and waited.

'Care to share?' Jessie asked him, after a beat. 'You don't have to, if you'd rather not, but I'm a good listener if you need an ear.'

And now Jason really had no idea where to start. For Karla's sake, he didn't want any of what he'd learned about his relationship with her to get out. There was no reason it should, but even so. 'I'm… not who my wife thinks I am,' he said, which sounded evasive – ominous, even – but he didn't know how else to explain it.

'Are any of us ever?' Jessie replied, sounding unfazed.

Jason shook his head. 'I guess not, no.'

'Do you still care for her?' Jessie asked intuitively.

'Very much,' Jason answered straight off.

Jessie hesitated. 'As in, you're still in love with her?'

'Honestly…' Sighing deeply, Jason kneaded his temple. 'I don't know. I realise that sounds ridiculous, but… The thing is, I found out something about her that means I can't love her, not in the way she needs me to.'

'Oh hell.' Jessie's voice was sympathetic. 'She cheated on you, I take it?'

'No. No, she didn't,' Jason said quickly, his stomach tightening into a fist. She hadn't before now, and he tried to hold on to that certainty – the one thing in this mess he thought he could hold on to.

'It must have been something bad though,' Jessie suggested tentatively. 'For it to have caused the two of you to split up, I mean. She's not a mass murderer, is she?'

'Definitely not that,' Jason assured her. Karla couldn't hurt a fly. She'd once cried when she found a dead mouse in the garage. She was terrified of mice, but she'd cried anyway, which had perplexed him. 'It's… something to do with her history.'

'I see,' Jessie said, after a thoughtful second. 'But you don't want to say what?'

Jason drew in a breath and then exhaled slowly. 'That wouldn't be fair on her.'

It all sounded nuts, he realised. It was nuts. If Jessie had any sense, she would end the call and cut her losses. Not that she would have lost much.

'Jessie, please accept my apologies,' he went on, after pausing to try and collect his thoughts. 'I didn't mean to string you along. I like you. A lot, as it happens. You're beautiful, smart, witty.'

'Keep going.' Jessie laughed uncertainly.

'My personal life is a mess, Jessie. I would very much like to offer you what you might be looking for, but I don't want to end up hurting you. If you'd rather not have anything to do with me, then… Well, I understand.'

Jessie went quiet again. She was obviously thinking it through, and thinking she'd had a close call.

'Definitely complex, isn't it?' she said, at length. 'Look, Jason, if you want to stop whatever this is we're doing, that's fine. I get it. But, just so you know, I like you a lot too. You seem nice, honest and caring.'

Jason laughed ironically. He doubted that would be Karla's estimation of him.

'I'm not looking to go golden rings here,' Jessie went on. 'I'm looking for someone to talk with, have a bit of a laugh with. I'm thinking you're looking for the same. What say we keep talking, and then, when your situation is less complex, maybe we can take it further? What do you think?'

Now Jason was definitely surprised. 'I think it's an excellent idea,' he said, relieved and amazed she would want to spend any time at all on him.

'Great.' Jessie sounded pleased. 'You might have to swim the Irish Sea to do the hooking-up bit though.'

'No problem,' Jason said, smiling. 'I think you actually might be worth swimming an ocean for, Jessie.'

'Oh, that I am,' Jessie assured him. 'Did I tell you I was a gift from God?' she said, her voice full of playful innuendo. 'That's what my name means.'

'You're definitely that,' Jason said softly. She was saving him from a life that seemed close to insanity.

CHAPTER THIRTY

DIANA

When Karla hadn't come over on Saturday with the children as she usually did, Diana had tried not to worry too much about it. Her daughter's life had been turned upside down, after all. She wasn't likely to be carrying on as normal with her marriage falling apart. She'd texted her on Sunday, receiving a short text back: *I'm fine, Mum. Just a bit off colour. Will call you later.*

She hadn't called. And now Diana was worried, especially after ringing her office that morning to be told she was off sick. Karla didn't do sick days. Knowing she might have to take time off at short notice if one of the children were ill, she would drag herself into work if required. Diana had begun to grow concerned when Karla told her she'd been vile to the people who worked under her. That wasn't Karla. Even as a small child, she'd been a considerate, gentle soul, less inclined to the attention-seeking that Sarah was prone to. Thoughtful to the point of introversion sometimes, and perhaps a little dominated by her sister. By Robert, too. Both girls were.

Immediately transported back to the awful day that had obliterated any feelings she might still have had for Robert, Diana closed her eyes, a familiar nausea sweeping through her as she relived the nightmare: Karla on her knees, hysterical, shaking uncontrollably.

Diana's gaze travelling past her to Sarah, lying so still and cold, she'd instantly known her soul had departed this world. Sweeping Karla up – a mother instinctively protecting her young – she'd squeezed her tight and tried to console her. She'd barely heard her choked whisper: 'He *killed* her. He *killed* her.'

Karla had never repeated it. To this day, Diana had never been able to persuade her to.

Attempting to vanquish the memory, she checked her phone again, hoping to see a text or missed call from her. There was nothing, which left her no choice but to ring Jason. Diana still hadn't managed to establish exactly what had gone on when he'd met with Robert, and therefore had no idea what reception she might get. If she didn't get answers from him regarding Karla's whereabouts and well-being, she would have to drive over to the house. She couldn't rest until she knew she was safe.

'Jason's phone,' someone answered, eventually. A female. A young female.

Diana checked her watch, noting that it was now well past five thirty, and her heart dropped. Surely he wasn't actually meeting up with the women Karla had claimed he was chatting to on dating sites? Diana had been sure that, no matter what was going on between him and Karla, he would never be cruel enough to do something like that. 'Sorry, who is this?' she asked tersely.

'Rachel,' the girl supplied. 'I work with Jason. He's in a meeting just now with a colleague. Can I get him to call you back?'

He was in his office. She'd imagined he wouldn't be, since he'd been forced to put the wheels in motion to sell the business, all thanks to her despicable husband. Diana felt a huge surge of relief. She hadn't wanted to be so wrong about him.

'Could you interrupt him for me?' she asked the young woman. 'It's his mother-in-law here. I wouldn't ask, but it is urgent.'

A minute later, Jason came on. 'Diana?' he said, his tone wary. 'Rachel said it was urgent.'

'I've been trying to get hold of Karla. She's not returning my calls and I'm worried to death,' Diana explained quickly. 'Jason, where are the children?'

'Here, with me,' Jason said, and Diana's heart settled clunkily back into its moorings. 'Karla's… got some kind of a bug,' he went on. 'Look, don't panic, Diana. I spoke to her not long ago about the kids. She's probably put her phone on silent since then. I'll finish up here and go straight home.'

'Thank you,' Diana said, her voice shaky. 'And you'll call me if there's a problem?'

'I promise,' Jason assured her.

Diana nodded. She hadn't been wrong about him. Whatever he was doing with these silly dating apps, at his core he was a good man, she was certain he was. 'Jason, about the meeting you had with Robert,' she said hesitantly, 'did he—?'

'I'd rather not discuss it, Diana,' Jason cut in bluntly. 'I'm sorry, but I'd prefer not to.'

'I see. It's none of my business, I know, but I just…' Diana faltered. She wasn't inclined to expose her vulnerabilities, but she needed to get to the bottom of what Robert had disclosed to him before putting in motion any wheels of her own, which she'd no choice but to do if she was going to help her daughter. 'I need to know, Jason. To understand what's going on in his head. Did he offer you the money?'

Jason didn't immediately answer, then, 'Yes,' he said simply.

'And you refused it?'

'That's right.' Jason's tone was short.

'But *why*? When you'd gone there ready to accept a loan, why would you turn it down?'

Again, Jason paused. 'You don't know about me then?' he asked curiously.

'Know what?' Cold foreboding travelled the length of Diana's spine.

'You should talk to Robert. You need to,' Jason said. 'I have to go.'

Realising he'd ended the call, Diana placed her phone on the breakfast table and stared at it. Surely, Robert hadn't done what the sick feeling inside her told her he had? *Why?* After all these years? *Damn* the man. Could he not just have let sleeping dogs lie?

Swallowing back the acrid taste of fear in her mouth, Diana pulled herself from her chair and headed towards the lounge. She didn't drink often, but she felt in need of a medicinal brandy. Up until these last few weeks, she'd bided her time, seeing Michael to keep her sanity alive whenever she could, and made preparations, sure that Robert's day of reckoning would come. She hadn't imagined she would have to be instrumental in ensuring that it did, and sooner rather than later. Diana had thought she'd prepared herself; that she would be emotionally ready for the fallout when the news broke, as she had always known it might. Now, she wasn't entirely certain.

But she had no choice, she reminded herself. She would have to find a way to establish that Robert had done the unimaginably callous thing she had long suspected him of. She wasn't sure how she would do it – he would lie through his teeth – but she would. And if he had opened that ugly can of worms, then *he* would suffer the consequences.

Passing through the hall, her attention was caught by a silhouette in the opaque glass in the front door. Someone hovering outside? Diana's heart leapt into her throat. A slim figure – a woman, it appeared – now turning away from the door.

Stepping closer, she made sure the chain was in place and eased the door open. 'Excuse me,' she called, as the woman walked back down the drive towards the road. 'Can I help you?'

The woman turned around. She was quite young – in her twenties, Diana guessed, squinting at her under the harsh glow of the security light.

'Sorry,' the girl said. 'I wasn't sure whether to knock.'

'Well, it seems a bit silly not to, since you're obviously here for a reason.' Diana smiled and released the chain. She looked harmless enough. Timid, almost.

'Yes.' The girl smiled nervously back. 'I wanted to talk to you.'

'About?' Diana asked curiously.

'Your husband.' The girl's gaze skittered down and back again. 'I work at Fenton's Bespoke Plumbing. I'm the receptionist there, and…' She paused and drew in a long breath, as if bracing herself. 'I've decided to report him, Mrs Fenton. The things he does, the way he treats people, it's not right.'

She stopped, her expression uncomfortable. 'I thought you should know. It might have implications for his family, and…'

'I see.' Diana nodded slowly. The day of reckoning could be fast approaching. 'You'd better come in,' she said, stepping back into the hall.

Half an hour later, Abbie, who'd been more in need of the brandy than Diana, had filled her in regarding her husband's behaviour, which didn't come as any surprise: his harassment of staff, his bullying, the sexual innuendo, inappropriate body contact, the touching. Diana knew the man she was married to. She was aware of his reputation. She hadn't loved him as a woman should love a husband, but finding herself pregnant, she'd chosen a life of luxury. It hadn't taken her long to realise she'd chosen unwisely.

'There's something else,' Abbie said. Though Diana had assured her that anything she told her about Robert and any consequences of reporting him wouldn't destroy her, she looked more worried than ever. 'It's about Jason. Your son-in-law…' the girl went on falteringly. 'You know he came to see Robert regarding financial backing for his company?'

Diana straightened in her chair. 'I do,' she said, keeping her tone impassive, though her radar was on red alert.

Abbie nodded, and then took a breath and continued, 'I'm not sure what he told him, but whatever it was, it knocked Jason sick. I mean, physically. He looked as if someone had punched him when he came out of Robert's office. He was obviously in a terrible state of shock. It was seeing that, seeing what he could do to his own son-in-law, that made me decide I should do something about him.'

Diana's heart froze. *The bastard.*

CHAPTER THIRTY-ONE

JASON

Coming in through the front door, Jason sighed despondently. The house was empty – cold and uninviting. Karla wasn't here. He'd known she wouldn't be, but he'd had no idea what to tell Diana when she'd rung him at the office. She'd obviously been worried, thinking her daughter was ill and not able to get hold of her. But telling her that she wasn't, that she was out – drinking, clubbing, staying out all night sometimes – and that he was worried too, about her state of mind… How was he supposed to tell her mother that? From their earlier conversation, he guessed Diana didn't have any idea about what her delightful husband had disclosed to him. As much as he would like her to see the man for what he was – someone who had no shred of humanity – he couldn't share the information. If Karla found out it would crucify her.

There was no way, therefore, to tell Diana why he'd refused the money Robert had so generously offered him – not for his company, but to disappear, preferably off the face of the earth. Robert Fenton hated his guts. At least Jason now knew why. Did he really still think he could buy him off – as if any amount of money could compensate for what he'd done? He wouldn't take a penny from him if his life depended on it, never mind his business, but he would gladly disappear. If it wasn't for his children, for the fact that he desperately didn't want to leave Karla like this, he would put as much distance between himself and that man as he could.

Ushering Holly and Josh into the hall, he focussed his attention on them. They needed him to hold it together, though Jason wondered how he could. If not for Jessie lifting him from his bleak moods, he wasn't sure he would be coping.

'Go get your PJs on, kids. I'll make us some hot chocolate,' he said, steering them towards the stairs. They were exhausted. Their routine was all over the place. So was their diet. Jason was going to have to do better than fast food if he wanted to feed them a balanced diet, as Karla always had.

Watching Josh slope towards the stairs, his scrawny shoulders drooping, Jason's heart sank. The kid's body language said it all. His son was worrying himself sick. Holly, too. Unsurprisingly. You could cut the atmosphere around here with a knife.

'I'll bring your drink up, Josh,' he called after him. 'Don't forget to—'

'Brush my teeth after I've drunk it. I *know*,' Josh threw moodily behind him.

Jason drew a hand over his neck. He was entitled to that. Jason couldn't help but wonder how the kids were holding it together either. He was grateful they were. 'I was going to say, don't forget you have your after-school coding club tomorrow,' he said. 'You'll need to make sure you have your notebook.'

'I'm not going. Don't fancy it,' Josh called back – and closed his bedroom door.

Right. Jason swallowed a tight knot in his throat. He wouldn't, he supposed, not now his father had shown him that running his own software company was a fast road to failure.

He really had lived up to Fenton's prophecies, hadn't he? He'd messed up his family's lives spectacularly. Where was Karla? What was she doing? Suppressing a combination of anger and fear, he took a breath and turned to Holly, who was loitering uncertainly in the hall. She would normally have dodged into the lounge and put the TV on – her usual ploy to postpone bedtime.

'Hot chocolate?' he asked her, with a hopeful shrug.

Holly didn't appear too enthusiastic but answered with a small nod, possibly to placate him. If there was one thing Jason had realised since his world started falling apart, it was that his kids were smarter than he'd given them credit for.

'I'll put the kettle on and bring yours up, too.' He attempted a reassuring smile.

Holly didn't look very reassured. 'Dad, where's Mummy?' she said, stopping him in his tracks as he took a step towards the kitchen.

Jason swallowed hard. That she'd referred to Karla as Mummy, rather than Mum, told him how scared his little girl was – and that almost tore his heart from his chest.

'Out with friends,' Jason answered, his voice catching. 'Work colleagues,' he quickly amended, hoping that might help to justify why she seemed to be out almost permanently. 'I expect she'll be home soon.'

Holly nodded again, her gaze dropping to her trainers, her expression 'not buying it'. 'When she does come home' – she looked up, fixing him with huge blue eyes that were so like her mother's, and so full of confusion, that Jason felt his heart crack another fraction inside him – 'could you tell her we're her friends, too?'

Stunned, Jason tried to answer, but the words got stuck in his throat.

'It's just, when Josh acts like a little kid, and I get a bit stroppy,' Holly went on awkwardly, 'she might not think we are, and…' She trailed off with a disconsolate shrug. 'Would you tell her?'

She was eleven. Josh was ten. *Jesus*. Jason sucked in a breath. 'I will,' he promised, and then reached out to her, yanking her close as she launched herself into his arms.

'We're your friends, as well, Dad,' Holly said into his shoulder, her voice muffled, as he crouched to give her a firm hug.

'I know, sweetheart,' Jason said, his throat hoarse. 'We both love you very much. You know that, right?' Such a fucking cliché, he thought, swiping a tear from his face and then hugging her tighter.

Half an hour later, with Holly and Josh safely in bed, Jason went back to the kitchen. It was a mess. Stuff everywhere, the washing basket and bin overflowing, yesterday's dinner plates stacked in the sink. The dishwasher still wasn't working properly. It was on his list, but he hadn't got around to it yet. It wasn't Karla's job to clean up during the week, but she always had. Jason wondered how she'd done it. How she hadn't come to the end of her tether – juggling her job, the house and the children; lunches, school runs, sick days, holidays. He'd always helped on Sundays with general housework, gardening and shopping, but with him working all the hours under the sun on weekdays, the load had fallen on Karla. He hadn't realised how heavy a load it was.

He was stuffing clothes in the washing machine when his phone beeped. Scrambling it from his pocket, he cursed as he almost dropped it, and then checked his messages. *Jessie.* Jason felt his spirits lift. Banging the washing machine door to, he read the message on his way back to the sink to tackle the washing up, and then stopped and raised his eyebrows in bemusement.

I've had a body piercing, he read. *Fancy a gander?*

Will I be shocked? Jason sent back.

Don't worry. It's not a nipple piercing.

Taken aback, Jason hesitated before answering, then, *Pity,* he typed.

Sex wasn't foremost in his mind. He wondered if it would ever be, given that his thoughts were constantly on Karla, on what they'd lost, which not so long ago, had been pretty special. Even knowing that Karla and he could never be together again, he felt guilty. He should be giving her time to move on without him before doing this. Except he needed it – someone in his life when there was no one else; someone who was easy to talk to and didn't make demands he couldn't live up to.

Bad boy, Jessie sent swiftly back, along with an attachment.

Viewing the photo of her torso, Jason's mouth curved into an appreciative smile, his own body responding to what was an undeniably erotic image, despite his conflicting emotions. What was it about the soft curve of a woman's stomach and hips that was such a turn on? His mind strayed to where it possibly shouldn't as he took in the jewellery adorning her navel.

A second later his phone rang. 'So what do you think?' Jessie asked him.

'Sexy,' Jason replied honestly. 'Why an anchor?'

'To keep me grounded, in case my fantasies run away with me. They're all about you, obviously,' Jessie said, a teasing edge to her voice.

Jason laughed, realising that that was why he could talk to her: because the conversation never got too heavy. She was aware the kids were struggling. He'd told her that much. She'd been empathetic, rather than just making the right noises. *I get it*, she'd written. *If you put yourself in their shoes, it's easy to imagine how hard this must be.* That had meant something to Jason, that she was a sensitive enough person to imagine herself in their position. Jason couldn't avoid doing the same; his own childhood had been spent dodging the crossfire between his adoptive parents.

'So, did it take your mind off your problems?' she asked.

'It provided a pleasurable distraction,' Jason assured her.

'Good.' She paused. 'You're on your own, I take it?'

Jason drew in a long breath. 'I am,' he said.

Jessie clearly heard the tension in his tone. 'Don't worry, I'm not about to propose phone sex,' she quipped. 'I just presumed you were, since you're talking to me.'

'Right assumption,' he said, with a sigh.

'And you've no idea where she is, your wife?'

'None.' Jason acknowledged the pang of jealousy he felt as he wondered whether Karla might be with another man. She was entitled to be, but still, the thought hurt like hell. The thought that she might be involved with someone who didn't give a shit about her caused his gut to clench. There was no point asking her. The answer was always the same: it was none of his business.

'And you're worried?'

Jason hesitated, torn now between guilt that he was talking about Karla to Jessie and guilt that he was burdening Jessie with his marital problems.

'Don't beat yourself up. I get it. It wouldn't be normal not to be, would it?' Jessie said, picking up on that, too. 'Although I must admit I'm amazed you care, after whatever awful thing she did that broke up your marriage.'

'She didn't,' Jason clarified quickly, concerned that he'd given Jessie the wrong idea. Whatever was happening between them, he would never rubbish Karla in anyone's eyes. He couldn't. 'It wasn't anything she did. Not knowingly, anyway.'

He paused. He couldn't say too much without sharing things that would devastate Karla. 'It's historical, something that was beyond her control,' he said, and left it at that.

'Well, she's definitely a girl with an intriguing past,' Jessie said. 'You've got me going mad here, trying to work out what it is. Maybe one of these days, when you trust me enough, you'll be able to share with me and put me out of my misery.'

Now Jason felt bad. 'It's not that I don't trust you, Jessie. It's just it's not something she would want made general knowledge.'

'God, the *suspense*.' Jessie sighed dramatically. 'Ah well, not to worry. I respect you for respecting her, to be honest. So you know though, I would never break a confidence. I've had that done to me – some eejit of a boyfriend telling all and sundry about things that were for his ears only. Like I say, some people can be real douches.'

Jason couldn't help thinking she might be listing him as one of them, after he'd as good as said he didn't trust her.

'So, how're the children?' Jessie changed the subject. 'Sleeping, I assume?'

'In bed,' Jason confirmed. 'I'm not sure they're sleeping though.'

'Poor wee angels,' Jessie said. 'You know, I was thinking, you should take a break. With the children, I mean. A long weekend, maybe? You could always bring them here,' she continued, before Jason could answer. 'There'd be loads for them to do. We could take them to the adventure centre just outside of Carlow. It's the largest in Ireland. They could have a go at karting, archery, soccer, wall climbing, roller skating, zip line...'

Jessie was on a roll, it seemed. Jason didn't interrupt. Just listening to her melodic voice, hearing her enthusiasm, somehow made him feel less stressed.

'There's tons of other stuff too,' she went on, 'There's the Chocolate Garden, that's a must for kids – a working chocolate and ice cream factory, with workshops, an ice cream parlour and play areas. If they're into more intellectually stimulating stuff, there's the visual centre for contemporary art, and there's loads of outdoor activities: canoeing, mountain biking, paintballing, cycling, walking...'

Jason found himself smiling as she stopped, possibly to catch her breath. 'You sound as if you're up for all of it.'

'Oh, I am.' She laughed, in that light, carefree way she did. 'But watch out for me on the mountain bike slopes. I'm hot stuff. And I'm a mean canoeist.'

'As long as your anchor doesn't weigh you down,' Jason suggested, his mind going back to the photo and the tempting expanse of bare flesh she'd sent him.

'Ah, see, that's where I'd be wanting my hero to come to the rescue.'

'At your service,' Jason assured her. 'You're definitely into outdoor activities then?'

'Absolutely. I like to keep myself fit, mostly on the way back from the Chocolate Garden. That's not to say I'm not into the odd romantic meal, too; walking in the rain, as long as I've got a brolly; barefoot on the beach and so on. I find that quite therapeutic. Do you like dogs?' she asked, at a tangent.

And Jason felt guilty all over again. They'd been planning to get one. The kids were desperate for one. They hadn't decided when yet, but they'd definitely decided on what: a Labrador. They'd even talked about taking long walks on the beach with it. Holidaying in Devon or Pembrokeshire maybe, both of which had dog-friendly beaches, where the kids could let off some steam. 'I do,' he said, a new heaviness settling in his chest.

'Excellent. I was thinking of getting one from the rescue place, to stave off the loneliness of empty nights on my own. We have a lot in common.'

'We do,' Jason agreed, trying not to let his mind linger on what could never be.

'Look, seriously, think about what I said about coming to stay,' Jessie went on. 'I have bags of room here at the cottage now my housemate's moved out. Well, a spare room anyway, so you and I might need to cosy up, but if you were up for that…'

'I think I could cope,' Jason said quietly, actually considering the idea and thinking that it didn't seem like a bad one. 'It sounds like a plan.'

'Let me have some dates,' Jessie said. 'I'm going to be coming to the UK to see my brother soon. He's working in Birmingham. I was thinking that maybe we could travel back together? What do you think?'

'I, er…' Jason hesitated, and then wondered why. 'Okay, why not?'

'Brilliant.' Jessie sounded pleased. 'Uh-oh, I'd better go back inside. My shift starts in five minutes. Looks like it's going to be a madhouse in A&E already. I'll call you tomorrow.'

'Speak then. Take care, Jessie.' Jason ended the call with a bewildered shake of his head. He felt as if he'd just been hit by a tornado. But he also felt better than he had when he'd come home.

CHAPTER THIRTY-TWO

KARLA

The last time I drank this much – in my youth, which now seems like a lifetime ago – it altered my perception of everything around me into something bearable. I felt exhilarated, uplifted and relaxed at the same time. Above all, I felt happy, filled with the overwhelming urge to dance. The lights were brighter, the colours more intense. I was locked into the music, confident on the dance floor. Free of the pain. Every and any sound was danceable to. Leaving the nightclub, I could have danced to the thrum of the rain on the pavement outside, the distant screams of a police siren. Hugged everyone and anyone.

Now, as I sit on the lowered loo seat, waiting for the walls to slow down, I feel nothing but cold and empty. In this club heaving with people, I am suddenly, irrevocably lost. A lonely, abandoned woman sitting on her own in a toilet – no one to reach out to, no one to hold me, no one to hold my hair back as I vomit into the bowl. Jason had done that once, when we were young, when being recklessly stupid was a rite of passage. He'd held me, carried me to bed, undressed me, carefully and respectfully, lain with me.

Stroked my hair softly until I'd fallen asleep.

Wrapping my arms about myself, I quiet a sob and try to still the fresh wave of nausea rising inside me, the acrid grief that grips me and won't let go. The jealousy. I love him. I miss him. I am mourning him – my husband, my lover, the father of my children. The man I am losing.

I have to go. I have to get out of here. I pull myself to my feet as the black-painted walls of the cubicle close in on me. The wine I drank before I came to the nightclub was a mistake, beyond reckless. I should have made sure to keep myself hydrated. I was dancing non-stop, until the floor shifted off-kilter. What was I thinking?

Holly and Josh are all I can think of, as I come shakily out of the toilets, desperately longing to be where I belong: at home with my babies, with Jason... But my husband doesn't want me.

My hook-up isn't too bothered about hanging on to me either, I realise. As I make my way to the exit, I see he's already hitting on a hot young thing, dressed appropriately for her age. That's okay. He's not my type anyway – too tanned, blonde and blue-eyed. Too arrogant. Not Jason.

Men half my age, no more than boys, look me over as I flag down a black cab. They don't comment. One of them even smiles. I don't flatter myself they like what they see. They're probably wondering what I'm doing here, a woman of my age, wearing spaghetti straps and lace and boots that belong on the thighs of a teenager.

Do you know why you're here? Sarah whispers.

After almost missing the seat as I get in, I give the taxi driver my address, right myself and close my eyes. *Playing the dating game. But I'm not sure I'm winning*, I answer, wishing I could sleep as I listen to the rhythmic swish of the windscreen wipers. Sleep until my nightmare is over. Or else forever.

Fifteen minutes later, I ask the taxi driver to keep going and stop a few houses past my own, take several slow breaths and try to still the wooziness in my head. I note as we pass that, apart from the mellow glow from the children's nightlights, all the lights are off. I breathe a sigh of relief, glad that Jason appears to have gone to bed. Sometimes he waits up for me, even though he doesn't know when I will be back – whether I'll be back. I have no idea why he does it, since he obviously cares nothing for me. I am disposable, interchangeable. He's bored with the marriage, the monotony, the responsibility; ready to reclaim his freedom and move on. Is it so wrong of me to want him to realise that I can do the same, if I choose to? If I want to. But I don't. I swallow back the grief that's now lodged like a stone in my throat. How will I bear it, having half of my soul ripped again from inside me?

The taxi driver's expression, as I fumble my purse from my pocket and thrust the fare into his hand, is one of ill-concealed disdain. 'You need to take more water with it, love,' he comments, as I turn to shove my door open and stumble to the pavement.

Steadying myself, I quash down my irritation. How dare he make assumptions? He knows nothing about my life, who I am. *I* don't know who I am. When I look at myself in the mirror, I don't recognise the person looking back. The photos I posted online, they're not me, but facets of me. In some, I look like Sarah, with her cropped hair and feisty attitude. In others, I can see my fun-loving, free-spirited self – someone who's got lost along the way. I'm fractured, falling apart. Will I recognise the body that lies on the ground when everything stops?

The house is still when I finally manage to manoeuvre my key into the lock and let myself in. After negotiating my way along the hall, I drop my holdall in the downstairs toilet until I can stow it away. My need to check on my children more urgent than satisfying the thirst that grips me, I go straight back to the stairs. I have no doubt Jason is looking after them; he will do that above everything else. Above temptation? Not that. Clearly, not that. He's already succumbed; will continue to succumb to whatever his online woman is offering him. How far might he go to distance himself from his past life? From me, or who he imagines me to be? From his children? I'm pushing him, but surely he must know that I want him to push back. I need him to. I desperately need him to realise he wants to.

Fear tingling my spine – fear of the unknown, of what my future might hold; fear of falling further into an endless abyss on my own – I climb the stairs, willing the floorboards not to creak. I have to open his eyes. I have to make him see the person he's forgotten exists inside me. I have to make him realise he doesn't want to lose *her*.

Finding Holly's door ajar, I nudge it further open and slip into her bedroom. My breath catches in my throat as I take in the form of my daughter in the pale light of her nightlight. Her pink Build-A-Bear – her childhood comfort toy – clutched to her chest, she is curled into a foetus-like ball, looking lonely and fragile and small.

Oh, sweetheart. My heart squeezing inside me, I wipe a tear from my face, lest it land on my baby girl's cheek to mingle with those I have no doubt she has silently cried, and lower myself to crouch down beside her. *We'll fix this, my darling.* Gently, I brush a strand of her beautiful blonde hair from her eyes, press a light kiss to her temple and ease the duvet up over her. *Mummy will make things right, make Daddy stay. I promise you, angel, I will make all of this go away.*

I'm tempted to lie down beside my little girl, curl my body around her and never let her go, but I caution myself not to. Holly needs to sleep. I need to check on Josh, who will be as bewildered by all that's happening as his sister. Easing myself up, I walk quietly to the door, pulling it to behind me, and creep along the landing to Josh's room.

Stepping inside his partially open door, my gaze goes instinctively to his bed and I stop dead. The duvet is thrown back and tangled. There's a soft hollow in his pillow, an empty space where my little boy's body should be. My eyes shoot to his bedside table, my panic subsiding a little as I realise his glasses are there. His iPad, too. He wouldn't go far without either of those. He's with Jason. Has to be. Backing out, I turn on my heel and fly to the main bedroom.

Please let him be there. Please, God, let him be there. My heart battering against my chest and terrifying scenarios screaming in my head – my ten-year-old son, wandering the cold, unfriendly streets on his own – I press down the door handle, and then I start breathing again. Relief flooding through me, I move quietly towards the bed. My husband is lying on his back, one arm thrown across his forehead. Tucked safely in the crook of his other arm is Josh, sleeping soundly, his head pressed against his father's chest, listening to the reassuring thrum of his heartbeat. As I so often did, feeling secure and needed and wanted.

Was that really such a short while ago?

I won't let him go. Can't allow him to. I have to make Jason see that, whatever it is he craves, whatever he thinks is missing in his life, he will find it right here, with his family. As long as we have each other we can survive. We can do more than survive; we can fly, if only I can open his eyes.

CHAPTER THIRTY-THREE

DIANA

Robert looked bleary-eyed when he came down to the kitchen – unsurprising, given the time he'd come in last night. He'd obviously been hard at it at work, which had necessitated time to de-stress at the golf club, the bar of which had closed a good hour before he'd arrived home. He'd driven, of course, despite the weave to his walk and the fact that he'd reeked of whisky when he rolled in. Diana curtailed her rising contempt, preferring to remain calm until she was certain her suspicions were correct. She'd been the epitome of calm throughout their marriage, skilled in the art of maintaining a composed façade. As the wife of a prominent businessman who liked to move in the right social circles, she'd played her supporting role well, tolerating his behaviour at first. After losing Sarah, she was so broken, and she didn't have the strength to walk away. Starting over, fighting him in court – it had all seemed too daunting a task. She'd stayed rather than cause any further upheaval in Karla's life. And then, once Karla was married, she stayed because it suited her to do so until she was financially secure. The bonus of being with a wealthy man who didn't care to notice her was that she could do exactly as she liked, which meant seeing Michael whenever she wanted, a fact Robert would wake up to one day. One day very soon.

'You're dressed early,' he said, blinking and looking slightly disorientated. Possibly because Diana hadn't dutifully brought him his cup of tea that morning, or his newspaper, the headlines of which he would browse before taking his shower and going off to his office to make his staff's lives completely miserable. She'd made a mistake in staying with him. A dreadful mistake. Robert's final cruel attempt to destroy Jason's life, thereby robbing his daughter of her happiness, had brought that sharply home.

Diana regretted not having the will to walk away sooner, but there was nothing to be done about it. She couldn't undo her life and get the years back. All she could do now was set her plan in motion. It was a pity, though, that she wouldn't have the satisfaction of seeing Robert's face when he realised the headlines were about himself.

'I had some things on my mind. I couldn't sleep,' she informed him, walking across to the work surface to fill up the kettle.

'Oh?' Robert said, behind her.

He sounded guarded, Diana noted. Clearly, he thought she'd been up half the night tearing herself apart about where he'd been until the small hours, and who with. That she might be about to demand explanations. As if she hadn't given that up years ago.

'Tea?' she asked him.

Glancing behind her, she noticed a flicker of surprise cross his face. Robert didn't take long to recover himself though. He rarely did. He was a man whose confidence bordered on intolerable arrogance. Diana often wondered whether he realised the young women he bedded wouldn't look at him twice if he wasn't flaunting his wallet.

'If it's not too much trouble,' he said, an exasperated edge to his tone, indicating his disgruntlement at not having his tea served to him in bed. The bed he'd made for himself, and which, Diana had decided, it was high time he was left to lie in.

'I had some things to do, so I thought I might as well come down,' she said, turning to face Robert as he seated himself at the breakfast table.

Diana watched him glance around with a perturbed look on his face, as if wondering why there were no breakfast preparations underway. 'Some old acquaintances to catch up with,' she added cryptically.

That got his attention. Robert was looking at her now, puzzled. And well might he be.

'What did you say to him?' Diana asked him bluntly.

Robert looked confounded at that.

'Jason,' Diana clarified. 'Karla thinks he's about to leave her.'

Robert furrowed his brow. He did his best to look perturbed, but Diana noted the glint of satisfaction in his eyes.

'She thinks it's because of something that passed between you and him at the meeting you had. What did you say, Robert, that had such a devastating impact on him and Karla?'

Now he looked dismissive. 'Not that again, Diana,' he said, with a heavy sigh, and reached across the table for the newspaper. 'I've told you, he—'

'What did you *say* to him?' Diana bellowed, causing his attention to snap back to her.

Taken aback, he eyed her warily for a moment and then shook his head in despair. 'You really are determined to paint me as the villain in all of this, aren't you, Diana? Did it not occur to you that "can do no wrong" Jason might have always intended to turn down the *substantial* amount of money I offered him?'

Diana laughed, disbelieving. 'Why? Because he wanted his business to fail?'

'Because he's been looking for a way out of his marriage,' Robert supplied, preposterously. 'Because he has been for some while, but being the weak specimen he is, he was looking for a way to blame everyone else for his own failings!' he finished, his voice going up several octaves. He stared angrily.

And now Diana was truly incredulous. Was he really going down this route? Could he not see that she was giving him an opportunity to redeem himself in one small way and tell her a truth she'd always known? But he would continue to treat her as if she were a halfwit, pile lie on top of lie and ruin Jason's life, Karla's life, in order to substantiate those lies and save his own miserable skin. *Unbelievable*. 'You bastard,' she said, shaking her head.

He pulled in a long breath, his nostrils flaring, and got to his feet. 'On the basis that you're obviously upset, I'm going to overlook that, Diana,' he said, his voice tight with suppressed rage. 'But please do not *ever* call me—'

'I know!' Diana took a step towards him, eyeballing him furiously.

He scanned her eyes, his ridiculous bluster faltering for a second. Then, 'Know what, exactly?' he said flatly.

He was bluffing. Waiting for her to spit it out. Diana could see the uncertainty in his eyes. Smell his fear. He knew damn well what.

'You've gone too far,' she said evenly. 'And this time, I will see that you pay.' Dragging her gaze disdainfully over him, she turned to walk away.

'Know *what*?' Robert shouted after her. 'Diana! *Fuck!*'

Diana heard the loud crash behind her, meaning that he'd taken his frustration out on whatever was closest to hand. Of course, he would then blame anyone and everyone for causing his frustration. Robert rarely felt that he was to blame for losing his temper, for any damage he caused, be it emotional or physical. For that, he would need to have a conscience. And a man who sailed through life, destroying anyone who might pose a threat to his business or his reputation – even his own children – clearly did not.

Diana didn't consider herself a vengeful person, but her fervent wish was that one day Robert might discover he did have a conscience. She wished more fervently that by then it would be too late. That he would already be on his way to the gates of hell.

CHAPTER THIRTY-FOUR

JASON

Waking with a jerk, Jason reached instinctively for his phone on the bedside table, only to find it wasn't there. Heaving himself out of bed, he checked the dresser and quickly scanned the rest of the room. He was sure he'd brought it up with him, ready to grab should, God forbid, there be an emergency phone call. But he'd been so bloody tired last night after another late meeting at the office to fine-tune the details of the sale of the company. He wanted the handover to go as smoothly as possible. Mark had been with him from start-up, when they'd worked together in one poky room. It was thanks to Mark they'd sold their first ever computer software package. Looking at the ideas he had for future expansion, the customers both he and Rachel were working all hours to secure, he deserved this to work.

The kids had also been exhausted, having spent the evening in the office with him, yet again. After talking to Jessie and then waiting up another hour, worrying about where Karla was, hoping she would come home, he'd been incapable of thinking straight. Then Josh had woken up with a screaming nightmare. The poor kid had been so petrified, Jason had tucked him into the main bed and then crawled in there with him. He could have left his phone anywhere. Possibly in Josh's room. Glancing in his direction, he saw he was still sleeping and decided he would give him ten more minutes, while he got breakfast.

Massaging the crick in his neck, he headed downstairs, turned towards the kitchen and stopped in his tracks.

Karla?

Fear twisted Jason's stomach. Cautiously, he moved towards the slim figure slumped on the hall floor, against the wall. What in God's name was she doing there, fully dressed and fast asleep?

Christ, he hoped she *was* asleep. Crouching beside her, Jason hesitated and then gently shook her. 'Karla,' he said softly.

She didn't move, causing his heart to almost stop beating. 'Karla!' He called her name more urgently and shook her again, relief crashing through him when she finally stirred.

'*Whoa*, hold on. Give yourself a second.' Jason reached out to help as, her eyes springing wide, she attempted to scramble up.

Karla relaxed a little when she realised it was him, gazing around as if not quite sure where she was. 'I'm all right,' she said.

Jason very much doubted that. She looked disorientated, out of it. 'What are you doing here, Karla?' he asked her, feeling sick to his gut that he was the cause of this.

Karla laughed – a small, defeated laugh. 'I live here,' she reminded him. 'I went to check on the children, and… I don't know. I sat down. I must have dozed off.'

On the hall floor? Because she'd drunk too much, Jason deduced, feeling her pain, her utter bewilderment. He wished he could communicate that much to her. That he felt it, too. That he always would.

'Did you not recognise me?' Karla added, with a heart-wrenching smile.

Jason swallowed. He guessed she was referring to her hair, which she'd worn sweeping her shoulders not so long ago. Jason tried not to recall the soft, silky feel of it, how he'd never been able to resist twining it around his hands as they made sweet love together. Now it was short, and dyed a striking auburn. It suited her face. She had beautiful bone structure, high cheekbones; she was perfect. He couldn't help feeling that this new look just wasn't her though.

Karla's fingers went to the nape of her neck. 'It's temporary, the hair colour – comb in and wash out,' she said, as if reading his mind. She'd always been pretty shrewd at that.

'I gathered.' Jason's mouth twitched into a smile. 'It's run a bit.' He nodded towards her neck; resisted reaching to wipe the tell-tale drip of watery auburn away.

'Ah.' Karla touched her fingers to it. 'I went walking in the rain,' she said. Noting the immense sadness in her eyes, Jason looked away. He had to. His mind had immediately gone to Jessie and the comment she'd made about romantic walks in the rain.

Looking back to Karla, his gaze strayed to her hand, now resting at the soft hollow of her neck. Her ring finger was bare, he noticed. He simply couldn't allow his mind to go there. 'You broke a nail,' he said throatily.

Her expression surprised, Karla turned the back of her hand towards her face, going slightly cross-eyed as she examined it. 'Oh,' she said, and shrugged. 'Not to worry. It's just another little piece of me.'

Jason drew in a breath. It stopped short of his chest. 'You need to lie down,' he said, carefully threading an arm around her.

'There are many pieces, you know, that make up the whole of me,' Karla went on, allowing him to ease her to her feet.

'I know.' Jason nodded. He did know. The carefree side of her, the woman who would let go of her worries and mesmerise people on the dance floor – she'd lost that part of herself because of him.

'Does she have nice hair?' Karla asked him, as he attempted to help her towards the stairs.

'Who?' he asked.

'Jessie, your girlfriend.'

Jason stopped walking.

'I like her belly button piercing.'

Jesus. Jason's heart dropped like a stone.

CHAPTER THIRTY-FIVE

KARLA

My heart beats erratically in a combination of fear and curiosity as I wait for Jason's reaction to my announcement that I've looked at his phone; that I know about her. *She's fake*, I want to scream. *Can't you see that this is a woman presenting what she imagines men want?* Is this woman, with her fake tan and body piercings, what Jason really wants? My heart thrums faster. Light-headed with nausea and nerves, I feel the floor shift beneath me.

Jason's eyes are agonised, his expression somewhere between deep shame and anger. 'Christ,' he utters, eventually, and slips his arm from around me.

But *who* is he angry with, I wonder, tears springing to my eyes. Me? *Why?* I made a mistake; I pressurised him. I didn't trust him. Sided with my deplorable father against him. I'm deeply ashamed, but was it really that bad? Was anything I did ever really that bad? Because if it was, then I must be completely insensitive, because I don't *remember* myself that way.

'She's obviously the confident sort, flaunting her body jewellery like that,' I say, my own anger rising as I bite the tears back. 'But then, perhaps she hasn't had her confidence crushed by a man too cowardly to tell her the truth!'

Jason looks away. 'We should talk about this later, Karla,' he says, uncomfortably. 'Not now.'

'Yes, *now*,' I demand, as he moves away. 'Does that do it for you, Jason?' I follow him, catching his arm and commanding his attention. 'Fantasising about what you're going to do to her when she sends you her teasing little photos, does that do it for you?'

Jason looks ill, so very tired, but still I can't curtail the fury festering inside me. Because I'm *hurting*. Can't he see that?

'Do you visualise her?' I ask him. 'Lying beneath you, as you—'

'Karla, *stop*,' Jason says, the blood visibly draining from his face.

'Imagine her piercings pressing into your skin?' I don't stop. With tears cascading down my face, though I try hard not to let them, and fury and humiliation driving me, I can't stop. 'Do you want to lick her flat belly, Jason?' *Mine's flat!* I want to shout. *I can't eat. I can't breathe. Do you even know what I look like?* 'Trail your tongue over her salty, wet skin? Push it into her mouth? Bite her? Work your way down her body and—'

'Enough!' Jason raises his voice, his face now rigid with anger. 'For God's sake, Karla, just stop this, will you?'

'Why should I?' I clench my fists at my sides, my fingernails digging painfully into my flesh. 'What do you *expect* me to do? Say nothing? Pay her a bloody compliment?'

Jason looks destabilised for a second, alarm flitting across his features, as I step towards him.

'You were concerned, weren't you, when you saw me sitting there?'

He kneads his forehead. 'Of course I was. You were damn near unconscious. I thought you were…' He falters, clearly unable to voice his fear – that he might have had to explain away how his actions killed me. And he has, on the inside; he's killed me stone dead. 'Karla, please… I'm begging you, don't do this now.'

'Begging?' I laugh, disbelieving. 'Would that have worked for me, do you think? If I'd begged you, would *you* have stopped?'

Jason says nothing. He sighs heavily instead, which only riles me further.

'I wonder how concerned my husband would have been on finding me semi-conscious if he'd known how I came to be in that state?' I push on. I can't help myself. My heart is fracturing, a thousand sharp shards of glass slicing painfully into me, because I know. I know that even if I did fall to my knees – right here, right now – he wouldn't stop. Emotionally, he has left me, and I can't bear it. I *can't*. 'I'll tell you how, shall I?'

Jason attempts to walk past me. I sidestep, blocking him. 'I was out dancing, Jason. You know that thing I used to do, when I had fun in my life? Dancing and drinking – with my very own dating site "hook-up", as it happens. As a prelude to having sex with him!'

'Jesus.' Jason looks heavenwards.

There's no one up there! I cry inside. I know this, too. I prayed so many times when Sarah died. When I realised my husband's love for me was dying, I prayed like I've never prayed before. No one *heard* me.

'Would you have been worried, Jason, if you'd known that about your wife, the woman you think you know so well? Someone who's just a boring mother, clearly a boring lover, too tired and worried to be adventurous in bed?'

Jason doesn't answer. One arm across his chest, his forehead resting now on his hand, his gaze is fixed to the floor.

'Someone who works to pay the bills, who can't afford to take risks, do something different with her life before it's too late! The mother of your children, Jason! The woman who gave up her dreams to be with you, and who *you* think you can casually cast aside for some slut you imagine will spice up your life and shore up your flagging self-esteem!'

I flail an arm out, stopping Jason as he tries again to walk around me. '*Why* was it flagging? Answer me that.'

Jason says nothing.

'Because you *failed*,' I answer for him, cruelly, almost wanting to goad him. I want him to shout back, to fight, to scream. I want him to fight *for me*.

Jason's eyes are full of hurt as he looks at me. His jaw is tense, but other than that, he doesn't react.

'*You're* responsible for your company going under. No one else.' Guilt tugs at my conscience as I blurt the words out. But even knowing how much I'm hurting him, still I can't subdue the monster inside me. 'You wouldn't have needed my father's money if you'd managed your business properly. You could've sold it before you had to and done something different – or else swallowed your pride and taken the damn money!'

Jason holds my gaze. His eyes are thunderous, so dark they're almost black. 'I did swallow my pride, Karla,' he says quietly. 'If I'd taken the money, trust me, that really would have made me a failure. Now, if you wouldn't very much mind, I'd like to get to my son.'

His gaze travels to the hallway beyond me, his line of vision lowering, and my blood freezes. Whirling around, I wish I could suck the words back. It's too late. My little boy has heard it all, every foul thing that has spilled from my mouth.

'Josh…' I take a tentative step towards him, but Josh steps back, darting a glance at his father. 'Josh, I'm so sorry baby,' I say tremulously. 'I'm not angry with you, sweetheart.'

Taking another step, I extend my hands, desperate to reassure him. To feel his small body close to mine.

Josh doesn't move. His little face is bewildered; his fists are balled defensively at his sides. I look into his eyes – rich brown eyes that mirror his father's, full of uncertainty and fear. He has tears streaming down his cheeks. I blink away a rush of shame-filled emotion as I realise it's me he's frightened of.

Jason steps sideways past me as I stand there, feeling impotent under the distrustful gaze of my innocent child. He places his hands on our son's shoulders. Then, looking me over with a mixture of disappointment and remorse, he turns his gaze to the stairs.

My heart sinks to the pit of my stomach as I realise Holly is there, standing uncertainly halfway down. 'You're a horrible person,' she whispers, fixing me with a defiant glare.

'Holly…' Jason says quietly.

Holly's eyes flick to his.

Jason doesn't say any more, simply shakes his head. It's enough. Heeding his unspoken warning, Holly drags her disgusted gaze away from me and turns to flee up the stairs.

'Come on, tiger.' His voice strained, Jason turns his attention back to Josh. 'Let's go and get dressed, and then we can grab breakfast on the way, hey?'

Josh's reproachful eyes stay on mine for a second, and then he permits his father to steer him away, guiding him up the stairs before him.

They're on the landing when I hear Josh ask, 'Do I have to go to school, Dad?' His voice is tearful and anguished.

'No, Josh,' Jason says hoarsely. 'You don't have to go to school. Not today.'

The day I broke my babies' hearts. I clamp my hands over my face and gulp back the wretched sob climbing my throat. He's stealing them, stealing my babies away from me.

No, he isn't. The voice that speaks the guilt I will carry forever echoes in my head. *It's you who'll be to blame if you lose them. You're driving them away.*

CHAPTER THIRTY-SIX

KARLA

It's not quite light when I hear the bedroom door open. Jason, I guess, bringing me tea. I'm not sure why, after the vile things I said to him – with my children in earshot. I don't think I'll ever forgive myself for that. I don't think my children will either.

'Are you okay?' he asks, as he places the cup on the bedside table next to me.

His voice is soft, concerned, and my heart breaks a little bit more. I don't answer. I don't dare, in case it initiates another argument. I don't want to fight with him any more. I'm not sure I have the will to. I haven't had the energy to do anything but stay cocooned in my bed, trying to escape the dark mood that hangs over me like a heavy grey blanket. I have no idea how to speak to him now, in any case. No idea whether there's anything left to say.

Jason has been awkward around me. Obviously, he would be. At one point, I felt like I wanted to die, but I don't want to leave my children. When I imagined that, I cried tears of raw grief. Silent tears. Jason was in the spare room, but I didn't want him to hear me crying, my children to hear my heart breaking. He would care for them if I simply ceased to be, I know this to be true. He would also have enough money from the insurance to provide for them until he discovered what he wanted to do with his life, now he's selling the business that ripped us apart.

I've no doubt his future plans include his notion of the perfect woman. Does he really imagine she exists? That I'm really so imperfect, since I adapted who I am to become a wife and a mother? Or did he think me imperfect before then?

'I've brought you some tea,' he says tentatively.

I nod, but I don't turn to him. I can't bear for him to see me like this. *I* can't bear to see me like this. I will rouse myself. I have to get up today and function on some level. Try to repair the relationship with my children, whose behaviour around me now is stilted, their looks guarded.

Hearing Jason's heavy sigh as he walks away, closing the bedroom door softly behind him, I close my eyes, burrow deeper into my cocoon and allow the fresh tears to fall.

My mind drifts for a while, searching for happier memories to latch on to. Try as I might, as horribly sorry for myself as I'm feeling, I can't seem to find any that aren't tinged with sadness. Somewhere between consciousness and slumber, I am in another time, another place, another bed, thin winter sunlight filtering through the gaps in the curtains. The house is quiet. Too quiet. I strain my ears for the sounds of birdsong, people stirring, the familiar soft sounds of my sister sleeping. Nothing. The stillness is profound.

'Sarah?' Glancing across to her twin bed, I whisper her name. She doesn't respond, even to grunt moodily, as she usually does, and wriggle away from me. Pushing my duvet back, a shiver runs through me as the icy air greets me. I hitch my legs over my bed and pad towards her, my small feet making no sound on the thick carpet.

'Sarah?' Goosebumps prickle my skin, and I whisper more urgently. She doesn't hear me. She is lying on her back, her eyes closed, her expression… serene. Her skin is pale, like alabaster. Obliquely, I'm reminded of the porcelain dolls we coveted when visiting a doll shop in Knightsbridge. Her lips are strangely blue.

'Sarah, wake up.' My voice is small. I'm growing scared, angry. I don't like this game. 'Sarah, *stop it*.' I reach out to touch her, warm flesh against cold, and my hand recoils in an instant. And then someone is screaming, loud, long and piercing. Seconds pass – firm arms encircle me, a voice tries to shush me – before I realise that someone is me.

Then I am startled by a nearer sound: my children's voices permeating the shrill noise in my head; the slam of the front door.

Hell! Panic-stricken, I throw back the duvet and stumble woozily to the window to see Jason walking our children to the car. Josh is lagging behind, as he always does, his eyes on his iPad. Holly has taken hold of Jason's hand. She's looking up at him, her little face serious, nodding thoughtfully as she digests whatever he's telling her. Most likely he's trying to reassure her about me. I'd overheard him telling them, 'Mummy's a bit poorly,' after my deranged behaviour the other morning. What does he say to them in private, I wonder. How is he convincing them that this nightmare will have a fairy-tale ending?

I curse myself for going back to sleep. I should have been up, hugging them close, assuring them myself that I would be well soon, back to normal. Though, in truth, I don't know that I ever will be. I feel as if I'm falling, that no matter how hard I flail out, there is no branch to hang on to, that when I land, the me I knew won't exist any more.

Watching my babies climb into the car, I press the flat of my hand against the glass, as if I might draw them to look up at me. They don't. They're both too preoccupied with their father. I would never have disillusioned them about him, rubbished him in their eyes, had my grief and anger not driven me beyond rationality. I would have lied for him, whatever the future holds, because I love my children. Because I love him still. I can't imagine a time when my heart won't feel as if it's bleeding steadily inside me. But the hateful words spilled from my mouth without process of forethought. Without a second's consideration for Holly and Josh, who were just upstairs. What kind of mother am I, really? What kind of person am I?

Imperfect. A monster.

My mobile rings as I'm making my way back across the room, willing myself to shower and get dressed. I don't want to answer it, but thinking it might be Mum, and knowing how worried she will be, I reach for it.

Not Mum. I note the number of the housing association I work for, and the knot of guilt in my stomach twists itself tighter. I've rung in, but I can't bring myself to go back to work. A shudder runs through me as I recall my bitchy behaviour towards the girls in the admin office, who haven't spoken to me since, other than out of necessity about anything work-related. I can't face them, any of my colleagues. Not now. Not like this.

Reluctantly, I take the call, guessing they're checking to see how long I might be off sick. Fervently, I hope it isn't the girl I reduced to tears. *Oh no.* My guilt multiplies as I realise it's the chief executive himself.

'Karla, how are you?' John asks, pleasant and cheery, as always. I wish he wasn't. I don't feel I can rise to it.

'Still a bit wobbly,' I say, not quite lying.

John tsks in sympathy. 'It's a nasty bug,' he says of the flu I'm supposed to have, which is going around. 'Well, don't you worry about rushing back,' he adds. 'Just take your time and make sure you're fully recovered before you return to work.'

'I will,' I say weakly.

'While I've got you, though – and I'm sorry to bother you with it while you're off ill – but do you think I could pick your brains about something?'

'Yes?' I say warily.

'Those pesky minutes for the last board meeting, you don't happen to know if the audio tape ever surfaced, do you?' he asks. 'It's just that the board are convening an emergency meeting due to lack of funding and, stupidly, I deleted my notes from my PC once I'd dictated them. We're going to be a bit lost without them.'

What? I blink, stupefied. Is he seriously asking me about something that happened aeons ago? In another lifetime, it seems to me now, when my bloody life wasn't falling apart?

'I don't know, John,' I answer, feeling irrationally agitated suddenly. 'Why don't you pop over to the admin assistants' office and ask them?' *As in, assert your authority and stop expecting me to do everything for you.*

'Oh well, not to worry.' He sighs expansively. 'I'm sure the board members will understand. I think I've committed some of it to memory. I'll just have to wing—'

'Alternatively, you could suggest that the board members drag themselves out of the dark ages and get online?' I say facetiously over him. 'You could send the minutes directly yourself then, couldn't you, instead of having to post them out?'

Shocked, clearly, John doesn't speak for a moment, then, 'Yes, well, thanks for your help, Karla,' he says abruptly. 'Like I said, don't rush back.'

Then he's gone. And I realise I might have just lost my job.

Holding my breath, I stare at my phone, scarcely able to believe what I've done. Cold fear settles inside me; a new fear. Fear that I might actually be deranged, intent on self-destruction, annihilating all that is dear to me. My life is falling apart. I'm blaming Jason, blaming my father, but is it me? I'm ruining my life, Jason's life, my children's lives. I am losing *everything*, and I have no idea how to stop it.

CHAPTER THIRTY-SEVEN

JASON

Having collected the kids from school at the end of the day, which he'd being doing for a while, with Karla being either out or out of it, Jason ushered them out of the car. He didn't mind doing the school runs. They were equally his responsibility, and he didn't have much to do in the office now that Mark was taking over the reins. He worried that Karla couldn't see the damage this disruption to their routines was doing though. The damage she was doing to her relationship with them. Wondering what the lie of the land was, how Karla was, since he'd left her, still in bed, this morning, he let the kids into the house before him, closed the front door and then swapped surprised glances with Holly and Josh.

'Mum's cooking.' Josh pushed his glasses up his nose and blinked at him, puzzled. Given that Karla had been obvious by her absence from the kitchen lately, Jason understood his confusion.

'Smells like meatballs,' Holly whispered worriedly.

Picking up the distinct aroma of garlic, onions and tomatoes, Jason guessed Holly was right. She was preparing the kids' favourite. *Damn.* He sighed heavily. She might have rung or texted him. How the hell was he going to tell her they'd already eaten?

'We're going to be in *deeeep* trouble,' Josh said, in exaggerated tones. Then he glanced sideways at Holly and sliced his hand demonstratively across his throat.

'Will you grow *up*,' Holly snapped irritably, giving him a swift nudge with her elbow.

'*Oi*, that hurt.' Josh scowled and rubbed his assaulted arm. 'Dad, tell her.'

'It was supposed to, moron,' Holly muttered.

'Kids…' Jason shot them a warning glance as he dropped their rucksacks onto the hall floor. 'Now's not the time.'

'Sorry,' Holly said, with an apologetic shrug. 'What do we do?' she asked, looking nervously up at him.

'We could always pretend to eat it,' Josh suggested helpfully.

Holly rolled her eyes and emitted a heavy sigh of despair. 'A moron, definitely.'

'We could take our rucksacks in,' Josh went on, unperturbed. 'And feed the meatballs into them, while she's not looking.'

Holly simply stared at him, astounded.

'Nice idea, Josh. Not sure what we'd do with the spaghetti though,' said Jason. He couldn't help but quietly smile at the image of Josh trying to feed spaghetti surreptitiously into his school bag, but he felt bad for Karla. She was clearly trying to make an effort.

'Come on,' he said. 'Let's go and say hello. Your mum will be okay. We can always have it for dinner tomorrow.'

Holly didn't look that convinced, but she nodded maturely and urged Josh on to the kitchen.

Karla turned from the pan at the stove as they went in. 'Hi, guys,' she said, smiling. 'Good day at school?'

'Normal,' Josh replied with a shrug.

'Did you remember your PE kit?' Karla gave him a knowing look. Josh tended to be so distracted by his iPad that he had to be told to do everything twice.

Josh shook his head, his eyes flicking guiltily down and back. 'No, forgot. It's okay though. Dad explained.'

'Oh.' Karla's smile slipped a little. She didn't look at Jason, but he guessed she wasn't impressed with his organisational skills. She was right. He should have reminded Josh last night, though he wasn't sure he'd actually remembered to wash his kit.

'Holly?' Karla turned her attention to her. 'How did your day go?'

Holly glanced quickly to Jason and back. 'Okay,' she said. Then, 'Did you go to work?' she asked her.

Jason sucked in a breath. Holly might only be eleven, but she'd thought that one through. Were things on the road to getting back to normal – that was what she was asking.

Karla turned back to the pan. 'Not today, no,' she said, with an uncomfortable shrug. 'I cooked your favourite,' she added, changing the subject. 'Spaghetti and meatballs.'

She reached for the herbs and stirred them into the sauce, then went to the oven to pull out the tray of meatballs, while the kids looked uncertainly on.

Karla glanced back at them. 'Go and wash up then, you two, and then we can sit down and catch up over our meal.'

'Er, will it keep, do you think?' Jason intervened, feeling as awkward as the kids looked. 'It's just that we've already eaten.'

Halfway through spooning the sauce over the meatballs, Karla stopped. 'Ah, I see,' she said tightly. 'So, what did you have?' Moderating her tone, she addressed the kids.

'KFC,' Josh supplied. 'Dad took us straight from school.'

'Well, that was nice of him. It might have been an idea if Dad had thought to mention it to me, though, *mightn't* it.' Karla placed the pan on the cooker top with a clang.

'Told you.' Josh sighed wearily, his shoulders slumping as he turned to trudge back to the hall.

'Sorry. I didn't think,' Jason offered.

'Obviously.' Karla reached to grab the spaghetti saucepan from the cooker. 'Well, the meatballs will keep,' she said, draining the water into the sink, 'but spaghetti's not likely to, is it? Honestly, you might have said, Jason. I mean, was it too much trouble to let me know? Or maybe you've already forgotten I exist? You're bound to be a bit preoccupied, after—'

She stopped as the kitchen door closed loudly behind Holly.

'Dammit.' Pressing a hand to her forehead, Karla placed the saucepan down, and then picked it up again and poured the entire contents into the sink. Jason sensed this might well be about to escalate into something. 'Thanks, Jason,' she said, chucking the saucepan in too. 'Point-scoring, are we?'

'For God's…' Jason closed his eyes, feeling weary to his soul. 'Don't be ridiculous, Karla. The kids were hungry. How was I supposed to know you were cooking? You haven't been here half the time.'

'You could have rung me,' Karla said. 'Texted me.'

Right. Jason shook his head cynically. And she would have answered? He'd texted her a million times – during the day; every evening when she went missing. He'd left messages. She never got back to him.

'But then again, I expect you were a bit busy, weren't you? Texting your tart!'

Jesus. Jason said nothing. She had every right. But with the kids nearby? Again? There was no way he was getting into this.

'Where are you going?' Karla demanded, as he headed for the door.

'To the lounge,' Jason answered quietly, his back to her. 'To get a drink. I'm not up for another argument, Karla. Not with the kids in the house. End of.'

Watching Karla walk past the lounge door to the stairs a minute later, Jason made his drink a large one. Massaging his neck, he sipped slowly, wondering what she might be about to do. He could hear her moving around in the bedroom overhead, but he really had no clue. She was so unpredictable. He hoped she didn't climb back into bed, crawling under the duvet and staying there, as if she'd given up. He couldn't stand to see her like that. Couldn't stand any of it. He had to try to talk to her. If he couldn't tell her the whole truth about what her father had told him, he had to try to reach out to her. She was hurting and he couldn't fix it. Though he might not ever have been able to fix things, even if Robert Fenton hadn't delivered the news he had. Mark hadn't used his PC while his was running a health check. He was trying to help him out of a hole, he'd told him. Which could only mean that Fenton had. In creating that false browsing history, the bastard had already as good as succeeded in breaking up their marriage anyway, fulfilling his long-held aim to do just that.

Anger boiling up inside him. Jason knocked his drink back. He needed not to be doing this – drinking too much with the kids to look after. He shouldn't have got paralytic that night, when he'd figured that if he was being accused of looking for other women, he might as well be. He'd regretted it, wondered what the hell had possessed him. Now though, he was beginning to feel differently. Without Jessie to talk to, he was sure he would have gone half out of his mind.

Seeing Karla come down again, carrying her holdall, Jason's gut clenched. *Christ.* She wasn't, was she? Going off on one of her jaunts to God only knew where? Some bloody nightclub. Not with girlfriends, he now knew.

'Karla, where are you going?' he asked her, walking into the hall.

'I told Holly the meal would be all right for tomorrow,' Karla answered. Unhooking her jacket, she looked back at him, smiling sadly. 'She's not speaking to me apparently. Again.'

Jason's heart ached for her. 'Don't go out, Karla,' he asked her, growing scared now – for her.

'I have to. I can't stay here, not tonight. I'll be back...' Karla laughed. 'I was going to say tomorrow, but I suppose you don't really care one way or the other.'

'Karla, don't. Please.' Jason caught her arm as she reached for the door.

Karla hesitated, and then she turned slowly back to face him. 'Stop me,' she said quietly, her eyes glassy with tears. 'Tell me you love me.'

CHAPTER THIRTY-EIGHT

JASON

With time on his hands now that Mark and Rachel were getting into the swing of running the company, Jason took the opportunity to use the office facilities over the next few days to job hunt. For Karla's sake, he knew he needed to move on – he would never forget the haunted look in her eyes when she'd asked him to tell her he loved her. Her heart had been breaking. It had cracked his wide open. There was no way he could stay. What was happening between them now was sheer torture.

He couldn't envisage actually leaving though. Up until now, he'd had no clue where he would go, what he would do with his life. He'd found himself leaning towards working in Ireland after Jessie's invitation to spend some time with her in County Carlow, and he'd made a few enquiries. Nothing much had grabbed his attention – his heart really hadn't been in it. On a whim, he'd called an extreme sports company based in Ireland. Mark and he had holidayed there a few times way back when they were both single with a view to taking microlighting lessons in Kildare. He'd been surprised when they'd rated his knowledge in the extreme sports field and told him they were looking for people on the team-building and corporate events side. It seemed like fate, almost. Yeah, and the way his luck had been lately, Jason couldn't help wondering what the sting in the tail would be.

Still, though, it was tempting. If he was going to have any kind of a life, he needed to get away from the lie he'd been living. He had no roots here, none that he wanted to acknowledge, apart from his sister, who he could probably visit as regularly as he did now. The issue, of course, was his kids. There was no way he intended them not to be part of his future. As things stood, however, he had nothing to offer them. He needed to sort out the practicalities: a decent income and somewhere to live.

Grabbing his mug of coffee, caffeine being the only thing keeping him awake now he was back to not sleeping – Karla hadn't come home again last night – he stopped as his phone alerted him to an incoming message. Realising it was Jessie, he checked his watch, surprised. They did most of their talking at night, while Jessie was on her breaks at the hospital, just before she went on shift or just after. Shouldn't she be tucked up in bed about now?

Taking a gulp of his coffee as he turned his attention to the photo she'd attached, Jason almost spat it out. *Bloody hell.* Feeling extremely hot under the collar, he perused the selfie slowly – a body shot, giving him a tantalising glimpse of stocking tops. He swallowed hard at the sight of white lace knickers stretched over her hips, above which was the new teasing belly piercing. *Jesus.* Taking another glug of his coffee, he was about to message her back to tell her that whatever she was trying to do to him, it was working, when his phone rang, almost giving him heart failure.

'Caught you looking,' Jessie laughed, when he picked up.

'You wear stockings?' was all Jason could manage.

'Hold-ups,' Jessie corrected him. 'For your delectation only. I don't send explicit pics to everyone, you'll be pleased to know.'

'Very,' Jason concurred, smiling. He had no reason to believe her, but somehow he did. There was something about her that was genuine, a lightness that was enticing. To say little of the 'explicit pic' she'd just sent him. Jason indulged in erotic thoughts of what he would like to do to her in those hold-ups, preferably with her white nurse's uniform on. Assailed, then, by the memory of a time he and Karla had indulged in acting out their fantasies, he found himself struggling with a sudden sense of gut-wrenching loss.

'So, did it cheer you up?' Jessie asked.

'Your timing couldn't have been better,' Jason assured her, his voice tight with a combination of deep guilt and grief.

'That bad, hey?' Jessie's tone grew sympathetic.

'That bad,' Jason confirmed, hating himself for it. But the fact was, it couldn't get any worse.

Jessie paused. And then, 'Do you love her?' She'd asked him once before. Her tone was still sympathetic, as if she got that he was struggling to know how he felt.

'I... don't know,' Jason answered honestly. 'I thought I did. I loved who I thought she was.'

'But not who she is now?' Jessie finished.

Jason sighed. 'Look, Jessie, I know this sounds like the biggest crap cliché ever, but it really is complicated. I don't even know where to begin to explain.'

'Ah,' said Jessie, with more than a hint of scepticism.

Jason sighed again, heavily. 'Is this where you tell me to piss off and stop wasting your time?'

'I'm considering it,' Jessie said sternly, causing Jason's heart to sink. 'But actually, no,' she added, her voice back to the light-hearted lilt he loved. 'I like you. You've been honest with me, so I'm trusting you not to mess with my emotions. I wish you'd learn to trust me a little more, though, and share this deep, dark secret about your wife's history. I feel kind of... shut out, I suppose.'

'Christ, Jessie, I don't mean to do that.' Jason immediately felt bad. 'It's just... it's not something Karla would want me to share.' He stopped, realising that now he actually did sound like he didn't trust her.

Jessie didn't speak for a second, then, 'Which I guess tells me my instincts are right. You're obviously caring, so as you're going through shit, I'll stick with you. We're not doing lifelong commitment here now, after all, are we? Just being friends – with possibilities.'

Jason breathed a considerable sigh of relief.

'We can sit down and have a good talk when you come over,' Jessie went on. 'Hopefully, things won't seem so complicated then. You are still coming, aren't you?'

'Wild horses couldn't keep me away,' Jason promised. And he meant it. Whatever did or didn't happen between them, Jessie was a tonic he desperately needed.

'Good,' she said, sounding pleased. 'Are you okay for the weekend we discussed?'

'Should be,' Jason confirmed. Jessie was coming to the UK to see her brother, and he'd made up his mind he was going back with her for a long weekend. He would need to talk to Karla's mother before then. Christ, that was going to be a difficult conversation if Diana didn't know what her delightful husband had told him.

'Brilliant,' Jessie said. 'You are still coming to pick me up from airport when I land, aren't you? It's just my navigational skills are so shite, I'm likely never to be seen again if I use public transport.'

'I am,' Jason promised. He couldn't wait to see her in person. Visualising the expanse of flesh he'd just seen, a definite thrill of anticipation ran through him.

'Great. Well, I'd better go and get my beauty sleep.' Jessie stifled a yawn. 'Before I do, though, bucket lists.'

'What?' Jason asked bemusedly. He had a hard time keeping up with her sometimes. But then, he liked that about her, too: the fact that there were never any awkward silences between them.

'Bucket lists,' she repeated. 'I want to get to know you a little better, so you tell me yours, and I'll tell you mine. Rapid-fire. Go!'

'Right.' Jason shook his head. 'Okay. Er, climb a mountain.'

'The Andes, Peru,' Jessie shot back. 'A trek to Cusco, the soul of the Inca Empire,' she added, as if she'd already half-planned it. 'My turn. See the Wonders of the World.'

'Ditto,' Jason said, in the absence of anything else coming to mind.

'No, you can't have the same as mine,' Jessie chided him. 'That's cheating.'

'Ah, er…' Jason furrowed his brow. He'd never really thought about all the things he'd like to do before he died. He'd thought he'd achieved one of his ambitions in life: to have a family, to belong. That hadn't worked out too well. 'I'm running out of ideas.'

'Already?' Jessie laughed. 'What about… scuba diving?'

'Been there,' Jason answered.

'Really? Oh, okay.' Jessie paused to ponder. 'Kayaking then.'

'Yep, done that too.'

'My, we are fit, aren't we?' Jessie sounded impressed. 'Okay, well…' She stopped to consider. 'If you could change your career, what would you do?'

Now Jason was definitely bemused. Was she telepathic? 'I am changing my career,' he said. 'Sort of. I'm looking at working in Ireland, as it happens. Nothing's certain yet, but there's an extreme sports company that might want me. I learned to microlight there, years ago now, but it's a possibility.'

'Well, I'll be damned. A man after my own heart.' Jessie laughed in amazement. 'Oh my God, we have to book some microlighting lessons when you come over. Ireland's coastal regions are a pure feast for the eyes. I don't think I've ever done anything so exhilarating. Well, apart from when I flew a helicopter,' she went on blithely, talking excitedly. 'I'm not sure I'll be getting my pilot's licence any time soon, though. My navigational skills really are rubbish. I'd probably end up being fished out the Irish Sea or else off the top of a bus. To be fair, it was lashing out of the heavens once I got up there. I swear the fella with me was almost having a heart attack with me at the controls.'

Jason shook his head, astonished, and wondered whether his luck might be changing, after all.

'Yikes, look at the time,' Jessie yelped. 'I have to go, or I'll be useless at work. You too. You'll get the sack before you've lined up your new job, at this rate.'

Jason hadn't yet mentioned it was his own company he was selling. There was a lot she needed to know about him. A hell of a lot. Maybe, in time, he could explain to her what his 'complications' were without leaving her as shocked as he'd felt when he'd found out.

'Speak soon,' she said. 'Keep your chin up, but watch what you're doing with your other body bits.'

'I will.' Jason chuckled as she signed off, leaving him somewhat dazed. She'd blown into his life like a whirlwind just when he needed her. He only hoped she didn't come to regret it.

He was heading for the outer office, thinking he ought to show willing and actually do some work, when his phone rang again.

Karla.

Swallowing back his now almost overwhelming guilt, Jason picked up.

'Do you love her?' she asked immediately, sounding tearful. 'Jessie, do you love her?'

Jason stumbled over his answer.

'Are you going to tell me it's not what I think it is?' Karla went on, before he could formulate any sensible thought.

'No,' he said, no idea what else to say. 'I…'

'I want you to tell me it's not what I think. You have to!' Karla cried forcefully. 'You *can't* love her. You love me!'

CHAPTER THIRTY-NINE

KARLA

The rain is relentless, drumming bullet-like off the pavement, icy daggers slicing into my clothes and wetting me through to my skin. My body is shaking. It's uncontrollable. My stomach lurches as I heave. I'm not sure what happened. One minute I was drinking, dancing, in another place, happy, bubbly me. The next I was crying as the walls tilted and the world seemed to close in on me. I tried to stay calm, inhaling deeply, exhaling slowly. It didn't help. My legs almost buckled beneath me as I blundered, disorientated, to the exit. Now I am bent over in the street, wearing a body-con dress that clings to my flesh and shows too much of my thin body, and I am so sick, so very sick. This time, I know I am in deep trouble. The rotating blue light that skims the shop window beside me confirms it.

The police are patient, though their despair is thinly veiled. The female police officer who assists me into the patrol car and seats herself next to me seems particularly unimpressed. 'Would you like to repeat that again, sweetheart?' she says, clearly struggling to understand my gabbled explanations as to why I'm wandering the streets in the dead of night, vomiting into the gutter. 'But a little bit more slowly this time, hey?'

I take a tremulous breath and try to articulate, desperately try to quash the queasiness rising inside me. She thinks I've taken drugs. I know she does. I can see the accusation in her eyes. But I haven't. I think it was the last drink I had, which I left unguarded on the bar. But I can't be sure. I can't remember whether I drank it, or how many drinks I had. I can't think. I can't remember.

I don't want to remember. I wish I could disappear into the dark, friendless night. That the rain would wash me away.

'Karla?' she prompts me, as another shudder shakes through me.

'My father, he's driving my husband away.' I try again to explain: why I'm here; why I've drunk so much; why I'm upset. Inside my head, I can hear myself saying it, but the words emerge from my mouth in a hiccupping, unintelligible slur. 'He's destroyed my marriage.' I try harder, grope for some coherence. 'He's stealing my children!'

'Who is, my lovely?' the officer asks, concern in her voice as she reaches to stop me attempting to open the car door, which refuses to budge.

'My husband,' I mumble, wrapping my arms tight around my midriff, trying to still the incessant shaking that seems to be rattling my body down to my bones.

'He's a bit of a git then, is he?' she says, taking hold of my shoulders and steering me towards her, peering narrowly at me.

'I won't let him.' I attempt to focus, but her eyes, her nose, her features all blend into one, and there is wet cotton wool in my head, and my own eyes are so heavy. So very heavy.

'Don't blame you, sweetheart,' she says, now sounding definitely unimpressed. 'Station or accident and emergency?' I hear her ask her partner, as if through a tunnel.

'The latter. Why not fill A & E with bloody drunks?' he mutters moodily. And my chest constricts as I drag another ragged breath in, try to stop the fresh tears erupting – tears of shame, pathetic self-pity and anger.

CHAPTER FORTY

DIANA

Noting that Karla still looked deathly pale when she went in to check on her, Diana's heart ached. It had almost splintered inside her when Karla had rung in the middle of the night from the hospital. She'd sounded so distraught; Diana had been terrified of what she might find when she got there.

Seeing her stir at last, she walked across to her. 'Feeling better?' She smiled, smoothing Karla's fringe gently from her forehead as she lowered herself to sit on the edge of the bed.

'Much.' Karla nodded and attempted to lever herself up.

Diana moved to help her. She didn't look better. If anything, she looked utterly exhausted, and so young and vulnerable, suddenly, that she could almost be the child who'd lain in this same bed twenty-five years back, not eating, unresponsive and unsmiling. She'd gone into herself after they lost Sarah, hardly talking for several weeks. In her sleep she would talk, cry out, her voice filled with anguish as she called Sarah's name. In her nightmares, Karla relived the horror of the bleak morning she'd discovered her sister lying dead, over and over. All Diana had been able to do was rock her gently back to sleep, try to softly reassure her, be there for her; hope that, even if she could never forget it, she would come through it. That she would eventually stop blaming herself. And

Karla had come through it. Diana had been proud of the way her girl had pulled herself up, determined to live life to the full and make something of herself.

When she'd first brought Jason home, confided she was pregnant by him, that she was in love with him and that they intended to have the baby and marry, Diana had worried for her. She'd hardly been able to sleep. Seeing that she'd found someone who quite clearly loved her back, who cared for her, someone who could make her smile again, she'd buried her worries. She'd thwarted Robert's attempts to interfere, and prayed that things would work out for them; that her daughter's marriage would be a better one than hers – a happy one, filled with love and, importantly, trust. And now this. Her marriage destroyed. Her confidence and belief in herself shattered, thanks to Robert, a man who imagined he was so important he was infallible, untouchable; that he wouldn't reap what he sowed. He would. If Diana hadn't achieved much in her own life, she was determined to succeed in one thing, and that was to ensure Robert's abominable behaviour caught up with him.

'Thanks, Mum.' Leaning back, Karla smiled sadly. 'For everything, I mean, as well as coming to collect me. I didn't know who else to call.'

Her husband would have gone to her, but Karla would rather have died than allow him to see her like that, lying emotionally broken on a hospital trolley. Diana's heart grew heavier. 'Did you think I wouldn't?' She gave her a mock scowl.

Karla dropped her gaze, and the unshed tears finally came. Pulling her tight to her, Diana held her while she cried, smoothing a hand over her hair. Her once beautiful, bouncy blonde hair, now shorn and coloured dark auburn – Sarah's colour, almost. When Diana had first set eyes on her at the hospital, while Karla was still woozy, she'd realised that her daughter was deeply troubled. That the ghosts from her past had never truly been laid to rest.

Feelings she'd never been able to process – her grief, her deep sense of loss – had resurfaced, been exacerbated by the prospect of losing her husband. Her daughter wasn't coping. Diana had no choice but to find a way to help her.

'I'm sorry, Mum.' Karla sniffled shakily. 'I didn't mean to be so stupid.'

Diana reached for her hands. 'You've nothing to be sorry for, Karla,' she said firmly. 'It happened. It's over. You reached rock bottom and now you have to climb back up again, for yourself, for your children. They need you. No man's worth this, sweetheart.'

Being arrested for killing a man of Robert's ilk might possibly be worth it, Diana couldn't help thinking, but slowly killing yourself, humiliating yourself, getting drunk at nightclubs over a man? Karla was worth more than this. It was about time she realised that.

'I love him, Mum,' Karla said, looking beseechingly at her, as if willing her to understand.

Diana did. More than her daughter knew. Her own heart would always bear the scars she'd inflicted on it the day she'd walked away from the man who truly loved her. Michael, though, had refused to let her go, staying in touch over the years. Diana was so glad that he had. Her life would have been intolerable without him to talk to. She needed to talk to him now.

'But how will this help?' Dismissing thoughts of Michael to concentrate on her daughter, she glanced worriedly across to the chair, on which were the questionable clothes Karla had been wearing in the nightclub: a minuscule black dress and thigh-high boots – a scream to be noticed. 'What are you trying to prove, darling?' she asked her, making sure to keep her tone non-judgemental.

'I don't know.' Karla shrugged, looking as miserable as it was possible to be. 'I suppose I wanted to remind Jason there was more to me than being a wife and a mother.' She paused, her eyes downcast as she absent-mindedly traced the flower pattern on the duvet with a forefinger.

'I'm not sure he ever really knew me, Mum.' She looked back at her, after a second, with such agony in her eyes, it tore Diana apart. 'I'm not sure I do. All of the pieces of me, I mean. I thought, if I could find them, that... Oh, I don't know... I thought that if he remembered there was more to me, he might learn to love me again.'

Diana swallowed back a hard knot of emotion. She might be wrong, but she was sure that Jason still loved her daughter. If he did feel differently, then it might be too late. But if they were to stand any chance of coming through this, then Diana had to make it safe for him to *keep* loving her. The consequences for herself would be life-changing, but then, wasn't that change long overdue? She should have done it years ago. Then she might not have been sitting here, watching her daughter's life fall apart.

Once the press got hold of it, the consequences for Robert would be catastrophic. Diana had considered that, and she realised she no longer cared. Once, she would have done. She'd made up her mind to be with him; been determined she would support him as a wife, told herself she would grow to love him. But, if his deplorable, misogynistic behaviour hadn't killed any affection she'd had for him, his lies had. The lies he'd told about the circumstances surrounding Sarah's death were the worst lies of all. There'd been no need, other than to preserve himself. Diana had realised, then, that that was what Robert was all about: self-preservation above everything else, even his own child.

'I should go,' Karla said suddenly, pushing the duvet back and attempting to heave herself off the bed. 'The children...'

'Will be perfectly fine with Jason.' Diana eased her gently back again. 'Stay here until you're feeling stronger. Indulge yourself and have a nice hot bath. Meanwhile, I'll get us something nice to eat. Soup,' she added, when Karla looked doubtful. 'You look like a sickly little pigeon. Though a very pretty one.'

Karla managed a small smile at last.

Giving her a warm smile back, Diana tucked up the duvet and walked to the door. She would feel better herself, doing something practical. To which end, she would ring Robert's receptionist, as she'd promised she would, and give her blessing for her to go ahead and talk to the newspapers. Abbie was a pretty young thing, and Robert, given his predilections, wouldn't have been able to resist. Diana was well aware of that.

Courgette and tomato soup, she decided, going into the kitchen. Her speciality – wholesome but not overly filling. Karla had lost far too much weight. She needed building up. She needed to fight back, but not like this.

Diana chopped the onions while she pondered, and then paused as her phone beeped. *Michael.* Her heart skipped a beat. He was always reliable, punctually phoning or messaging her when he said he would. With the distance between them, the occasions they could be together were rare, but cherished and more special because of it. There would have been no distance between them, if only… Quashing that thought, Diana downed her knife. She had no time for regrets. The past was the past. Her focus now had to be on her daughter's future, whatever the emotional cost to herself.

Picking up her phone, she checked the text.

Still on for next week?

Desperate to meet, Diana replied.

Naturally, he sent back. Not conceitedly. Diana knew he wasn't an arrogant man.

Obviously, she said.

Shall I call you? he asked.

Not a good idea. Karla is still here.

Ah, no problem. How is she? he enquired, aware of why she was there.

Hurting, Diana answered honestly.

You need to talk to her.

Diana took a breath. *I know. I just have to be sure.*

You know where I am if you need me.

Diana wished he was there. Ireland suddenly seemed so very far away. *It will keep until we meet.*

I look forward to it, Michael assured her. *Whatever the outcome, I'll be there, Diana. I should always have been.*

But he couldn't have been, could he? Diana had loved him with her whole being, but as a married man with a small income and a two-year-old child, Michael had struggled with his conscience. Diana had eventually made his decision for him. She'd chosen Robert, fancying that a comfortable life where her child would be abundantly provided for might soften the pain of her loss. Perhaps living this life of purgatory had been her just deserts? Diana had pondered that often, but there was nothing to be done about it now, other than what she had to.

See you soon. She signed off with a kiss, and then, cursing the onions, wiped a tear from her eye and went back to her recipe. She was chopping the courgettes when her phone pinged in another text. Diana had been expecting this one too.

Are you still sure you want me to go to the press? Julie had sent.

Positive. Diana replied.

But I thought the payments were to ensure I didn't. Julie was obviously concerned. *Are you positive he won't try to sue me?*

Absolutely. He'll be in no position to, trust me. And it's high time Robert found out what it's like to be bullied and blackmailed, don't you think? Ask him for one more payment and then go for it.

I'll email him now. Do you want me to transfer your share of the payment to the usual account? Julie asked.

That would be perfect. You're an angel. Diana smiled, pleased that she would have a little extra to add to the quite considerable sum she'd already accumulated. Having to sleep with Robert's accountant had been an odious chore – the man was a lecherous old reptile, definitely one of Robert's ilk – but necessary in order to achieve her aim. It really was quite amazing what a man was prepared to do in order to prevent his 'indiscretions' being found out.

That's what friends are for, Julie assured her. *Take care. X*

You too. X

Diana then set about chopping the courgettes with new vigour. Yes, doing something practical definitely made her feel better.

CHAPTER FORTY-ONE

JASON

Replacing the phone in its cradle, Jason glanced up the stairs, glad Karla hadn't heard the phone ringing, or worse, answered it. It had been a reporter. There'd been rumblings in the papers, hints about a certain businessman's nefarious activities. It wouldn't be long before the story broke, the guy had said. Did Karla have any comments, he'd wanted to know? Jason had said he thought not, but had given him a choice one of his own.

Christ, how would she handle it when it did break? Robert Fenton deserved all he got, but Karla didn't deserve any of this. Their kids didn't. He'd have to warn them about answering the phone.

Checking his watch, he realised they were late – again. He headed back to the kitchen, fetched the juice from the fridge and slammed Josh's porridge into the microwave. He was retrieving cutlery from the useless dishwasher to wash when he realised he'd forgotten to time the porridge correctly.

Dammit. Jason swung around to grab it before it was cremated, and then – '*Shit!*' He cursed loudly and shook his burned fingers as the hot dish hit the floor.

'*Daddy*, language,' Holly chastised him, from where she sat at the breakfast table.

'Sorry, sweetheart.' Jason shrugged apologetically. She looked tired, he noticed. Her hair was a mess. She'd had two buns on top of her head when she'd come down, which Josh had felt obliged to point out made her look like Mickey Mouse. Holly had growled at him and decided on two braids instead, which she'd asked Jason to help her with. She might as well have asked him to knit her a jumper.

Unimpressed with his hairdressing skills, she'd finally settled on a simple headband instead, dragging it through her hair without actually utilising the brush. She wasn't looking any more impressed now – unenthusiastically stirring her porridge, which had probably solidified.

Grabbing up the milk, Jason carried it over and tipped some in her dish. He noted the despairing roll of her eyes as he did. 'I'll do better tomorrow,' he promised, giving her shoulders a squeeze.

Answering with a small nod, Holly dropped her gaze and gave the unappetising sludge another stir. She was upset, wondering what was going on with him and Karla. The arguments they'd been having lately were loud, the silences in between louder. Jason felt his heart ache for Holly and Josh, both. They didn't want him to make breakfast tomorrow – or any day, for that matter. They wanted their mother doing what she always had, being her efficient self, feeding them edible food. Karla was the epitome of organisation, or she had been. Jason had tried, but more often than not he failed, setting off with the kids for school minus their lunchboxes, forgetting half the stuff on the shopping list. They didn't need him; they needed Karla, joking with them or chivvying them on when they dawdled, issuing threats if they didn't 'get their skates on', threats they knew she wouldn't carry out. Their children wanted familiarity, normality. With Karla lying in bed, recovering from another hangover, they were about as far from that as it was possible to get. He'd begged her not to go out.

'Tell me you're not leaving me, and I won't,' she'd said, her tone weary with exhaustion, her eyes… haunted.

Jason hadn't. He couldn't. 'I'll stay for a while,' he'd said use-lessly instead.

Karla smiled; a smile filled with such defeat and such soul-crushing sadness, he'd almost blurted out there and then why he couldn't. What would that have done to her?

'Sorry, tiger.' Swallowing back his guilt, Jason offered Josh an apology for his failed porridge. 'Fancy some toast instead?'

'Coco Pops. I'll get them,' Josh said, sliding off his chair with a world-weary sigh and heading for the cupboard.

'Cheers, Josh.' Jason went to grab a cloth to clear the mess from the floor. 'Can you leave a drop of milk in the carton for Mum?' he asked him. 'She'll be thirsty.'

Dehydrated, no doubt. It had gone three o'clock when she'd arrived home last night – or rather, this morning. They didn't share the same bed any more, but Jason hadn't been asleep. He'd come through from the spare room to see what was happening after he'd heard the front door open, followed by a crash in the hall. 'Karla, everything all right?' he'd called down, concerned when he saw that she was unsteady on her feet.

'Fine,' she'd said, precariously repositioning the upturned statue on the hall table and retrieving one of her boots from the floor. 'Couldn't be better. Been nightclubbing.'

Waving the boot vaguely around, she'd then attempted to tiptoe up the stairs, almost falling up them as she did. Worried she was going to stumble backwards down them when she wobbled at the top, Jason had gone to try to help her.

'Don't.' She'd recoiled in an instant, staggering and very nearly doing what he was trying to avoid. 'Just don't. Please.' That had hurt, that she found his touch so unbearable.

She wouldn't even look at him.

Trying not to imagine how she would feel if she knew all there was to know about him, he sucked in a breath and concentrated on his cleaning endeavours, glancing up at their son as he did. Josh was doing as he'd asked, pouring the milk carefully on his Coco Pops and then shaking the carton close to his ear to check he'd left enough milk for his mum. He didn't ask where she was. Neither of them did. They knew she would make an appearance eventually.

'We'll be late, Dad,' Holly reminded him, collecting up her bowl and heading for the bin to scrape most of the contents away. Jason felt for her. He hadn't realised how useless he was at this. He'd never had to do it, other than the odd few times. He would improve. He had to. Wherever he might end up, he had no intention of losing touch with his kids. At one point, he'd felt they were all he had to live for.

'I know. Don't worry, I'll ring the school and explain.' Straightening up, Jason mustered a smile. 'Go up and brush your teeth, sweetheart. I won't be long.'

Sighing, Holly walked across to the dishwasher. 'Are you going to shave?' she asked him, a concerned frown crossing her face as she looked him over.

'I'll do it in the office,' he assured her, aware that his own dishevelled appearance was probably as destabilising for them as everything else. 'Go on, scoot. You, too, Josh. And don't forget to brush properly – with toothpaste.'

'I won't,' Josh said through a mouthful of Coco Pops, as if he didn't regularly forget. 'I'm still eating.'

'Well, hurry *up*.' Holly shot him a despairing glance as she headed for the hall. 'Dad has to go to work.'

Watching her go, Jason felt his heart sink. She was sounding more grown up every day, because she felt she had to be, that it was her responsibility to be adult around grown-ups who were acting like children. Having felt exactly that way as a child, it was the last thing Jason had wanted for his kids, but he had no way to fix it.

'Oh.' Holly stopped at the kitchen door. 'Morning,' she said, sounding majorly unimpressed.

Following her gaze, Jason could see why. Karla had made an effort, pulling on tracksuit bottoms and a T-shirt, but the fact was she looked pale and drawn, and more dishevelled than he did. Jason's heart sank another inch. As much as he would like to undo all that had happened and take away the horrendous hurt he knew she was feeling, he couldn't. It simply wasn't within his power.

'You'd better get your skates on,' Karla said, with a cautious smile, 'or you'll be late.'

'Like you care.' Her forehead knitting into a scowl, Holly eyed her mother reproachfully.

'Of course I *care*.' Karla laughed, taken aback. 'I'm sorry I wasn't up, sweetheart. I wasn't feeling too well.'

'Again.' Holly stepped away from her pointedly. 'Maybe you should stop drinking so much, and then you might feel better,' she suggested, oozing sarcasm.

'*Holly…*' Bewildered, Karla spun around as Holly flounced past her to the hall.

'I can smell it, Mum,' Holly informed her, her tone flat as she thumped up the stairs.

Turning back, Karla glanced dazedly in Jason's direction and then wrapped her arms about herself and dropped her gaze to the floor.

'All right?' Jason asked, taking a tentative step towards her.

'Fine,' Karla snapped. 'Why wouldn't I be?'

Josh scooped the last of his cereal into his mouth and scrambled off his chair in record time. 'I'll go grab my rucksack,' he mumbled, wiping his hand over his mouth and skidding out after Holly.

'Don't forget to brush your teeth,' Karla called after him.

'I *know*,' Josh said over his shoulder. 'You don't have to keep bloody well *telling* me.'

'*What?*' Karla whirled around again. 'Josh, come back here.'

'I can't! I'm late,' Josh shouted back.

'*Now*, Josh.' Her expression disbelieving, Karla started towards the stairs, and then stopped as Josh's bedroom door slammed resoundingly overhead.

Sighing, Jason kneaded his forehead. 'Go easy on him, Karla,' he ventured, as she came back to the kitchen. 'They're struggling to understand—'

'*Really?*' Karla grabbed up the kettle and shoved it under the tap. 'You do surprise me. I mean, why on earth would their worlds be falling apart, I wonder. Oh yes, now I remember. That would be because their father has chosen to take up with a *trollop!*'

Jesus. Glancing upwards, Jason drew in a sharp breath. 'Don't Karla. The kids…'

'Don't *what?* Tell the truth? Disillusion them? Don't you think you've already disillusioned them enough for *life?*' Karla turned tearfully towards him. She looked worse than he'd realised. Drawn, almost. She was losing weight. She really was beginning to look ill, and Jason had no idea what to do. What he could do. If she asked him to go, he would have to. As things were, though, he was too scared – scared for her, for the kids.

'I know I have,' he said quietly. 'I wish… I'm sorry.' *Christ.* He ran a hand over his neck in frustration. How pathetic and inadequate did that sound?

'I bet you are.' Her eyes, burning with anger and humiliation, searched his.

No idea what to say, Jason looked away. If only she knew how sorry he was. How much he wished he could turn back the clock, only then to be consumed with guilt when he realised he was wishing his children away.

'Just go, Jason,' Karla said defeatedly, after a minute's loaded silence.

Jason nodded tiredly. 'I'm dropping the kids off on the way,' he reminded her.

Her gaze focused on the mug she was heaping sugar into, Karla didn't answer.

'Will you be all right?'

Wiping the back of her hand across her eyes, Karla sniffed and nodded.

'Do you need me to pick anything up?'

'Something for the children's dinner,' she said, her voice strained. 'I'll be at Mum's.'

'Right.' Jason hesitated. 'How is she?'

'How do you think?' Karla's tone was flat. 'I bet you're enjoying this, aren't you? Finally seeing my father humiliated?'

Not half as much as I should be, Jason thought. She'd seen the first reports in the newspapers, claims made about a recipient of various UK Business Awards abusing his staff. He guessed she thought it was him who'd leaked information to the media. He hadn't, though he'd been sorely tempted. After all Fenton had done to him, Jason had desperately wanted some kind of revenge – it wouldn't have been human not to. Fenton had always aimed to take away what it had taken Jason his whole life to find: the family he'd never had. That had become emphatically clear on the day the man had delivered the news he'd known would bring him to his knees. Jason had wanted the ruthless bastard to know how it felt to lose everything that mattered, the things that money couldn't buy. Now though, counting the casualties, he dearly wished he'd done what his so-called father-in-law had wanted and walked away years ago.

'I have no feelings one way or the other, Karla,' he said, heading to the hall for his car keys. He didn't, he realised with surprise. It was only a matter of time before Robert was named by the press. When he was, Jason would gain no satisfaction from it. He simply couldn't be bothered wasting any more emotion on the man.

'No feelings full stop,' Karla threw after him.

CHAPTER FORTY-TWO

ROBERT

'*Bastards.*' Dabbing at the nick on his chin with a towel, Robert peered furiously through the curtains at the bay window of their bedroom, to find the press already baying for his blood on the street outside. Did they have nothing better to do than harass upstanding members of the public? To hound a hardworking businessman and valuable contributor to society, solely because a few of his staff had had the temerity, despite the rewards of working for him and the astronomical salaries he paid them, to make ridiculous accusations?

Christ almighty, they'll be branding us sex fiends if we so much as smile at a woman soon. Fucking *MeToo* campaign, ruining lives, bringing great men to their knees. Attention-seekers and gold-diggers, the lot of them.

Fuming, Robert dropped the curtain, pulling the white towel, which was now stained crimson, away from his face as he walked back towards the bathroom to continue his shave. The mob out there would probably be ecstatic if he did cut his throat, trampling each other to death in their rush to get a photo opportunity and try him by press after his death. Tossers. Robert would like to see any one of them attempting to do half of what he'd done. He'd bet there wasn't a single person amongst them who'd ever done a real day's graft, working his fingers to the bone to set up a business, which provided *employment* to people and shored up the flagging economy.

Did that ever occur to them? That, in putting him out of business, they would be robbing the people they were supposed to be informing of their jobs?

Not a chance. They earned their fat salaries off the backs of people like him, destroying them and their families without compunction before going back to their cosy little homes to tuck into their dinners. God only knew how they slept at night.

'Bloodsucking parasites.' Turning to toss the towel into the corner of the bedroom, on top of yesterday's washing, he caught his wife's eye as she came through the bedroom door. Diana glanced from him to the pile of dirty laundry and back, with that indifferent expression she wore permanently around him. She'd looked at him like that for years, like she didn't even see him. It had been bad enough before the appalling circumstances surrounding their loss, and then that had caused her to withdraw from him completely. Up until then, she'd stood by him. She'd never quite forgiven him for the silly affair he'd had prior to their wedding, and he couldn't blame her for that – he'd been playing far too close to home – but she'd accepted that it was a momentary weakness, that he'd given in to a temptation of the flesh. She'd been aware that her enticing little friend, Julie – who he'd hired out of the kindness of his heart – had her sights set on him. In a close office environment, sadly certain women did develop fixations on their bosses, he'd pointed out. He'd let Julie go, of course, with compensation for her trouble, which he continued to pay out on a regular basis – and which Diana had no knowledge of – but naturally the friendship between the two women had soured. There had been no further questions asked and the episode was consigned to history, which is where Robert considered it should stay.

'I suppose you think I deserve this?' He sighed heavily and watched as she bent to scoop up the washing, wishing she would look at him now with a hint of sympathy in her eyes. That she would offer him a small smile of encouragement. It was her smile that had attracted him, lighting up her features and cheering his day as he passed through the bookshop where she worked, before he descended into the bowels of the building beneath the shop to toil and sweat and build up his business. She'd been supportive of him then, typing up his correspondence, listening as he'd told her of his plans, his hopes and his dreams. She'd been beautiful when he first met her, and she was still a fine-looking woman. Always paying attention to her diet, she'd kept her figure well. Robert had to admire that in a mature woman. He'd been tempted to tell her though, on many occasions, that the scowl would only age her prematurely.

'I don't think anything, Robert,' she said, walking past him to the bathroom to put the dirty laundry in the washing basket. 'At least nothing you would want to hear.'

'Which means what, exactly?' Robert eyed her with despair as she came back. 'That you *do* think I've done something to warrant this shit descending on me?'

'I think we both know you have, Robert,' Diana said, not even glancing in his direction as she headed for her walk in wardrobe.

'Such as *what*, exactly?' Watching her reappear, carrying a suitcase, Robert was uncomprehending for a second, and then a sharp knot of panic tightened inside him.

'Where are you going?' he asked her, his throat suddenly parched.

Her back to him, Diana placed the suitcase down on her dressing table, and picked up her handbag, casually flicking through the contents. 'I'm leaving you,' she said matter-of-factly, snapping her handbag shut and turning to face him.

Only then did she look at him. She looked at him full on for the first time in a very long time. And what Robert saw shook him to the core: hatred, unadulterated hatred, her ice-blue eyes hardening to flint.

'But... why?' he stammered, fear gripping his insides like a vice. But he knew. It wasn't about this nonsense in the newspapers, which he'd tried to reassure her would disappear once he had his injunction in place. This simmering anger went back to the harrowing events of twenty-five years ago. She'd turned away from him in the bleak days following the funeral, making it clear that she couldn't have cared less about his pain, the fact that he'd felt as if his heart had been ripped out of him. He'd needed her then, like never before. He'd needed to hold her, if nothing else, but she hadn't been there for him. Instead, she looked at him with growing disdain if he came home late at night, as if a man was supposed to remain celibate all his life.

Every day, he'd acknowledged a quiet dread in the pit of his stomach that she might leave him. But not now. She *couldn't*! The media would have a field day with it. It would be proof positive that he was guilty, in the eyes of the public. She *knew* that. He couldn't do this on his own. Face the press, who – if, God forbid, he wasn't granted an injunction – would dig mercilessly through every aspect of his life, seizing on anything to paint him as a bully and a sexual predator, no matter how baseless. Face the police, if these ludicrous claims were taken seriously. The courts! God help him.

'It wasn't true, Diana!' Sweat wetting his forehead, he repeated what he'd always maintained. 'I have no idea why Sarah's friend would claim I did such a thing. She was a child – confused. A little liar, obviously. Karla was *there*, for God's sake. She corroborated my story. I was nowhere near her.'

Diana didn't move when he stepped towards her, his hands outstretched, desperate to feel her hands in his, to be held by the woman who was the one constant in his life. She just kept right on looking at him, right down into the depths of his soul.

Robert glanced away. Closing his eyes, he was assaulted by harsh memories of the day of Sarah's death, one he would never forget: Diana turning from the phone, her face distraught, her eyes awash with tears. 'I have to be with my mother,' she'd said. 'Please, Robert…'

'I know.' He'd nodded, his heart sinking. Bloody woman, he'd thought. Could she have chosen a more inconvenient time to die? 'Of course you do.' He heard himself saying it, his voice sympathetic, his irritation immense, knowing he would stand little to no chance of getting his tender for a huge contract in.

A tight band of tension tightening between his temples, he'd been sweating profusely in the stifling heat of the long summer, playing childminder while he attempted to work from home. Nausea – he felt it again – swilled around in his belly from the vast amount of brandy he'd consumed at the golf club the night before, the whisky he'd imbibed before lunch. The children – he heard them, above the distracting whine of the lawnmowers. The neighbour's unruly kids too, screeching and screaming right outside his study window. The phone ringing incessantly: his new secretary, pissing about at the office rather than getting her arse over to the house, where he needed her.

Utterly fucking useless.

The children, their noise escalating – unacceptable, raucous shrieking – grating against the inside of his skull. His rage, building steadily inside him.

Sarah calling him a miserable bastard as he strode into the garden, bawling at them to keep the noise down. This from the mouth of an eight-year-old *child*? His temper had exploded. He hadn't meant to do it. It was if a switch had flicked inside him.

Picturing the shock on Sarah's face when he'd lashed out, her hand clutched to her cheek as she backed away from him, falling as she did, Robert felt afresh his shame and deep, deep remorse. His horror, when he'd realised what he'd done. He heard it now, the sickening crack as her head made contact with the garden path. His heart had stopped beating as she lay there, unmoving. When her eyes had finally fluttered open, and he'd been able to breathe again, she'd looked at him as if he were some kind of monster.

He'd only wanted to apologise to her that night. To have Sarah forgive him, not look at him as if he were something abhorrent. He recalled stumbling home after several brandies at the club. He'd needed them. Knowing he'd be highly unlikely to get a warm reception if he went to his own bedroom reeking of alcohol, he went into the girls' room – he could remember that much. After that, nothing.

'I don't know what happened. I don't remember,' he said, his voice a hoarse whisper as he looked again at Diana, his heart leaden with the weight of the guilt he'd borne since that night. Would always.

'She was your *daughter*,' Diana seethed. 'I *loved* her. Karla loved her. She was her sister! She never knew her as anything but. And you had her blaming herself for her *death*, you despicable bastard!'

'I didn't want her to do that.' Robert took a faltering step towards her. 'I—'

'You *lied*!' Diana's voice was shrill, her face tight with fury. And now Robert was truly scared. She'd never spoken to him like that before. 'You made Karla lie for you! Have you any idea what that would do to a child? The guilt you caused? The heartbreak?'

'It broke my heart, too.' Desperate, Robert took another step. 'I didn't mean to—'

'I'm going,' Diana stated flatly. There was no compassion in her expression. Not a smidgeon. Just a pitying look in her eyes as she walked past him to the door.

Robert felt his chest tighten, his heart rate quicken. He would have a heart attack before the day was through, he swore. He breathed in hard, feeling his fury at the unjustness of it all, the suffering he'd endured at the hands of other people, mounting inside him. 'You won't get a penny from me!' he yelled, whirling around after her. 'Not a penny! Do you hear me? Don't even bother trying, Diana!'

Diana stopped, and faced him. 'I don't need to. The house is half mine and I have investments of my own, Robert; something you wouldn't be aware of.'

'What investments?' Robert scoffed. He gave her a monthly allowance – a generous one, he considered. He permitted her access to certain accounts, but she would never have been able to stow away enough to afford the lifestyle to which she'd become accustomed. Unless… Recalling the discrepancies on his statements, funds not showing that should have, Robert blinked, stupefied. Had *she* somehow accessed his business accounts? Was his accountant *aware* that she had?

Diana didn't answer; she simply studied him for a long unnerving moment, then, 'I know what you did,' she announced. 'I know why Jason turned down the loan.'

Robert felt the blood drain from his face. 'What are you talking about?' His voice came out a croak.

'I imagine this will add fuel to the press pyre,' Diana replied calmly. 'I haven't informed Karla yet. Naturally, I want to do that sensitively. Goodbye, Robert.'

Cold foreboding clutching his stomach, Robert stared at her. Then, as the implication of what she was saying began to sink in, he felt something snap dangerously inside him. The rage that consumed him was so blinding, so all-encompassing, he had no awareness of crossing the room. He was appalled when he realised what he'd done. He hadn't meant to. He'd never laid a hand on her before. He didn't realise he had, until he saw the terror in her eyes.

'Oh, God, Diana… I'm sorry. I didn't…' he stuttered, reaching for her – but Diana recoiled in an instant, that same shocked look on her face he'd seen on Sarah's.

Robert watched hopelessly, powerless to stop her, as Diana grabbed up her things and fled. He'd only ever cried twice before in his adult life. Once at the funeral. Once afterwards, when he'd realised his wife would never again look at him with affection. By then, he'd accepted that things had fizzled out sexually between them – he'd had no choice – but he'd still needed her affection. He'd sought an outlet for his needs, of course he had, but he'd loved her still, in his own way. She must have known he did. Must have known that, as intolerable as things had sometimes seemed, he'd never envisaged a life without her. Why else would he have bothered working day after day, working himself into an early grave?

How could she do this to him? Feeling a tear spill from his chin as he stood amongst the ruins of his life, he reached to wipe it away. Attempting to compose himself after a while, he walked to the bathroom, where he extracted a bandage from the medicine cabinet and wrapped it round the hand he'd cut while retrieving large slivers of glass from the carpet. Going back to the bedroom, he paused, surveying himself in the shattered mirror. He didn't recognise the broken person looking back: a worry-worn, defeated man with tell-tale ruddy cheeks and sagging jowls. A much older man than he perceived himself to be. That wasn't him. Pulling himself taller, Robert squared his shoulders and braced himself to face those who would see him fall.

Moving back to the window, he looked out, feeling deep loathing for the money-grabbing rabble outside who would revel in his humiliation. *Human flotsam.* Robert peeled his disgusted gaze away and went to attend to the necessary clearing up. Minutes later, he descended the stairs with his stained dressing gown and the duvet cover. It took him a while, but he managed to work out how to put the washing machine on. The newspaper plopped through the letterbox as he walked back. Tiredly, Robert bent to pick it up.

UK BUSINESSMAN NAMED IN #METOO SCANDAL, blazed the headline.

His chest constricting painfully, Robert read on: 'Robert Fenton – who grew his hugely successful plumbing and bespoke bathroom business from the basement of a bookshop and is now worth an estimated £50m – is reportedly seeking to obtain an interim injunction preventing the press from publishing allegations of sexual harassment and abuse of staff. Fenton, who has "categorically" denied the allegations, is accused of using non-disclosure agreements in an attempt to prevent staff speaking out…'

Robert folded the newspaper, placed it on the hall table, sucked in a deep breath and held it. He should clean the bedroom carpet, he decided, and then get dressed. The premium wool suit in blue or the grey tailored fit, he pondered, as he went back to the utility for whatever cleaning paraphernalia he might need. Impressions were important, after all.

All-important, to Robert. One of six kids, brought up on an estate notorious for petty crime and drug dealing, he'd fought hard to free himself of his roots. He'd built his business with nothing but the sweat of his brow, better than his competitors, bigger and infinitely more successful. Finally establishing himself as one of the UK's leading businessmen, he'd made sure to leave poverty behind him. He'd worked equally hard on his image, dressing stylishly but not flashily. He commanded respect amongst his peers, and had been paid substantial amounts to head up seminars and give inspirational talks. He'd *been* someone. Yes, he'd made mistakes along the way. Might have misread one or two signals, but what's a red-blooded man supposed to do when a lithe young thing smiles coquettishly and encourages him on? He would never have overstepped any boundaries had he not thought a little harmless flirtation was on offer. He'd had one or two women making silly noises after the event, forcing him to pay them off and remind them of the stipulations of their contracts. Overall, though, Robert considered he'd been more than reasonable. Generous, even.

Now it appeared that those who had benefitted from his generosity were determined to bring him down. Robert only had to look and see the great men falling around him to realise that eventually they would destroy him, too. He wouldn't wait for the ignominy of that, for kiss-and-tell stories in the tacky tabloids. Lies. Unflattering photographs portraying him as a lecherous pervert.

No, he wouldn't let them see a beaten man. His pride simply wouldn't allow it. He would do as he'd always done: maintain his image, dress for the occasion and exit in style.

CHAPTER FORTY-THREE

KARLA

'Were they late?' I ask Jason, as he comes back after dropping Holly and Josh off at school. I know they will have been, because I overslept again and didn't have time to prepare their lunches, meaning they would have had to stop and buy something on the way. But I overslept because of him, what *he's* doing to this family. Yet still he plays the martyr to the children, the hard-done-by party. He's painting me as the villain, trying to win them over. He's stealing them away from me. I can't let him. My heart thrashes, palpitating inside me.

'A bit,' he says, closing the door. 'I had a quick word with their teachers though, so the kids were okay.'

'A quick word communicating what?' Anger surfaces above the fear twisting inside me. 'That their mother is incapable of looking after them?'

Emitting a heavy sigh, Jason turns to face me, though he doesn't look at me.

'No doubt the poor harassed father dashing in with his children earned himself some sympathy?' I add, my tone facetious, because I know that's exactly what he would invite. Tongues will have been wagging, heads shaking and hearts going out to a lonely-looking man who's suddenly started bringing his children to school.

Jason shakes his head wearily. 'I have no idea what you're talking about, Karla.'

Yes, he does, Sarah says knowingly.

Of course he does. Won't he be milking it? Wouldn't I, in his shoes? 'I'm not sure they'd be giving you any father of the year awards if they knew the truth,' I go on, a toxic mixture of bitterness and cynicism simmering inside me, 'that you're the sort who picks up cheap little—'

'Jesus Christ, Karla, will you just stop!' Jason shouts over me. 'I can't *do* this again.'

'You stop!' I yell back, my anger rising. 'Pretending you're the victim in all of this. As if you've been *driven* to it. You're *cheating* on me! With some—'

'We're *both* victims!' Jason yells, louder. 'For fu—' Banging the heel of his hand against his forehead in frustration, he stops and meets my gaze at last, and then emits a ragged sigh. 'It's better for you if you don't know.'

'Know what?' Goosebumps prickle my skin as I note the wariness in his eyes.

Jason scans my face tiredly for a second, then, 'Talk to your mother, Karla,' he suggests quietly, turning back to the front door. 'You need to.'

Destabilised, with apprehension creeping through me, I don't try to stop him going. There's no point demanding explanations. He will refuse point-blank to discuss anything to do with my father, and this has to be about him.

Grabbing my phone from my bag, I call my mother, my tummy clenching with a combination of nerves and nausea as I wonder whether she knows something I don't. Something Jason has confided in her? Something she's been keeping from me? She wouldn't, surely?

Her phone goes to voicemail. Impatiently, I text her. And then, receiving no response, I call her again. Nothing. Ten minutes later, I'm halfway to my car when my phone beeps. I read the message twice, and then stare at it, stupefied.

I've left your father, it says. *I need to get away from the attention. We need to talk, darling, but first I need a little time. Can you give me that?*

Time? For what? My hands shake as I text quickly back: *Where are you?*

The airport, she replies, after a pause. *Going to stay with a friend for a while. Will be in touch soon.*

The airport? Which airport? What friend. *Where?* I try again to call her. Again, her phone goes to voicemail. And now I'm growing desperate. I don't want her to 'be in touch soon'. I need to be in touch with her now. I need her to be here. I have no one else. *No one.*

Throwing myself in my car, I drive frantically to my parents' house. Something's happened. Is this what Jason meant? Is he aware of something I'm not? Yet more worms crawling out of the woodwork regarding my father? Even with the press interest, the stories in the papers, my mum wouldn't just go. After all this time staying with him, she wouldn't go now unless something awful had happened to make her.

Turning into my parents' road, I slow, glancing towards their house with deep apprehension. It's beautiful, a grand three-storey Georgian house, with picturesque views overlooking the park from the back windows. When she was alive, Sarah and I had shared the attic bedroom on the third floor, the room with the best views. We used to sit outside on the wide window ledge on hot summer days, telling each other stories, dreaming and dangling our feet. It should have been paradise. It turned into a nightmare. For a second, I'm back there, waiting outside the house on the day of the funeral. But the people congregated here now are not here to mourn, to stand and watch the hearse arrive in respectful silence. Jostling each other, running towards me, this crowd is hungry, ready to close in for the kill.

My heart rate escalates. I am hot and clammy under my too-heavy parka coat, a bead of sweat snaking its way down my throat to trickle over the soft hollow of my neck. I should have approached the house from the back, snuck through the garden gate adjoining the park and gone in through the conservatory. It's too late now.

Inhaling deeply, I clutch the steering wheel and ram my foot down on the accelerator, causing the bloodsuckers with press badges to scatter as I screech to a stop.

'Mrs Connolly!' One of the reporters follows me through the un-gated drive and pushes a microphone in my face as I spill from the car. 'How do you feel about the allegations made against your father?'

'Karla!' a female reporter shouts, nudging him aside. 'Can you give us a brief comment? It would be invaluable to the MeToo campaign.'

'Piss off,' I hiss. Key poised, I make my way to the front door. He's my father. What do they want me to say? I'm not here to comment. I have no idea how I feel about him, the man who robbed me of my sister. The man who played a part in the failure of my marriage; who has almost been a third person in my marriage. I'm not sure what he did, what he said to Jason that finally drove home the last nail, but I felt my husband withdraw from me that day. I knew it was only a matter of time before he walked away.

My father categorically denied having said or done anything, according to my mother. I don't believe it. I don't trust him. All of my life, I have wondered about him. When I was younger, looking at him through a tiny child's eyes, I couldn't conceive of the possibility that this big businessman in his smart blue suits, the man I revered, might tell anything but the truth. As I grew up, I learned differently, and I simply stopped looking. Mum turned a blind eye to his 'indiscretions', indiscretions which I came to realise had gone on for longer than I could remember, and I did too. And then came the tragedy that rocked our world. I stopped listening to the voice in my head that whispered the word 'liar'. I shut it down.

I'm not sure how much of what the press is accusing him of is true. I'm not sure of anything, other than that it's not my father

I'm here for. I'm here because my mother is not. Perhaps all of this, the clamouring reporters who will undoubtedly dig up the past, is the final straw that's driven her to do what I never imagined she would. But for her not to have discussed it with me, with all I have happening in my life? For her not to have at least rung me? I don't understand. She's left so suddenly, and I need to know why. I need to know where she is.

Shit. I curse silently as my key jams in the lock. They're still on me, right behind me, still shouting, making my head spin. 'Think of the victims, Mrs Connolly,' one of them bellows. 'How would you feel?'

I don't know how I feel! I want to turn around and scream. *My husband is cheating on me. My father is accused of things I can't bear to contemplate. My mother's not here, and I need her. I need something tangible to hold on to, and there's nothing! How would you feel?*

Pulling my key from the lock, I stuff it back in and wiggle it, and finally the front door gives. Stumbling into the hall, I slam the door behind me and stand still for a moment, trying to take stock. It's quiet. No clangs of baking trays and pans from the kitchen. No radio drifting from inside.

It's as still as the grave, Sarah whispers.

'Dad!' I yell, panic twisting my stomach. '*Dad!* Where are you?'

Gathering my courage, I head down the long hall and through the kitchen towards the utility – and the pulse of tension in my throat tightens. The washing machine is on. Dad doesn't use the washing machine. He's never used the washing machine. I'm not sure he knows how to. But it's not this incomprehensible oddity that causes my heart to palpitate like a trapped bird in my chest. It's the next load, waiting on the floor in front of the machine. The dark crimson stain on the duvet cover. The spatters of blood on the floor.

'*Mum!*' Whirling around, I retrace my steps. My eyes glued to the floor, I notice a steady trail of rich red droplets – *splat, splat,*

splat – along the hall carpet and continuing on up the stairs. I pause at the foot, my mouth dry, my thoughts a chaotic jumble.

Clutching hold of the banister, I heave myself up and charge to my parents' room, where I hesitate, and then, terror climbing my chest, I shove the door open – and freeze.

My father is on the floor. On his hands and knees on the floor. A bowl to his side, a brush in his hand, he's scrubbing at a stain on the cream carpet. Bewildered, I look from him to the candy-pink froth forming on top of it. 'Dad?' I murmur, my voice small and tremulous.

He pauses, brings the brush around again and then pulls himself up. Sitting back on his haunches, he wipes an arm across his forehead and then turns his gaze towards me.

'What's happened?' I ask, my voice emerging a dry croak.

My father's gaze lingers, searching my face as if he doesn't know me. He looks older, smaller somehow, his eyes rheumy and uncertain.

'Dad! What's *happened*?' I yell. The house, too silent, even with the low rumble of voices and car doors slamming outside, seems to close in on me.

Dad's expression changes as I step towards him, hardening to the aggravated, impatient look I've so often seen him wear – when dealing with 'imbeciles'.

When Sarah challenged him on that long-ago summer's day, talking back to him, disrespecting him, he'd worn that look then. My stomach churns, as I hear it over again, Sarah's shrill shrieking, the sharp slap. The soft thud. Silence.

Oh, dear God. Did my mother challenge him? He would undoubtedly have been trying to lie his way out of this latest soul-crushing debacle. 'Dad, *talk* to me. Where's Mum?'

'Gone,' he says, and goes back to his cleaning.

'Gone *where*?' I shout, louder, careless of who might hear. '*How*? They would have seen her. The reporters.' If my mum was injured, they wouldn't have failed to notice. They would have been baying like dogs over a bone, gleefully relaying that information to me, trying to extract information from me. Through my rising terror, I realise this fact.

Pausing again, he studies me curiously, clearly registers my incomprehension. 'She called a taxi to pick her up at the park entrance,' he says, his tone flat.

I scan his face. *Liar.* The word ricochets around my head.

'Do you honestly think she would have left by the front door?' he asks me. 'Run the gauntlet of that pack of wolves out there?' Sighing in despair, he looks away and continues to try to clean the stain from the carpet.

I stare hard at him, trying to digest. 'Was she hurt?' I ask him, forcing the words past the dry lump in my throat. *Don't lie to me. Please don't lie to me.*

Straightening up, he looks again in my direction. 'You really do have a low opinion of me, don't you, Karla?' he says quietly, his expression a combination of hurt and regret.

I don't answer. There's no way to answer.

'You're referring to this, I assume?' He nods down at the stain on the carpet. 'I lost my temper,' he admits, causing my chest to constrict. '*After* she'd left.' Breathing in hard, he indicates the tall free-standing mirror. 'Fucking gutter press,' he utters. 'She wouldn't have gone if not for them.'

My gaze shoots towards the mirror. In the shattered glass I see several fractured images of my father. I turn my gaze back to him as he raises the hand that holds the brush. It's bleeding, my stultified mind registers. He has a bandage wrapped haphazardly around it, soggy and wet with a mixture of water and blood.

He smashed the mirror. In his anger and frustration, he lashed out and punched it. This makes sense. This is something my father would do. Giddy with relief, I close my eyes, suck air deep into my lungs and start breathing again. Still, though, through the clearing fog in my head, the ceaseless voice resonates. *Liar.*

CHAPTER FORTY-FOUR

KARLA

I have no one to call. No one I can talk to. No one left in my life who wants me. I don't know, any more, whether I was responsible for driving Jason away or whether he would have gone anyway. But should I have done nothing? Just watched him go? Allowed him to destroy my life? Our children's?

It's you who's destroying their lives. Sarah pipes up. *That's why he's stealing them.*

They don't want me. I ignore her persistent voice in my head and continue on into the nightclub, where I will be able to block all of this out. The low thud of the bass coming through the huge sound system reverberates through my chest cavity as soon as I enter. An aphrodisiac, resonating through my entire body and down my spine, it heightens my senses. At one time, back when I was single and carefree, the music would have whetted my desire – not to sleep with the first reasonable-looking man I saw, but to live, to love, to experience all that life had to offer. Now, it allows me to disappear.

It's an art I have perfected. When I was at acting school, I seized on one golden rule that we were told we needed to follow in order to succeed: to beware of personal issues, which would be highly corrosive to our creativity. Personal issues shouldn't creep into any rehearsal or casting, we were instructed as eager new students. I got that. When a personal issue took over, you were no longer telling the character's story. 'Introducing personal issues into a scene will take you out of the moment,' our tutor informed us. 'We need to cast them aside.'

So that's what I did. What I do still. If my emotions threaten to engulf me, I switch them off. I become someone else. I smile when I want to cry. I turn my attention to the children, to my husband, or to my job. To whatever crisis that might need dealing with. I handle things efficiently, mostly, and calmly. Or at least I used to… when my children wanted me. When I had a husband who wanted me. I'm not sure the housing association wants me back either.

Attempting to quash the grief that kicks in ferociously, I refocus, reminding myself why I'm here: to detach from the pain. My husband is leaving me, walking away from all that we have together, as if it means nothing. As if I mean nothing. My mother has gone. I've no idea where, or when she will be back. If she will come back. I'm a grown woman, I shouldn't need her, but I do. So badly. My father… I don't think he ever cared for me. How could he?

Do I care for him? Yes, for the man I once imagined he was. But he only ever existed in my mind. Banishing thoughts of him, which immediately invoke a new wave of impotent anger, I squeeze through the mass of gyrating bodies that seem to move in slow motion under the strobe lights. The usual overabundance of beer and perfume assaults my senses, and tonight I feel at ease with that, as if I belong. I don't need alcohol; I've had plenty. I can already feel the little rushes of exhilaration as I move to the music, my physical senses, touch and smell, becoming keener. The music is louder, sharper within me. I am more aware of the moment. Soon my inhibitions will loosen. I will be free of the hurt. Does Jason know how deep my hurt runs? The uncertainty I now have about who I am, my sexuality?

He does. He would have known as soon, as he contemplated leaving me, what that would do to me, but he didn't care enough to stay. This is my unpalatable reality. I am unloved, unlovable.

Unwanted, unless by a stranger. The ache in my heart grows unbearably heavy as I move closer to the man whose Tinder profile I swiped right on. My 'date' for tonight. He's younger than me, but he doesn't seem concerned about that. And I think I'm past caring about anything anymore. We exchange meaningful eye contact, but we don't speak. We can't compete with the music, and words are superfluous anyway. We both know why we're here. I feel the heat of his gaze travelling over me as I turn around. I'm aware, as I raise my hands in the air, gyrating my pelvis to the pulsating rhythm, that my short dress is creeping higher, revealing the bare flesh of my thighs above leather boots. I know it's a come-on. I don't protest as he pulls me suddenly towards him, my back pressed close to his body, his hands anchoring my hips hard to him.

He searches my face as I twist around, his eyes communicating his question. He finds his answer in mine. He grasps my hand, leading me away from the dance floor. This is okay. This is what I want: someone to want me, whoever 'me' is.

Who are you? I ask the painted-on face that stares back at me through the over-sink mirror as he thrusts into me. This person who is not me, but another part of me. I'm not embarrassed at being taken like this. I want it – to go back to basics, to see love for what it really is: a lie. A primal need to fuck, that's all, dressed up to mean something. It means nothing. My marriage, what I thought Jason and I had, all lies. My father, who was supposed to care for me... a liar, a misogynist, a cheat. My mother, disappeared. I understand, to a degree, why she would need to separate herself from all that's happening – this is the same urge that drives me: the need to not be here, in this life. But to not contact me, talk to me. Does she truly care, the only person I thought I could depend on?

And me, I am nothing. I watch a tear spill down my face. Someone who is worth nothing.

But you are. Sarah. Her voice is frightened. An urgent whisper. Am I? Another tear falls silently. I don't believe her. How can I?

CHAPTER FORTY-FIVE

JASON

Where in God's name was she? Ending the call as Karla's phone went to voicemail, Jason tried to bury the dark thoughts rattling around in his head, as they did every time she stayed out. There was nothing he could do. He couldn't stop her. All he could do was wait and pray she was safe.

Checking on Josh, he lifted the iPad from his bed, carefully removed his son's glasses from his face and then reached to flick off the bedside light. Josh had taken to leaving it on at night lately. Up until recently, he'd claimed he was 'too big' for night lights. Four foot six being a little short of the average height for a ten-year-old, he wasn't actually that big. Right now, he looked exactly like what he was: a vulnerable, confused child.

Swallowing back his guilt at the part he'd played in turning his children's worlds upside down, Jason tucked the duvet around Josh and then headed back to the landing. Aware of his son's propensity to see shadows in corners if he did wake in the small hours, he left the door open a fraction then went to check on Holly.

Her lamp was also on, he realised, as he noticed the light spilling from under her door. He eased the door open and peered around it, and his heart sank. She'd fallen asleep with her earphones in. They would both be exhausted in the morning.

What the bloody hell was Karla thinking, he thought angrily – and then pulled himself up sharply. He had no right to be angry. No business judging her. He might not have left physically, but emotionally he had, as Karla had pointedly reminded him. It was none of his business where she went or who with, she'd said before she'd gone out that night. In fact, she'd added, it would probably solve a few of his problems if she were found dead. Those words were ringing loud in his head now. It was almost two in the morning. Jason hoped she was only out dancing, 'setting her spirit free', as she called it. It was something she'd done regularly when they'd first met. She hadn't done enough of it since she'd become, in her own words, a 'boring wife and a mother'. In fact, they hadn't done much of anything together since the children had been born. Was that her fault, she'd challenged him? The weeks had turned into months and the years had slipped by, him working all hours, Karla working too, and doing the stuff he wasn't around to help with in between. Jason had never thought of her as boring. He'd thought of her as incredible: juggling her job and the kids far better than he ever could; supporting him when he made one bad business decision after another. He would never forgive himself if anything happened to her.

Trying to still the fear gnawing at the pit of his stomach, he went across to Holly to ease her earphones from her ears, careful not to get them tangled in her hair, which she'd spent an hour trying, and failing, to coax into a bun earlier. Placing them alongside her phone on her bedside table, he noted the bottle of nail polish. A pot of body glitter stuff she'd been given for her birthday was there too. Right next to that was a unicorn pendant, the sort eleven-year-old girls wear. Her bedroom was a stark reminder that she was approaching a fundamental milestone in her life. She was growing fast from a child into a young woman. The leopard print leggings and bare-shoulder crop top thrown on her wicker chair was evidence of that. It seemed like only yesterday he was holding her hand while she tested out her first pair of roller skates. She'd worn her long, blonde hair in a simple ponytail then, her cheeks always flushed with the excitement of childhood. Now she was getting into cool hairstyles and make-up – 'sculpting her cheeks', she'd told him when he'd caught her in front of the mirror.

He'd noticed that Karla had taken her make-up bag with her when she'd gone out, so clearly it was a night on the town she had lined up. He just wished she had mentioned if she was intending to stay out the whole night. Jason closed his eyes and prayed again that she was safe.

He switched off Holly's light and pulled her door quietly to, and then, checking his watch, wondered what to do. He badly wanted to touch base with Jessie, but she would be at work, halfway through her night shift.

Jason debated for a second and then, hoping he wouldn't catch her at a bad time, he texted her. He'd barely pressed send when his phone rang. *Jessie.* He swore she had a sixth sense. She seemed to know him better than he did himself, sometimes. But then, she could probably guess things weren't great here if he was texting her in the middle of the night.

'Hey,' he said. 'Are you busy?'

'Unfortunately, yes.' Jessie sighed apologetically. 'I've barely had time to draw breath. I think every club-goer in the vicinity of Carlow has descended on accident and emergency tonight. I'm up to my armpits in it, I swear, but I'll spare you the details.'

Listening to the light, melodic lilt of her voice, Jason couldn't help smiling. He loved her Irish accent. It always seemed to lift him.

'Are you not sleeping?' she asked him.

'Not yet, no. Karla's out, and I, er…' He stopped. Did Jessie really want to hear all this?

'You're worried about her,' she finished intuitively. 'It's okay, Jason. You can talk about her, you know? She's the mother of your children. I'd hardly expect you not to be worrying about where she is.'

'I wish she'd bloody well remember she had children.' Jason sighed despondently.

'You're angry with her?'

'A bit,' he admitted. 'More with myself, to be honest. The marriage is over, but… I could have handled things better.'

'I don't think there's any good way to handle the breakdown of a marriage,' Jessie offered sympathetically.

Jason pulled in a breath. 'No,' he acknowledged, with another heavy sigh.

'She'll be back,' Jessie assured him. 'She's proving she has a life without you, that's all.'

Jason supposed she was right. It was what kind of life that was worrying him. Karla's life had been her kids. This. Him. And he'd screwed it up. 'You'd better go,' he said, remembering Jessie was busy. 'Attend to the needs of your club-goers.'

'Oh joy,' Jessie said, sounding not very joyous. 'I'd better get back, I suppose, before I'm for the high jump. Meanwhile, you go to bed. Lie down, at least, or you'll be fit for nothing in the morning. Just imagine I'm giving you a nice slow massage, and if your imagination runs away with you, I'll talk dirty to you tomorrow.'

Jason laughed. 'You're incorrigible, do you know that?'

'And you can't get enough of me, I know. Uh-oh, clinical lead on the warpath – gotta go. Sleep! That's an order. We'll talk tomorrow.'

'Night, Jessie,' Jason said softly, his emotions ricocheting between relief and guilt. Talking to her kept him sane, but also reminded him that Karla had no one to confide in – unless things had developed with the guy he'd seen her with. Had they? Try as he might not to let it, Jason's gut twisted at that thought. Where the *hell* was she?

Running a hand tiredly over his face, he made his way to the spare room, supposing he should take Jessie's advice and lie down.

He wouldn't sleep. He rarely did when Karla was out. He intended to go in to the office tomorrow, to tie up some loose ends, but he'd already told Mark it might be late morning, so that wasn't a problem. Mark was pretty much running the place now anyway. He would probably run it a damn sight better than he had. He'd given Jason the option to buy back into the business at some future point, if things didn't work out at the extreme sports company he'd approached in Ireland. Jason didn't envisage going back. He'd had it with ecommerce. He needed a clean break, a new future, to be able to live a life that hadn't been built on a lie. That future may or may not be with Jessie, but her cottage in County Carlow made Ireland seem like a haven – for a few days, at least, while he tried to sort things out.

Jessie had been thrilled for him about the job. Jason guessed he was pleased too. Assuming they offered him a position, it would give him the chance to indulge his passion. Sadly, extreme sports weren't something he'd done much of since he'd been married. He hadn't really minded, figuring that, as a father, one of his responsibilities was not to risk life and limb thrill-seeking.

But wasn't he doing just that? His marriage was over – it couldn't survive now – but didn't making plans to build a new life so far away mean he was taking risks with his children's future? He was their father. He was responsible for them, their health and happiness. He had yet to tell Karla he was going. Having made arrangements to meet Jessie's incoming flight and then fly back to Ireland with her, once she'd visited her family here, he had no choice now but to tell Karla.

Whether he would get on the flight, though, he wasn't yet sure. The way Karla was behaving now, he wasn't confident he could leave Holly and Josh safely in her care, particularly with her mother having left her shit of a father for a safe haven of her own away from the media.

Dammit. He needed to talk to Karla, but how, when they were barely speaking? When they did, it was only to argue. He would have to find a way, assuming she came home before he left for the airport tomorrow, that was. He wouldn't come back to the house while Jessie was here. That wouldn't be fair on Karla or Jessie.

CHAPTER FORTY-SIX

KARLA

I wake with the stale taste of alcohol and cigarette smoke in my mouth. My stomach churns, but I'm too queasy to trust myself to make it to the bathroom. Prising my grainy eyelids open, I squint towards the window. I'm in the Travelodge, I realise. I grope for some recollection of how I got here and then squeeze my eyes closed, mortification crashing through me as I recall stumbling drunkenly into a taxi, spilling from it here with a beer bottle in my hand.

I fell. I swallow back my shame as an image of an out-of-control, brazenly dressed woman weaving across the car park assaults me. I lift my hand. The sharp shards of grit embedded in my palm confirm it.

My eyes stray to the window. It's still early. By the thin blue light filtering through the blind, I judge that it's approaching dawn. There's no birdsong to greet it; just the distant rumble of traffic on the dual carriageway. But then, there's been no birdsong in my life since my marriage began to crumble; no sunshine. Just this cold, empty bleakness that surrounds me and seems to reside inside me.

My gaze travels to the bland, cream-coloured walls. The room is still spinning, though not with the nauseating merry-go-round momentum it did last night. More like a slowly turning roundabout in some sad, forgotten park. I can almost hear the haunting laughter of the children who've abandoned it.

Gulping back the acrid taste in my throat, I twist my head to the side. He's lying on his back, his face turned towards me, one arm crooked under his head. His hair is dark, military-cut, with just a sprinkling of grey. His eyelashes are long, luxuriant, sweeping his high cheekbones as he sleeps. He's obviously well groomed. I try to take some small comfort from that. He reminds me of Jason. I feel my insides knot. The same sharp spasm I feel every time I realise I've almost certainly lost him: my husband, the person who is fundamentally part of me. This man is not Jason. Jason doesn't have tattoos. Jason doesn't like rough sex. I know this person intimately – my body, sore and raw, tells me I do – but I don't know him at all.

Did I have sex with him at the nightclub? My heart thumps in my chest; broken thoughts leap around in my head. I see the overly made-up face of the woman looking back at me in the mirror and my stomach recoils, rebelling against the memory, as well as the wine I poured into it, so easily, so carelessly. God, what am I doing?

Who am I? I don't know any more. This person lying here with a stranger is not me. Not the me I used to be: a mother, a wife. A good mother, I'd thought. A good wife. But not good enough. Inhaling, I hold my breath, try to stop a silent tear sliding from my eye.

Did Jason miss me last night? My heart stalls at that thought. Jason doesn't try to stop me going out. He knows that, in choosing to throw away what we had, he forfeited the right to interfere. He asked me not to go one night. I told him he could stop me by telling me he wouldn't leave me. He didn't. I bite back a low moan. He doesn't want me. He's not jealous. Why did I imagine he would be, when emotionally he's already left me? He's staying for the children. He doesn't want to rock their worlds. He will miss them if he goes, that much I do know: Josh, his scrawny ten-year-old son, who's already decided he wants to do computer science, to grow up to be clever and big and strong, just like his father. Poor Josh. How badly will his illusions be shattered? Holly, the baby I refused to abort, despite my father pressurising me to. His granddaughter. Even now, knowing the truth about the kind of man my father is, I struggle to believe he would have had me snuff out her life.

Jason worships her. He has loved her ferociously since the first time he glimpsed her tiny form on the monitor. He swore he would die to protect her when he first cradled her gently in his arms; that he would kill anyone who dared hurt her. Would he die for her now? Would he stay if he realised that, by leaving, he would be killing part of his daughter, crushing her childhood innocence and showing her how cruel life can be? How cruel love can be? Does he realise that he, *her* father, would be the man who would hurt her most of all?

Just like my father, he will destroy the child he created. I never imagined Jason capable of that. There's part of me that still hopes he won't, that somehow I can make him believe that our love for each other is strong enough to endure. He has been sidetracked by an illusion of his perfect woman, that's all. I have to make him see that the person he wants to be with is me. But it's not me, is it? I reach to wipe away another slow tear. What would he think if he could see me now: this sad morning-after creature, lying under sheets that smell of sex, next to a complete stranger?

Is he still in bed, I wonder? I picture him, his arm thrown across his forehead, lying next to the ghost of me, dreaming of a new life without his wife.

He stirs, my military-haired stranger, grunting slightly as he does, reaching for me in his drowsiness. He probably doesn't know who it is he's reaching for – soft flesh, female flesh, that's all. Wriggling away from him, I ease myself woozily to a sitting position and realise dawn has turned to day. And then it occurs to me: I don't know *what* day. Is it a school day? Frantically, I sift through my alcohol-induced haze. I can't remember. Panic engulfs me, and I wonder again whether I might be losing my grip on reality. I'm drinking too much, thinking too much, struggling to keep track. *Friday.* I seize on it. It's Friday. Breathing a slow breath, I feel calmer for anchoring this piece of knowledge in the sea of madness my life has become.

God, what time is it? I fumble for my phone on the bedside locker. Eight a.m.? But *how*? I would have sworn it was only six o'clock a moment ago. And then I hear the unmistakable spatter of rain outside, which explains the drab blue-grey start to the day. Instantly, I am transported back to the dark, defining days of my childhood – the rain lashing the windows, the cloying air of the steamy kitchen.

My dad is circulating, shaking hands with the funeral guests, sombre black-clad figures with pitying faces. He is stoic, despite the cross he bears. And my eight-year-old self watches him. And she knows. She knows the secret that will stay forever hidden within the walls of that grand house, the house my sister should have grown up in. His cross to bear is that the small body in the ground lies there because of him.

My mind fast-forwards, jerking through the images I try to keep stored away. I'm at Mum's sixtieth birthday party. My father's talking to Jason as I watch from the dance floor, belittling him, humiliating him. Always doing that. *I* humiliated him that night, not once, not twice, but three times: dancing with the toy boy, bringing up the subject of the loan, finally turning him down in bed. I see Jason's frustration. I *feel* it: a sharp painful knot right at the core of me. That was when I realised the foundations of my marriage had truly been rocked. One final push from my father ensured it would topple. He'd known it. He set Jason up, and then sat back and watched while we fell apart.

I have to go. I pull myself to my feet. I have to try to reassure my sweet little girl, who's not much older than that lonely little girl at the funeral. But Holly's not me. She's extroverted, confident, bright and sassy. Innocent. Blinking away the tears, I head shakily to the bathroom, pee quickly, gulp tap water into my mouth, spit it out. I think of Josh: the constant reminders to brush his teeth, his confusion, his palpable anger. I have to go. I collect up my scattered clothes, my cheeks burning with shame. They will be missing me. I'm not the same mummy I used to be. I have seen the bewilderment in their little faces. Things are not running as smoothly as they were when I was organised – smiling and caring, not ranting and raving, slightly insane. But my children still love me. This is my one certainty in a life that's unravelling around me.

I should be there. I hastily tug on my underwear.

My mum, she was always there. And now… I so wish she would call. There are many words unspoken between us, secrets we've both chosen to bury, but she must realise I need her. Wiping my nose with the back of my hand, I grab my phone. My thumb hovers over her number, but I hesitate. What if it goes to voicemail again. What will I do then?

I'm about to call Jason when my phone pings: *Hope you had a good night. Taking the kids to school*, he's sent. There's no sign-off, no 'see you soon'. The three kisses he would normally send are obvious by their absence. They're an expression of love, after all, and he no longer loves me.

But he *does* – if only he would believe it. I have to make him. I have to make him realise he wants *me*. I reach to smooth back my hair before I remember it's no longer there. Short is easier to keep while I live my double life: mother when I'm home, a bad mother now, no longer a wife; and someone the complete opposite of me when I'm not. Will the fragmented sides ever come together, I wonder? Would Jason find that person enticing, exciting?'

'Hey.' I feel an arm snake around my waist as I pick up my holdall. 'Where are you off to in such a hurry? It wasn't that bad, was it?'

I clamp my mind down on the memories – jagged memories, incomplete and broken: a woman's body going through the motions, somewhere else in her head. 'Home,' I say. I unfurl his arm and step away from him, then drag my change of clothes from my bag – clothing more suitable than the ridiculous outfit I was wearing last night. 'I have to get back to my children.'

'Children?' I hear the surprise in his voice.

'Two,' I tell him, tugging on my jeans. 'A girl and a boy, aged eleven and ten.'

'Blimey, you must have had them young,' he says. 'You're married then?'

'Yes.' Pulling my jumper over my head, I turn to face him.

'Right.' He smiles a *c'est la vie* smile and shrugs. And I thank God he appears to be quite reasonable. It could have ended differently. Badly. I didn't care last night. I truly believed it wouldn't matter if I ceased to exist. *How* could I have thought that? However unbearable my life has become, how could I have been so selfish I hadn't considered my children?

Guilt twisting my stomach, I retrieve my pumps from my bag and push my feet into them. 'See you around.' I give him a small smile before I leave. I don't owe him anything. The room was already paid for. And he owes me nothing; I think he's aware of that.

He nods and then cocks his head to one side. 'You look different without the make-up and stuff,' he observes.

'Better or worse?' I ask, curious as to how other men perceive me.

'Just different,' he answers.

Yes, I am. Giving him another smile for his tactfulness, I collect my bag and turn for the door. *I'm not the woman my husband imagines I am.*

I am reminded of something as I leave: 'Paradox of the Actor', an essay written by prominent historical philosopher Denis Diderot. Abstractedly, I recall a class on the subject. Diderot believed the actor should be 'free of sensibility', likening him to a blank slate. Waiting to be drawn upon, the slate sits unblemished. An empty vessel, it becomes filled by observations which are then poured into the performance; the actor has the ability to shape his observations to become anything or anyone.

I liked that metaphor. But what happens when you strip away the personas, I wonder, as I wait for my taxi. When the performance is poured into the audience and the vessel is empty, where is the person beneath?

CHAPTER FORTY-SEVEN

JASON

After fumbling to open the front door and get into the house, Karla came into the kitchen. 'I thought you'd be gone,' she said, clearly surprised to find he'd come back after dropping the kids off at school.

Stifling a sigh, Jason continued to unload the dishwasher to make room for the detritus that still littered the breakfast table. It was fairly obvious why Karla had struggled to get her key in the lock. He could smell the alcohol on her breath. She'd had a good night then, out with the 'friends' she didn't care to share details about.

'There's fresh coffee in the jug,' he said, assuming she could use some.

Prising her pumps off and kicking them into a corner, Karla didn't answer him. She didn't look at him as she headed towards the coffee machine. Jason didn't pursue it. There wasn't much point when they couldn't even communicate civilly for the sake of the kids any more. His fault. He hadn't meant it to be this way, but he couldn't change things any more than he could change who he was. At least he now knew why Fenton had always seemed to openly loathe him. The feeling was mutual. It was small compensation that the world's smuggest fat cat and self-proclaimed 'entrepreneurial genius' was getting his just deserts for the destruction he'd caused.

How the mighty had fallen, Jason thought, a sour taste in his mouth as he recalled how he'd seen him in action that day at his offices. If he hadn't been appalled by the sheer obnoxiousness of the man before that, there was now no doubt in his mind. The media had finally named him, thanks to Abbie's courage in outing him. In so doing, other people felt encouraged to come forward, which had started a ball rolling that Jason guessed would only gather momentum, injunction or not. Naturally, Fenton was still denying the allegations, but while Karla and her mother had closed their eyes to his odious behaviour, Jason had been on to him for years. Even without knowing what he now did, he'd always thought Robert Fenton was a pitiless and ruthless bastard. People simply didn't matter to him. If he had to trample them underfoot in order to preserve what he'd 'fought for', so be it, even if those people were his own flesh and blood.

Jason supposed he should be feeling some kind of satisfaction. Strangely, he still didn't. All he felt was battle-worn. He simply wanted out. Closing the dishwasher door, he braced himself to make his announcement. He had no idea what her reaction would be. Apathy or anger? Relief? He just couldn't read her any more. 'I'm going,' he said quietly.

'And coming back when you feel like it, no doubt,' Karla said, pouring coffee into her mug.

'No.' Jason pulled in a long breath. 'I won't be back, Karla,' he continued carefully. He had to do this now. He'd searched his conscience over and over, but his mind was made up. He'd stayed home specifically to catch her and deliver the news. He hoped it wouldn't destroy her, but this, being in a relationship that couldn't survive, should never have been. She needed to be free of him. To be able to move forwards without him.

At least selling the business would leave her debt-free and with some funds in the bank, though he doubted he would get much credit for that. Jason prayed that his kids would understand, that they would realise nothing could ever diminish his love for them. But the raw reality was that he was about to turn their world upside down, no matter how hard he tried to rationalise what he was doing. It had to be better than them hearing the arguments, feeling the antagonism, though, didn't it? With Karla seeming more unpredictable lately, determined to do her own thing, and him basically miserable, this environment couldn't be good for them.

Karla put down her mug and turned to look at him as if she hadn't quite registered what he was saying. 'You're... leaving?' She laughed, her expression a mixture of disbelief and bewilderment.

Closing his eyes, Jason nodded regretfully and supressed an urge to go to her and hold her.

'To be with some online... *slut*?' Karla stared at him, her eyes now a kaleidoscope of emotion, from shock through to heart-wrenching, palpable hurt.

Jason kneaded his forehead. He didn't answer. There was nothing he could say that wouldn't lead to yet another argument.

'When?' Karla demanded, lifting her chin, her eyes narrowing.

'Soon.' Jason glanced guiltily away. Whether or not there was any future with Jessie, he had no choice. How the hell was he supposed to tell Karla that? 'Today.'

'*Now?* While the kids are at school? Without telling them?' Karla's expression was one of astonishment, and then her eyes darkened. '*Coward!*' she screamed suddenly, causing him to step back.

The coffee jug she launched across the room missed him by millimetres, splintering against the wall to send sharp slivers of glass shooting across the floor. The mug hit its target, white-hot pain searing through his cheekbone as it glanced off his face.

'Karla! Stop!' Raising his hands to defend himself, Jason backed into the hall.

'Get out!' she seethed, raising the milk bottle, the next thing that came to hand.

'Karla, don't,' Jason tried. 'Don't do this. Please, for the kids' sakes, can't we just—?'

'The kids?' She stared at him, her blue eyes wild. 'The *kids*? Go!' she screamed, louder. 'Now! You complete bastard!'

Jason was shaken. He'd hurt her, in the worst possible way a man could hurt a woman, but he hadn't considered she would be capable of actual violence. Seeing her gaze sweep the kitchen, probably searching for a more suitable weapon, he backed further away, pressing the back of his hand gingerly to his cheek.

He hadn't intended to take much. Essentials, that was all. A couple of hastily packed bags were already in the boot of his car. He'd aimed to stay at a hotel while Jessie was with her family. Now, he was wondering whether he should contact her to let her know he wouldn't be able to pick her up from the airport. He couldn't leave Karla like this. *Jesus.* He stopped on the stairs, panic rising inside him, as he heard cupboards opening and slamming, crockery smashing. Drawers opening, contents spewing out to clang noisily to the ceramic floor. Cutlery?

Shit. Imagining her selecting the sharpest knife she could find, he debated whether to call someone. Who? Her mother had gone off somewhere, seeking sanctuary from the press. Should he ring the police? God, no. He couldn't do that. Hearing her sobbing downstairs as he reached the bedroom, Jason felt the guilt he'd been carrying threaten to rise up and choke him.

A slow swallow sliding down his throat, his antennae on red alert, he waited, and then, hearing nothing but sudden stillness from down below, he moved quietly across to the wardrobe, yanking the case from the top to pack the last of the things he needed in.

He was grabbing stuff from inside the wardrobe when he heard the creak of a floorboard on the landing. Glancing quickly towards the door, he saw Karla standing there, not moving. Her face devoid of any particular emotion, she was simply watching him;

continued to watch him, calmly, as he pushed his clothes into the case. Jason wasn't sure which was more worrying, the explosion of anger downstairs or this, the ominous silence of suppressed fury.

THE LAST CHAPTER

KARLA

I should be following him. I should be there when he arrives. Instead, I stand frozen to the spot, dry-eyed with shock. I tried to prepare myself for this, but I prayed he wouldn't actually do it. Prayed *so* hard. Hatred settles like ice inside me. Not for the man who's leaving me, but for the man who's responsible for his leaving. The man who should pay for the unbearable pain he's caused me, caused my family. The guilt and the shame. Listening to my husband reversing his car swiftly from the drive, keen to be gone into what he imagines will be the safe embrace of his Jezebel, and with my arms wrapped tightly about myself, the knife still in my hand, I make my decision. I can't follow him. I have something more pressing to do. Jason will find out what a terrible mistake he's made. He can't fail to.

I'm about to turn from the door when a newspaper rattles noisily through the letterbox. I glance at it and then stop. A laugh of bewilderment escapes me as my gaze alights on a photograph of myself and Jason. My mouth running dry, I crouch to retrieve the paper from the floor and register the headline emblazoned across it – *DAUGHTER OF OUTED UK BUSINESSMAN IN DODGY RELATIONSHIP*. My heart freezes.

Scanning the photograph, my mind skittering feverishly from thought to thought, I try to work out how they'd managed to get hold of it. It's one taken in Paris, grabbed from Instagram possibly? Below it, there's a photograph of my father, his arm draped about a young woman, his hand brushing her breast. Noting his smile – a smile of triumph, almost – and the licentious look in his eyes, I emit another slightly hysterical laugh and brace myself to read on.

'Robert Fenton, the latest multimillionaire businessman accused of implementing non-disclosure agreements, used by some employers to gag employees from reporting allegations of sexual harassment and abuse, appears to have passed some of his dubious traits on to his son.'

My blood runs cold. Dimly, I am aware of the telephone ringing as, my hands trembling, my knuckles white, I clutch the paper tight.

'In an exclusive interview, Jason Connolly's birth mother, Julie Ferguson, a former employee of Fenton's Bespoke Plumbing, reveals that the private adoption of her son was organised by none other than his father, Robert Fenton…'

I stop breathing. My emotions reeling, I glance up at the ceiling, trying desperately to assimilate. It's still there when I look back at it, the same ridiculous, ludicrous… *fucking lie*! My mind races as I try to digest this. Nausea curdles my stomach. Icy fingers of realisation tug at my heart, at my mind, dragging me back to that long-ago day when my father tried to make me 'see sense'.

I hear him, his voice oozing paternal concern: 'I understand you want to be with him, princess. I know love isn't choosy. I won't try to influence your decision, sweetheart, I wouldn't dream of it, but you can postpone motherhood for a while, surely? You're young. You have plenty of time to have children…'

He'd been standing over me, his eyes full of sympathy. And something else, something I couldn't read at the time: panic. I see it now, the cogs of his despicable mind going round as he looked away, groping for a way to save his own skin, his company, which meant more to him – means more to him – than his own children. He'd decided to sacrifice me. He'd decided to sacrifice his grandchild. He'd tried to make me abort my baby.

All these *years*? I quash the scream rising inside me. The lies he's told. The lie I've been living. The indescribable hurt… *Jason!* He *knew*. My heart lurches painfully. How long has he known? Surely he hasn't always? *No!* That's inconceivable. My thoughts come rapidly now, a mad rush in my head. But *when*…?

But I know. I know exactly when. Robert engineered it. Promising him financial backing, he set Jason up, and then cold-heartedly delivered the news that would destroy him, destroy us. Meanwhile, thanks to the insidious seeds of doubt he planted, he ensured that I would be in Jason's office, checking his internet activity. Closing my eyes, I see Jason's face, his incredulity, his bitter disappointment. I might as well have driven this knife through his heart.

He walked away from me. Chose not to tell me. He chose to leave me. My father chose not to tell me, making a conscious decision instead to crush all that was dear to me. To allow me to live with *this*. My children to live with it.

Swallowing back the bile climbing my throat, my thoughts swing to my mother. Where is she? Is this why she's suddenly unavailable, uncontactable? Hiding away, too ashamed to face me?

They *all* knew. Fury explodes inside me. They… all… fucking… well… *knew*!

I snatch up my car keys and fly through the door, ignoring shouts from reporters as I scramble into my car. Careering it off the drive, not caring if I reverse over any of them, I thump so hard against the kerb that I bite the side of my tongue. The pain is sharp. I relish it, the salty, sour taste of blood in my mouth, hold on to it. It detracts from the unbearable pain in my chest. Does Jason know, now, that I know? Has he seen this morning's shitty, trashy headlines yet? What will he do? Will he care? The questions keep coming as I drive, the knife – a Japanese stainless-steel chef knife, eight inches in length – comfortingly on the passenger seat by my side.

He won't care. He never cared, another part of me, my sister, answers.

'He did, once. I know he did,' I say confidently. He *did*. No one can take that away from me.

But not any more. You tested him. He failed you. He left you.

'He still loves me,' I fume. 'I just need to open his eyes.'

But he's our brother. Forbidden fruit.

Wrenching the handbrake on as I arrive at my destination, I don't acknowledge her last comment. I pick up my knife and climb out of the car. I haven't processed this yet. The enormity of it. The impossibility of it. Of us. But it doesn't have to be impossible. It wasn't before. If we'd never known… I flail out for something to hold on to. But I am floundering, drowning in a dark sea of hopelessness.

The gate adjoining the park is locked. Locating the same footholds I used as a child, it doesn't take me long to scale it. Finding the back door open, I swipe the tears from my face and step quietly in to slip through the utility and across the kitchen. I pause as I step into the hall and listen. I have no idea where in the house my father is. His study, possibly. I want to surprise him. I'm absolutely sure he will be surprised, once he realises the scared little girl he intimidated into silence isn't scared any more.

Treading carefully, I walk towards the study, press my ear to the door – and then pause. Now *I'm* surprised. The wanderer returns. The hard knot of anger tightens inside me. My mother, it seems, is home. Come to clean up now the shit has hit the fan? I smile ironically. She never could stand a mess.

I swap the knife into my other hand and wipe my sticky, wet palm on my jeans. Then I swap the knife back and reach for the door handle. I'm about to push the door open when my mother's voice, filled with venom, freezes me to the spot.

'I knew about your arrangement with Julie, you bloody fool,' she sneers. 'About Jason. Did you honestly not wonder why she kept coming back to you for more money? Because *I* told her to.'

'You… blackmailed me?' Robert's voice is shocked.

'*Ha!* I'd say it was you who was doing the blackmailing, wouldn't you? Buying people's silence, paying people off. Threatening them. What did you tell Sarah's mother when she was forced to leave the child you undoubtedly refused to acknowledge on your doorstep?'

'I'm not listening to any more of this,' said Robert, his tone agitated.

'You *will* damn well listen.' My mother's heels are sharp against the wooden study floor, her words… incomprehensible.

Sarah? But… she's my twin. We were inseparable. Two sides of the same person.

Do you think that's why he killed me? Sarah's voice is small, tremulous.

I am too shocked to answer. Too shocked to breathe.

'How old was she? Eighteen? Nineteen?' My mother snatches me back to the conversation unfolding behind the closed study door. The conversation I'm not supposed to hear. The conversation she should have had with *me*! 'What did you threaten her with, Robert, after *compensating* her for ruining her life? She didn't sign one of your silly contracts, did she? Did you tell her to keep quiet or she would never work again? Did you threaten to tell her parents?'

'Diana, you need to stop this,' Robert says tightly. 'You're upset. You need to think about what you're—'

'Upset? I'm not *upset*.' My mother laughs derisively. 'I don't *care*. I *never* cared. Do you honestly think I was sitting at home nursing a broken heart while you were entertaining other women? I've been seeing Michael for *years*.'

Silence for a second. Loud. Ominous. Then, 'You're… sleeping with someone else?' says Robert, sounding choked. 'Since when?'

'Oh, before we were married,' says my mother, her tone almost flippant. 'And after we were married. *Now*.'

Cold trepidation prickling my skin, sweat wetting my armpits, I step closer, press my forehead against the door.

'And you stayed with *me*?' Robert emits an incredulous laugh.

'Played dutiful wife!' my mother counters. 'Cleaned for you, picked up after you, put up with you. And every single day was sheer—'

'Spent *my* money, lived a life of luxury,' Robert seethes, his tone menacing, dangerous. '*Stole* my money! And all the while you were fucking—'

'She's not your daughter!' my mother bellows.

It falls silent again. A silence so charged I can feel the static crackling between them as I flail to grasp the enormity of what she's just said.

'*Michael* is Karla's father. Do you understand?' My mother goes on, forcing the shock hard home.

I'm not my father's daughter? My heart beats frantically in a combination of confusion and disbelief. Michael? Desperately, I sift through my memories. He's there, on the periphery. And I realise that, somewhere inside me, I've always remembered him. A man who was often part of our lives, when we were too small to wonder why.

I see him. I see Sarah and I skipping along beside him, our small hands trustingly clutching his big ones as he led us through the park, pointing out dragonflies and butterflies, a kingfisher by the water. His twinkling eyes and dark chestnut hair. His warm smile and his lyrical lilting brogue as he entertained us with tales of Ireland, telling us of rich, green landscapes that were a 'feast for the eyes'.

He's my father. Even as the penny drops sickeningly into place, it's as if part of me already knows, has always known.

'It was all for nothing!' my mother screams it. 'Your attempts to pay Julie off, your lies, your cruel, *cruel* deceit… You've destroyed her life, your son's life, for nothing!'

Jason. My stomach churns with sick realisation. His pitiless persecution of him, the hurt he'd caused him – it *was* all for nothing – other than to protect his reputation.

Unsteady on my feet, I reach shakily for the doorframe. A bead of sweat drips from my hair, tickles my eyelashes. Using the back of my hand, I wipe it away, rest my forehead harder against the door – and then freeze as I hear the low growl beyond it.

'*Bitch*' – my father snarls it again and I snap my head up, my hand reaching unbidden to wrench the door handle down.

His back is towards me, his wide shoulders hunched over my mother, who is forced against his desk; his hands – hands that lash out and destroy – clutched hard around her throat.

For a second, I am petrified, uncertain, everything inside me frozen. And then a rasp, like a dog coughing, escapes her, and rage – red-hot, all-consuming – erupts, and I am behind him.

Sinews tensed, the knife held high above, a toxic mixture of anger and raw grief broiling inside me, I am poised to drive the blade between his shoulder blades when he crumples.

Bemused, I step back as he flops forwards, landing heavily, his bodyweight on top of my mother.

Uncertain what to do, disorientated, I take another faltering step back as she shoves him off. And another, allowing him space as he buckles at the knees and slides limply to the floor. I look down and see the crimson flower blooming slowly beneath him, the paperknife protruding at a right angle from his neck. I don't move. Watching in fascination, I see his splayed arm twitch, his fingers crawling along the carpet – a vain attempt to escape – and then I snap my gaze back to my mother.

She has a hand to her throat. It's bruised and sore. 'Karla,' she croaks, her voice raw. She is crying, upset, stepping towards me, reaching out for me.

Who is she? I back away.

'Karla!' she cries, desperation in her voice.

Clamping my hands over my ears, I don't answer. I am not listening. I don't want to hear. I can't listen to any more lies. I *can't*.

'I did it to protect you!' she calls, following me into the hall as I turn to flee.

'Liar! You did it to protect *you*!' I scream, pausing to glare at her as I thunder up the stairs. 'Was it worth it? All the secrets you kept, the lies you told, the people you sacrificed so you could feather your *fucking nest*, was it worth it?'

'Karla, *please*… Let me explain.'

'No!' I keep going, past my parents' room and the room beyond it, which became mine, and on up to the third floor, where I bang open the door to a room that has rarely been ventured into since the funeral. As I hear my mother hurrying along the landing, I turn the key in the lock. It's a sturdy lock. It will keep her out for a while. I wish I'd turned the key all those years ago. I wish I could turn back the clock.

And be with me? Sarah asks hopefully.

I don't know, I answer silently. I don't fit anywhere. I've no idea who I am. Who anyone is. I don't want to be… anywhere.

'Karla,' Mum says tremulously outside.

Ignoring her, I head for the window. Sarah and I used to look out over the park from here, telling stories of charming princes and wicked witches, sharing our dreams.

The sharp wind cuts through me as I throw the window open. The heavy rain that's now steadily falling spatters my face. I can't stand outside without stooping any more, but I can sit comfortably enough on the wide window ledge. The man who thought he was my father said he would build a balcony here, once, so we could all eat together, looking out over the park. He said he wanted to do it himself at the weekends. He never did. He was always too busy nursing his hangovers on Sundays.

Shifting slightly, once I've lowered myself, I clutch my knees tight to my chest and rest my head. I can see Sarah, smell her, smell my mother's Poison perfume. We would sneak into her bedroom and steal a spray sometimes.

I can smell the alcohol, too, that wafted from his body the night he killed her. He'd been drinking all day before he'd gone out to his club; drinking to forget what he'd done. I squeeze my eyes closed as I see his face, puce with rage, his eyes, bloodshot and bulbous, as he strikes out at Sarah. I hear it: the dull thud, as her head smashes heavily against concrete.

I smelled the brandy on his breath when he crouched down in the garden beside me, trying to wake her. Later, up here in the bedroom, I could smell it when he lay his heavy bulk on her bed. I tried to tell him about her odd breathing. He wouldn't listen to me. 'Go back to bed,' he slurred, and then grunted and rolled over. Rolled onto her.

'Karla, please open the door, darling,' my mother calls again, as I press my hands hard to my ears, trying to block out his snoring, which is reverberating in my head. 'Please come out and let me talk to you.'

I was unconscious, Sarah says.

But did he hurt you? I ask the question I've asked over and over that's driven me halfway to madness. *Did he touch you?*

I couldn't breathe. That's why I died. He suffocated me, but he didn't touch me, Sarah finally answers me. *I didn't die because of you. I died because of him.*

I close my eyes, relief flooding every vein in my body. I'd thought that he… For so long, I'd wondered. Even in my childhood, it occurs to me, I must have known that my father was a man who was deeply flawed. Did he deserve to die for what he'd done? For causing so much hurt? For killing Sarah? For killing me?

I don't know. I'm so tired of searching for answers. Keeping secrets. The tears and the lies and the arguments. I crave sleep; deep, dark and dreamless. Escape from my conscience.

Will I hurt when I land, I wonder? Will the physical pain be harder to bear than the emotional pain? I can't endure that any more. I glance to my side, down to the bone-crushing ground below. I'm watching a leaf curl and flutter gently in the wind when my phone rings, causing me to jolt.

Jason. Hope rises inside me as I recognise his ringtone. He will have seen the papers or heard the news. By now, he will know that this latest story has broken. How will he feel when he realises how twisted a story it's become? What will he do then? Stifling the sob climbing my throat, I pull my phone from my pocket, and accept the call. I don't speak.

'Karla, where are you?' he shouts, his voice frantic.

Lost, I want to cry. *I can't find me. I don't know me.* 'Watching the leaf,' I say weakly instead.

'Watching the leaf where, Karla?' Jason asks carefully.

I hesitate. Why does he want to know? He's not likely to come to me when he's halfway to the airport to meet his fantasy.

'Karla, please…' he begs, his voice filled with emotion.

'In the window,' I tell him. He won't come. He's salving his own conscience, that's all. Checking to make sure I'm functioning. He will lie to me, probably. Tell me he's not going to try to steal my children. But he *is*. I know he is. He was going to take them to her. I *know* this, I want to rage at him. But she's not there. I'm not here. *Don't you see?*

I gulp back a sob. *Jessie is me!*

'Which window, Karla? Please tell me,' he asks.

'The bedroom. Our old room,' I supply. 'Sarah's here with me.'

'*Fuck*,' Jason utters. 'Stay where you are, Karla. Don't move. Promise me you won't move.'

'I'm cold,' I say instead.

I don't move though, even when I see my mother appear from the front door, her face horrified as she looks up at me.

'Karla, please…' she says wretchedly. 'Get down, sweetheart. I should have told you; I know I should have. We'll talk now – I'll tell you anything you need to know – but… Please get down from there, Karla. For Holly and Josh…' She breaks off, her voice catching.

Holly. Josh. My babies. My heart constricts. I'm no good to them. They don't want me. They want their father. But… they need *me*. I need them. I can't live without them. Without anything or anyone. 'He's taking them,' I cry. 'He's stealing them.'

'He's not,' my mother assures me. 'I've spoken to him. I told him about Michael, Karla. He's on his way here now. He— Oh, thank God.'

I follow her gaze and my heart rate spikes. He's here. My husband. A good husband. Was. Once. I look down at him, raw grief flooding through me at the thought of losing him. That I might already have lost him. I thought I could make him love me again, if he remembered who I was. Instead, I've made him loathe me.

His face deathly pale, Jason looks up at me. 'Karla?' he says softly, and I feel as if my heart might fracture completely.

'Jason, please do something.' My mother flies towards him. 'She won't budge. The bedroom door's locked. I've tried—'

'Where the *hell* have you been?' Jason snaps, catching hold of her arms and moving her aside.

'With Michael,' she answers ashamedly. 'He has a wife. I needed to talk to him. I… Jason, none of that matters now. Please—'

'Christ, you and your fucking husband deserve each other, do you know that?' Swiping the rain from his face, Jason turns back to me. 'Karla, please look at me,' he says, his voice choked.

I don't answer. I can't look at him.

Jason takes a step towards the house. 'Karla, I'm coming in,' he warns me, a determined edge to his voice. 'Just stay—'

'So you're not coming to meet me then?' I ask him tauntingly, making sure to accentuate the lilting brogue I know he loves so much. 'And there was me thinking I'd found me a nice, honest man. Ah well, it's back to the douches and bad pick-up lines, I suppose.'

'*What?*' Stopping, Jason shakes his head, confounded.

Look at me! I stare down at him, will him to look at me properly, to open his eyes and to realise. 'You know, you really shouldn't be going making promises you can't keep, Jason Connolly.' I stop – and wait. Watch the colour drain from Jason's face as he tries to process this, to comprehend that his fantasy, his illusion of the perfect woman, is me.

'*Jesus Christ.*' Emitting a stunned laugh, he squints hard. 'Jessie?'

'The woman you want me to be,' I answer. 'I was coming to meet you at the airport. I was going to surprise you, but…' That was my plan, before I got sidetracked by the urgent need to kill the man who is not my father. Would Jason have been disappointed, realising that Jessie was me? I think he would. Perhaps fate intervened for a reason. I don't think I could have borne that.

'Karla?' he asks confusedly. 'I… Karla, please listen to me. Please, don't…' He trails off, struggling, clearly, to know what to say. The rain is spattering his face, wetting his hair, running in rivulets over his high cheekbones. My man. So handsome.

A heartbreaker.

I don't reply. How can I, when it's not me he wants.

'Karla,' he calls, more forcefully.

It's Jessie he wants. This part of me, but not all of me. 'Why are you taking my babies?' I ask him, pulling my arms tighter about myself, trying to compress all that's inside me.

'I'm not taking them,' Jason assures me. 'They're in the car, just around the corner. They're waiting to see you. Karla, *please*…' He stops, his voice cracking. 'Get down from the window.'

'Why? You don't want me,' I remind him of this painful fact. 'You've forgotten I existed.'

Jason closes his eyes. 'I didn't forget you,' he says hoarsely. 'I could never – would never. I thought I had to, for the children's sakes, for your sake.'

Sarah's not happy with that. *Bullshit*, she hisses.

'Not for your own sake?' I ask him.

Drawing in a ragged breath, Jason nods slowly. 'I ... was lonely,' he admits, now sounding as defeated as I feel. 'I didn't know how to be without my family. Didn't want to be. *Don't* want to be. Please... climb down. I'm begging you.'

'Seems to me that you did,' I point out. 'You were going to teach me to skydive, do you remember?' I add pointedly. 'And sail and windsurf and abseil. We were going to go on adventure holidays. Didn't you tell me we would always stay invested in each other; that we were going to scale mountains together, you and I?'

Jason swallows hard. 'Yes,' he says ashamedly.

'I like the idea of the Andes, in Peru.' I fix my gaze hard on his. 'Do you?'

'I do.' Jason kneads his eyes with his forefinger and thumb. 'I'd very much like to climb those mountains with you. You're my wife, Karla. The mother of my children. Please come down. Holly and Josh would very much like to see you.'

'Would they?'

I doubt this. Poor, sensitive little Josh is scared of the monster, and Holly positively hates her.

'They would,' Jason says, his voice tight with emotion. 'They don't want to wake up crying in the night any more, Karla. Please, for them, climb down.'

I focus on him, my heart thrumming wildly as I try to read his expression – to see whether he might really want me, his imperfect wife – and then I tear my gaze up sharply.

'Mummy!' Holly screams, staring aghast at me from the street. 'Come down, Mummy – *please*.'

She's crying. My baby. She needs me! 'I'm coming, sweetheart.' I push my hands against the ledge, the heels of my shoes scuffing for purchase as I attempt to lever myself up. 'I'm—' But my words are lost on the wind. My heart flips as my hand slips, and my scream is drowned out by the sudden wail of a siren.

I feel my bones move jarringly as I land. The thud, it's softer than I thought it would be. I feel nothing at first, and then a tingling sensation through my body, but it doesn't hurt as much as I imagined it would. I can't see very much past the blinding white light. Snapping teeth with sharp, jagged edges dance across my vision.

Concussion, Sarah whispers.

I hear, though, my husband weeping; feel his warm breath next to my cheek. He has me, his strong arms gently encircling me. 'You caught me,' I whisper, incredulous, because somehow, I realise, he must have.

'I let you fall,' Jason murmurs. 'I should never have… I am so sorry. So, *so* sorry.'

Shh. 'I know.' I try to reach out to him, but things don't quite seem to be functioning. 'So, would you swim the Irish…' I stop, emit a short, sharp cough, and swallow back the metallic taste in my throat.

'All of the seas,' Jason assures me, wiping the blood from my mouth with the pad of his thumb. 'Don't leave me, Karla,' he begs, a tear falling from his eyelashes as he lowers his forehead gently to mine. 'I can't climb this mountain without you. Please forgive me.'

Can I?

EPILOGUE

DIANA

His lips had still held the sweet piquancy of forbidden fruit: Michael Kinsella. Karla and Sarah had adored him. In her mind's eye, Diana could see the girls walking with him on one of their outings. Just five years old, they'd placed their tiny hands trustingly in Michael's as they skipped along beside him, chattering excitedly as they went.

Robert had been away, on one of his business trips, where he would no doubt wine and dine and bed his latest conquest. They'd been going on the popular Blossom Trail that day. She hadn't talked of Robert. Michael hadn't talked of his wife. They'd simply enjoyed each other's company, the ice cream, the picnic she'd prepared.

Closing her eyes, Diana recalled Karla and Sarah sitting opposite Michael, their earnest eyes fixed on his, their faces a picture of studiousness as they'd watched him. Michael's melodic laughter – she heard it as Karla emulated him, carefully enunciating each roll and lilt of his accent. She'd been a budding little actor even then: inventing stories; performing plays in the back garden and inviting the neighbourhood children. And charging them for the show, Diana remembered, her mouth curving into a smile. Robert had said she was taking after him.

Diana's heart saddened at the thought of her husband. His reputation had meant everything to him, more than any woman ever could. That was gone now. She still didn't know the whole truth about what had happened on the night Sarah had died. She wished she hadn't banned Robert from the marital bed whenever he'd been drinking. But it was what it was. She couldn't undo it. She'd carried her guilt. He'd carried his. Perhaps, when Karla was stronger, she would be able to visit her at the hospital and ask her.

Assuming Karla would talk to her. Assuming she wasn't in prison. Would Michael visit her if she was, she wondered? He would. He'd always been there for her. That was the thing about love, she supposed: it knew no restraints. She wished she could have learned to love Robert a little better.

At least now the media couldn't hound him to his grave. That was one small mercy.

Wishing he might rest peacefully in death where he never had in life, Diana slipped on her coat – and turned to accompany the police officers through the throng of reporters to the waiting car.

A LETTER FROM SHERYL

Thank you so much for choosing to read *The Marriage Trap*. I really hope you've enjoyed it. If you did enjoy it, and want to keep up-to-date with all my latest releases, just sign up at the following link. Your email address will never be shared and you can unsubscribe at any time.

www.bookouture.com/sheryl-browne

Beginning a book with the end of a marriage wasn't the easiest place to start. My aim was to examine how a seemingly solid relationship ended up so fractured. What influences came to bear? No one can truly know the person they live with, the secrets they might keep, the lies they might tell, the experiences in childhood that shape who they are. I've endeavoured to strip away the layers and share with readers a little of what lies beneath the surface. *The Marriage Trap* looks at the impact a manipulative or bullying parent can have on a child, and the resultant emotional vulnerability that child will carry into adulthood and inevitably into their relationships. It looks at the lengths someone will go to to preserve themselves at whatever cost to those around them, even those they're supposed to love and protect. It also looks at the strengths people might find within themselves to try to rescue their relationship. Sadly, there are people in the world who abuse or use other people. Often the people on the receiving end of that abuse feel powerless, blaming themselves in some way. They keep secrets because they are ashamed of what they imagine was their culpability. I started with a broken marriage therefore, and tried to find out what broke it. What effect a domineering parent might have on a child, a misogynist on a woman. The consequences for his family – and, ultimately, himself.

As I write this last little section of the book, I would again like to thank those people around me, who are always there to offer support, those people who believed in me, even when I didn't quite believe in myself.

To all of you, thank you for helping me make my dream come true.

If you have enjoyed the book, I would love it if you could share your thoughts and write a brief review. Reviews mean the world to an author and will help a book find its wings. I would also love to hear from you via Facebook or Twitter or my website.

Keep safe everyone and Happy Reading.

Sheryl x

sherylbrowne.com

SherylBrowne

SherylBrowne.Author

ACKNOWLEDGEMENTS

Massive thanks to the fabulous team at Bookouture without whose expertise, dedication and patience *The Marriage Trap* would never have made it onto paper. Huge thanks, too, to the cover designer. Bookouture covers are simply divine. I've totally adored all of mine. Special thanks to Helen Jenner for her faith in the book and loving it from outset. Without her amazing editing skills, I suspect I might have got a little lost along the way. Special thanks also to Kim Nash and Noelle Holten, the dynamic Bookouture Publicity Managers, for their hard work and unstinting support. You two are phenomenal. We would definitely be lost without you. To all the other super-supportive authors at Bookouture, I love you. Thanks for your ears when I needed them and the cheers every step of the way.

I owe a huge debt of gratitude to all the fantastically hardworking bloggers and reviewers who have taken time to read and review my books and shout them out to the world. Your passion simply leaves me in awe. I think all authors would agree we could not do this without you. Thank you!

Final thanks to every single reader out there for buying and reading my books. Authors write with you in mind. Knowing you have enjoyed our stories and care enough about our characters to want to share them with other readers is the best incentive ever for us to keep writing.